BUCKSKINS AND BROADWAY

Amber Carlton

MENAGE AMOUR

Siren Publishing, Inc.
www.SirenPublishing.com

A SIREN PUBLISHING BOOK
IMPRINT: Ménage Amour

BUCKSKINS AND BROCADE
Copyright © 2009 by Amber Carlton

ISBN-10: 1-60601-482-X
ISBN-13: 978-1-60601-482-0

First Printing: September 2009

Cover design by Mark Luedtke
All cover art and logo copyright © 2009 by Siren Publishing, Inc.

PUBLISHER
Siren Publishing, Inc.
www.SirenPublishing.com

DEDICATION

To Della, who always has the best ideas.

BUCKSKINS AND BROCADE

AMBER CARLTON
Copyright © 2009

Chapter 1

Washington, D.C.
September, 1890

"Galahad!"

Every face in the lobby swung in her direction, but Olivia Raines focused on the tall, dark-haired man. A wide smile spread across his face as he strode across the marble floor. Livvie lifted her skirt and tore down the grand staircase of the Willard Hotel, barreling into a man on his way up. She ignored his annoyed glance as she side-stepped around him laughing. When she reached the bottom, she vaulted over a stray suitcase and hurtled straight into the man's arms. Martin Travers swept her up, whirling in a circle then dropped her to her feet, holding her out at arm's length. He plucked a black curl from her shoulder.

"You look more like Jessie every day."

She wrapped her arms around his waist and cuddled close. She couldn't resist him—her adopted brother, her uncle. She couldn't explain their relationship to most people and had stopped trying. "The Fathers say that all the time. We all know Mother's far prettier than I am."

He cupped her cheeks and lifted her face toward him. "No, not anymore. You've grown up since I last saw you, Livvie. You're a beautiful young woman and you've clearly left your tomboy ways home in Kentucky."

He eyed her evening dress, a beautiful gold and silver gown, a gift from her mother for her birthday. The dress felt far less confining and restrictive than so many of her clothes. It bared her shoulders and swept down low, exposing the tops of her breasts. His brow rose at the amount of cleavage she displayed. Her shoulder lifted as she blushed. So, perhaps it wasn't the wisest choice of dress for an unescorted lady but she liked it.

"Washington might be a dangerous place for a girl like you. Jessie's probably going to have my head for encouraging this assignment."

"Only after she lops off mine," she murmured.

Martin peered at her, his green eyes perusing her face. A scowl settled on his handsome features. Livvie's glance darted away for a moment. *Oh, oh. Here it comes.*

"Livvie…"

His quiet voice forced her gaze back to his. She took a deep breath. "Well, I didn't exactly ask permission. And I didn't exactly tell them I was leaving."

"*What*?" Several curious faces swung toward them at the tone of his voice. Oblivious to the shocked stares and questionable looks, Martin grabbed her arm and maneuvered her through a contingent of businessmen. She smiled at their appreciative glances. He yanked her to a private area in the corner and practically tossed her onto one of the velveteen sofas. She oomphed and bounced, landing in an unlady-like sprawl, and blew a lock of hair away from her eyes.

She huffed. "Is this bit of insanity coming from a brother's perspective or an uncle's?" She eyed him up and down, pulling off her gloves. She hated gloves. "It seems like a brother's."

Martin took a step closer, his hands clenching at his sides. His eyes blazed as he stared down at her. "It's coming from a man who hopes to keep his balls intact. What the hell were you thinking? You just left Kentucky without telling anyone?"

She sniffed. "I'm twenty-one now, Galahad. I can pretty much do what I want."

"You most certainly can not."

"Stop the big brother act. I get enough of that from Jake. I don't need it from you too."

Sitting up straighter, she wiggled to adjust her skirt then plucked at her neckline, smoothing the fabric and pulling it down to expose more cleavage.

"You have enough skin showing," Martin snapped. "Now, does anyone at *all* know you're here?"

Livvie rolled her eyes. "I'm not a complete idiot. Of course they know." Her glance darted around the lobby, touching on the front desk, the chandeliers, the fireplace, the door, several ladies adjusting their hats in a mirror. She hated hats. Finally, her gaze skimmed across Martin's face, settling firmly as she smacked her lips and tilted her head. "I left them a note."

Martin's head dropped to his chest. "Damn it."

He flung himself onto the sofa, his head whacking with a thud against the back. He ran his hands through his dark curls, tugging, as he stared at the ceiling. "A note. Wonderful. Cutter will be here on the next train and your ass *and* mine will be his." He twisted his face toward her.

Livvie smiled and patted his knee. "Don't be silly. I have a mission, remember? I'll be gone on the train to Kansas by the time he arrives. You'll have to deal with him."

The corner of his mouth lifted in an almost-smile. "Apparently you've thought of everything. As usual."

She laughed. "I have to plan in order to get anything I want. Mother's not so bad, but the Fathers are vigilant."

Martin nodded. "Cutter and Billy have always been on to your antics."

"Yes, well, they've taken it to a new extreme. They've not been overly happy with me lately. Seems they don't like me seeing Jeremy Hicks and actually had me confined to the house! Can you imagine?"

Martin's lip curled. "No, I couldn't possibly."

"Like that would stop me anyway." Livvie smoothed back another strand of wayward hair. "It's not as if I wasn't careful. And it only happened a few times. I did like it though. Mostly. Jeremy could stand to be a little more…something." Martin gaped at her, a blush rising in his cheeks. She should have shut up, but she'd always had a hard time with that. She laughed, cupping his chin with her fingertips, and snapping his jaw upward with a click. "Don't look so shocked, Marty. I'm a progressive woman. There is no reason a woman can't enjoy sex as much as a man. Mother enjoys sex. She's told me so. Someday I'd like to enjoy it too but the way Jeremy—"

He held up his hand. "Stop. I refuse to discuss your sex life. You shouldn't even have one for Christ's sake. Jessie is a *married* woman so she's allowed to have a sex life. You, on the other hand, should—"

"Mother is a married woman who doesn't exactly have a *regular* sex life, or married life for that matter. Perhaps half the world doesn't realize that, and perhaps the other half ignores it, but you must admit things have always been different in our house. Do you know of any other families who have one mother and two fathers? We haven't had a normal family, a normal life. Why should I lead *my* life with normalcy?"

Martin shook his head. "You're too young to be thinking of these things."

"Am not. I told you I've turned—"

"Yes, twenty-one, I know. Twenty-one or one-hundred-and-twenty-one means nothing where Cutter is concerned. He's not going to be happy about any of this."

She waved her hand. "Oh, he'll get over it."

Martin sighed. "Good luck with that, Liv."

"He and Billy have two other children to concentrate on. They should be able to leave me alone, but apparently having one perfect daughter is not enough for them. Abigail this, Abigail that. The Fathers sing her praises daily. Abigail is often so perfect it makes me want to puke."

She made a face as she pretended to gag. A handsome young man walking past the sofa chuckled softly. His gaze swept her décolletage and he winked. She smiled sweetly then made another face just for fun. The man burst into laughter and Martin groaned.

"Please, Livvie. I know that man."

She wiggled. "Sorry. Don't ruin your reputation or anything by being seen with me." She waggled her fingers at the man and he turned around and came toward them.

Martin held up his hand. "Don't come any closer, Timothy. This is my *insane* niece."

Timothy winked at her and pantomimed dancing.

Her head bobbed enthusiastically. As the man headed up the stairs her gaze followed him. He looked promising. Blond, blue-eyed, good sense of humor, charming... She planned to dance continuously tonight with Mr. Timothy Whoever.

"Liv, must you encourage every man you see?"

"Apparently I must." Livvie licked her lips then she turned back to Martin. "Abbie's teaching now, did you know that? Quite the little schoolmarm. The Fathers are so proud of her and determined I be a lady with a future as well. They want me to learn in Abbie's shadow. Seriously, Marty, can you see me as a schoolmarm? Really!"

"They want the best for you."

"I don't want the kind of future they see. I want to create my own."

Her lips pushed out in a pout. Martin took her hand.

"You are creating your own." His hand swept out to encompass the lobby. "You're here in Washington. Isn't this what you wanted? A mission of your own?"

"Yes! But I'm forced to go behind their backs because they don't want me following in their footsteps. They insist being an agent, *spying*, is too dangerous. I said that Mother did it, but of course, Cutter has an argument for everything."

"It runs in the family," Martin muttered.

"Cutter says Mother had them to protect her."

"And what does Billy say?" Martin asked.

"Oh, well, you know Billy. He wanted me to go into theater. He says I'm far too intelligent and creative to do government work." She ducked her head to avoid his gaze. "Sorry. No offense. I'm sure he didn't mean anything against you."

Martin smirked. "They begged me to study medicine. Guess we're both disappointments to them."

Livvie threw up her hands. "And Mother—who should be on *my* side—said I had too much curiosity for my own good. Ha! How can someone have too much curiosity? She can look in a mirror and see the definition of curiosity. But no! She put her foot down and took their side."

Martin chuckled. "They always did stick together where we were concerned."

"They're impossible to break once they've created a united front. So, I'm making my own choices. After your note and the letter from Mrs. Harrison, I just plain up and packed and here I am. Ready to do my patriotic duty in Kansas." She squared her shoulders then tilted her face and stared up toward the ceiling. "I wonder what Kansas is like…"

"I hear it's far different from Kentucky but you'll find out more when you meet—"

She pounced forward, hands clasped in her lap. "Can you tell me anything about the mission?"

Martin rubbed the back of his neck. "I know the basic mission, Liv, but Mrs. Harrison's designed the operation and I'd rather she give you the details. She's made all the arrangements and—"

"I'll wait 'til tomorrow then. I'm looking forward to seeing Caroline again. She's a great lady. Will I get to see the president as well?"

"President Harrison is very busy, Liv, which is why the First Lady has undertaken this project. He—"

She winked at him. "Never mind, Marty. If you were any more vague, I'd accuse you of being a politician."

"I'm hardly a politician, Liv. I'm more of a glorified personal assistant."

"Either way, you fit right into this town. I'm very proud of you for defying the parents and living your own life. You're my personal hero."

"Damn, Liv." Martin shook his shoulders in a pretend shudder and Livvie laughed. "Don't say things like that. Jessie'll skin me alive. Then Cutter will do it again just for fun."

"He's not as scary as all that." Livvie snatched up her gloves, jumped to her feet and grabbed his hand. "Let's go have dinner. I'm starving. You'll have to tell me about Timothy. Do they have lobster here? I've been dying to try it. And I'd love a glass of champagne. Since the Fathers aren't around to stop me..."

Chapter 2

After locking the door behind the chambermaid, Livvie let her dress drop to the floor. Stepping out of the shimmery pile of fabric, she yanked off the corset and hurled it across the room where it thumped against the wall before landing in an opulent wing chair.

"Damn thing," she muttered. "Might as well wear a straight jacket."

She shook herself like a wet dog, her shift grazing her skin with a delicious freedom. Gathering the hem, she snapped it over her head, and tossed it away. She rolled her shoulders then ran her hands up and over her breasts, loving the feel of them simply bouncing the way they'd been meant to. Whoever had invented the corset—or any one of the numerous articles she was forced to wear—should be shot dead. They were obviously men and she'd be more than happy to arrange for the firing squad to put them out of their miserable existences. She kicked off her shoes, rolled down her stockings and let everything drift to the floor. She wiggled her toes against the carpet then began yanking the pins out of her hair, dropping them one by one onto the dressing table.

She fluffed her curls, enjoying the way they swirled down her back, soft, silky, caressing waves of heat. She stared at herself in the mirror. There was no doubt she was Jessie Raines' daughter and that pleased her. Her mother had always been a beauty. Her youngest daughter had been blessed with Jessie's black hair and green eyes and her body as well—a petite frame with creamy skin, full breasts, slender hips, shapely legs. Livvie sighed. Not a man in sight. What a waste of a great body.

She ran her hands down her hips and wiggled. She loved being naked. Laughing, she whirled around, diving onto the bed. After bouncing for awhile, simply enjoying the liberating sense of being alone in a big city, she rolled around on the soft comforter and snuggled against the pillow. It felt good against her skin. Timothy had felt good against her skin too, at least as close as they could get on the dance floor without Martin's constant interruption.

Marty hadn't been too happy with her toward the end of the evening because four glasses of champagne had made her a little loopy and when she got loopy, she also got a little bit grabby. Timothy hadn't seemed to mind. But the Fathers certainly would have, which is why they had initiated a "no-champagne-for-Livvie" policy. She didn't think Martin would tell them. At least she hoped not. Even if he did decide to be a tattle-tale, she wouldn't have to pay that piper until she got home to Kentucky and that might not be for awhile. She'd be taking a trip to Kansas. She stretched luxuriously.

She rose from the bed and grabbed her wrap, pulling it around her shoulders and shoving her arms into the sleeves. Though she knew she should go to bed to be fully awake and, more importantly sober, for her meeting tomorrow, the warm breeze drew her to the window like a lure. Her second-story window overlooked the back courtyard, a triangular park lined by windows on two sides. She wondered what lay beyond those windows. Each one would hold a small world of another excited traveler or weary businessman, and she'd love a peek into their lives. But the hotel guests either slept or still caroused in town because she saw only empty darkness.

Twinkling lights spread across the cityscape of the capital. Even after midnight, the city seemed alive and vibrant, so much different from home where an outside light seemed a rare occurrence. Beyond the courtyard and a tidy alley stood several buildings of varying sizes, though the Willard dwarfed each. One seemed especially busy. Several carriages and buggies dropped off passengers, singly and in pairs, and a group of young men chatted loudly as they strolled through the back door, their voices carrying in the muggy air.

She leaned against the casement and glanced up as the flickering rays of a gaslight stuttered and flared. She had a clear view into the third-story window of the tallest building across the courtyard. It appeared to be a bedroom, but the ornate and rather tawdry wallpaper and bed linens contrasted sharply with any hotel décor Livvie had ever seen. Her face puckered in distaste. She watched as a pretty blond woman unwound the wrap from her shoulders.

Livvie started to pull the drapes, but paused when another figure appeared in her view. A man, his face shadowed by the brim of a hat. He wore a long coat of some sort. He shed it with a sinuous grace, like a snake shedding its skin, and tossed it onto a chair. When he removed his hat long strands of black hair fell around his face and over the collar of his shirt.

Livvie leaned forward, trying to get a better view. Her waist dug into the window sill. She held her balance, waiting breathlessly for a glimpse of the man's face, hoping she wouldn't end up as a dead crumbled heap on the flagstones below. She wouldn't have moved for the world.

When he tossed his hair he revealed sun-darkened skin stretched across hard planes and angular features. A day's growth of beard shadowed his jaw. He looked dangerous, dark… but she couldn't see his face well enough.

"Damn, damn, damn!" She held up a finger to admonish her mystery man. "Don't move."

She scurried to the dressing table and pawed through her train case, flinging ribbons, hat pins, necklaces, broaches and lip rouge into a growing pile. She finally pulled out a pair of spectacles and slipped them on. She hustled back to the window and focused her gaze on the window.

"Dangerous, dark…" Livvie fanned herself with her hand. "And delicious."

She'd seen a lot of dangerous creatures in Kentucky, but most were of the four-legged variety. This man was unlike any she'd ever met and a wave of jealousy consumed her. She wanted to be that woman. She wanted to know what it would feel like in the shadow of a man like that. She shivered slightly.

The man moved closer and the features of his face became more pronounced—wide cheekbones, a straight nose, generous lips that curved bow-like when a soft smile touched them. His eyes, well, she couldn't see the color. She'd need a telescope for that. She closed her own and imagined them—deep dark blue, kind of like Cutter's, only more dangerous. Livvie laughed. Sometimes, when she'd done something particularly stupid, Cutter's eyes could blaze with a spark of danger, but Cutter was a doctor, and a father to boot, and exuded confidence, strength, and compassion. If Cutter had ever been dangerous like this man, those days were over. Yes, a deep, dark, dangerous blue, like the waters of Lake Michigan at night.

She blinked, pushing the spectacles closer, and focused back on the lighted window. She'd almost forgotten the woman existed because her gaze locked on the man. He wore some kind of light brown pants with matching shirt. It looked like some sort of animal skin and rather like the costumes she'd seen in a Wild West show. Perhaps he was a performer of some kind. Either way they were unacceptable in polite society and would not be appreciated somewhere like the Willard Hotel. She shouldn't have worried because he didn't wear them long. Within moments he yanked the shirt over his head, his boots flew past her field of vision and the woman slid her fingers into the waistband of his pants.

Livvie clasped her hand over her mouth as a small noise escaped. Her gaze roamed to another group of men entering the building, then to a smaller window on the bottom floor that shone with light. Several women walked around a table, their hands caressing men who played a card game. One woman plopped into the lap of a player and his arms settled around her as she viewed his hand. When his fingers slipped into the bodice of the woman's dress, Livvie's eyes snapped closed.

A bordello.

She tentatively lifted one lid, her face scrunched. Her mother might laugh but her fathers would tan her hide if they knew she'd been peeking into the windows of a whorehouse. Face blazing with heat, she tucked herself behind the curtain, and peeked around it anyway, her gaze focused back on her dangerous man.

His naked body nearly burned her eyes. Though she knew parts of a man's body, she'd never seen a completely naked man before and what she'd seen of Jeremy Hicks seemed nothing compared to this man. Wide, muscled shoulders, a chest sprinkled with dark fur that trailed down his body into the triangle between his legs. His manhood grew before her eyes and lunged toward the woman. Livvie's hand tightened into a fist around the fabric of the drape.

"Oh, dear God. That's what a man should look like."

The woman's clothing vanished in the blink of an eye. The man's hands consumed her flesh, running down the blonde's tall, curvaceous body with a controlled predatory hunger. The woman's head fall back as his lips roamed the column of her throat with a searing heat Livvie felt to her bones. The woman's arms fell to her sides when his wrapped around her waist and yanked her against him.

They fell on to the bed, and Livvie gasped, falling to her knees.

The man's mouth traveled from the woman's throat to her shoulder, settling deep, long kisses over every inch of flesh until he reached her breast. He pulled the nipple into his mouth, sucking hungrily, and she arched her back, aching to be closer. The woman wrapped her legs around the man's, straining toward him. Livvie scooted on her knees to the center of the window, and her fingers curled around the window sill. She rested her chin against the frame, staring shamelessly into their private world.

When he moved his mouth, the woman's breast was wet, slick, her nipple a hard, smooth stone. He latched onto the other and Livvie slipped her hand inside her wrap and touched the tip of her own hardened nipple. Her fingers skimmed her flesh then pressed tight against the sudden ache that flared through her breasts. A piercing pain stabbed deep within her body, her inner muscles clamping violently. Shoving both hands between her legs, trying to ease the ache, she shot to her feet. Her chin scraped against the wood.

"Damnation!"

It hurt like hell.

The man lifted his head from the woman's body, shaking his hair away from his eyes. His face twisted toward the window, and for a moment, his dark brows drew down as a frown skimmed his face. His stare seemed to lock directly on her then a smile touched his perfect mouth, lifting one corner in an adorable way that made her heart flutter. Hands still pressed hard between her legs, Livvie's face flared with heat. She flung up her hands, shaking them as though to dislodge something disgusting and lurched away from the window. She stumbled on a wayward shoe and the pointed heel bit into her foot.

"Goddamn it!"

A string of curses erupted from her mouth. She kicked at the shoe and hobbled backward, pressing against her wounded chin. A smear of blood stained her fingers.

She twisted around, trying to find the other shoe before she stepped on it as well. Her wrap tangled around her legs and slid off her shoulder. The sleeve dropped over her hand and the blood spread across the pink silk.

"Shit!" She rubbed at it, making the stain bigger, and turning the wrap into a worthless hunk of trash. She dropped her arm in disgust. "Nice move, Liv."

When a warm breeze hit her breast, she realized half her body was exposed. Panicking, she fought the fabric, desperately trying to pull it around her. She glanced toward the window. The man was laughing! His body shook and the sound drifted toward her like a midnight serenade.

She took a hurried step backward. "He can't see me," she murmured. "He can't possibly see me."

You can see him.

She ducked down, squatting down in the middle of a first-class suite in the Willard Hotel like some sort of deranged jack-in-the-box.

"You're an absolute idiot, Liv. Some spy you'll make."

She plopped onto her ass, rubbing her hurt foot. With her other she kicked at the shoe again, sending it flying across the room.

"He couldn't have heard me."

You heard the men in the courtyard. And they were just talking. You were cursing like a sailor. And loudly, I might add.

"Shut the hell up. You're not helping."

She scooted across the floor on her ass and hooked her fingers into the sill. Cautiously, slowly, like some kind of timid forest creature, she lifted up and peeked over the edge.

"Oh dear God," she whispered.

She dropped to the floor and leaned against the wall. Her heart raced. She pressed her hand against her chest and felt the thundering beat. She pulled several deep gulps of air into her lungs then twisted around, rising to her knees. Folding her arms on the sill, she rested her hurt chin in the soft cushion, trying to ignore the sting. She had no intention of not watching. She'd never seen anything like it in her life, had never even thought anything like that could ever happen.

What the hell kind of lover is Jeremy anyway?

"Bad," Livvie whispered. "Jeremy is a bad lover. This man…this man is a god." She leaned forward, pressing her lower body tight against the wall.

The man had forgotten about what he'd seen or heard and had completely stopped laughing because he had far better uses for that mouth. His body had slid down the woman's and he had buried his face between her legs. His hands clutched her thighs, spreading them wider, and she wrapped her lower legs around his back, her heels digging deep into his muscles. He moved his hands under her bottom, lifting her hips and pulling her private areas tighter against his mouth. The woman's eyes closed and her teeth bit into her bottom lip. Livvie heard a moan and realized it had come from herself. She pressed her mouth against her arm.

His tongue lapped at the flesh between the woman's legs, licking as he would the most delicious ice cream treat. She'd had ice cream tonight after the lobster and it tasted wonderful. Livvie licked her lips wondering what a man would taste like. Probably better than ice cream. Musky, heady, satisfying.

"Stop thinking of things like that," she whispered.

She held her breath watching the long, smooth, rhythmic strokes of his tongue. The flesh between Livvie's legs pulsed and tiny flutters twitched the muscles inside like she needed to pee. She wanted that wonderful mouth on her skin, touching the throb between her legs, dipping into the wet warmth that seeped from her. She slid her hand between her hips and the wall and pressed her palm against the ache, curling her fingers against her body. Her privates were damp, hot and swollen. That ache had turned into a burning itch. Her breasts throbbed.

The man withdrew slightly, just enough to allow Livvie to see his next movement. He thrust his tongue inside the woman's body. Her lips pressed into a tight line and her jaw clenched. Her legs clamped tighter around him, rising higher along his back. His mouth settled on her and sucked. His jaw line flexed with the movement of his mouth and Livvie stared at the stubble on his face, wishing she could feel that rough texture brushing against her thighs, wishing that mouth sucked on her.

"Stop thinking of that too."

She rubbed her palm between her legs, trying to ease the burn.

Livvie couldn't pull her gaze away from the window. The woman's body bowed upward as she shuddered. Shivers ran rampant through her body and the man held her hips as his mouth continued to devour her flesh. When she collapsed onto the bed, he crawled up her body and Livvie saw his manhood skim the rumpled bedspread. Thick, hard, swollen, it seemed to pulse and throb even from the distance. Her mouth dropped open.

"Jeremy is a *very* bad lover."

Without a word, the man shoved that thick, hard length inside the woman to the hilt. Their bodies smashed together. She cried out and the sound of her pleasure spilled across the alley and the courtyard and caused Livvie's stomach muscles to clench and tighten. Moisture leaked into her hand. She pressed her mouth against her arm to stifle the sound that threatened to explode from her.

The man lifted. Arms braced on each side of her, he pumped into his lover again and again, ramming into her with enough force to slide her along the spread. Both of them glistened with sweat, and each time his manhood withdrew, the damp sheen of her juices covered his flesh. Livvie closed her eyes for a moment as that sharp ache once again tore through her privates. Her hand rubbed at the area, enjoying the tingles it caused. It reminded her of the tiny flutters she got when riding Stardust at home. She moved her hand higher and slid across a tiny piece of flesh that pulsed. A shiver went through her whole body.

"Oh!" Her eyes flew open. "That felt...nice."

She'd touched herself plenty of times but had never gotten a reaction like that. She stroked her finger several times over the swollen nub. More moisture pooled between her legs. The more she stroked the more attention it craved. So, she gave it, her finger tracing a wet circle between her legs. She focused on the body of her dark man, standing up for a better view.

His movements became rougher, demanding. The pounding of his manhood became harder and deeper. The woman's cries, guttural, primal sounds of pleasure, spiraled on the damp, muggy air of the Washington night and invaded Livvie's private world, taunting her with what she could not have.

"That is fucking," Livvie murmured. "Not intercourse. Not lovemaking. Pure fucking. Pure desire."

Her body tensed as she watched them mate with enough energy to make a stallion jealous. Waves of ticklish delight coursed through her privates, all centering on the small area she rubbed with her fingertip. Livvie's body floated in the sensations that coursed through it but her gaze remained riveted on the man as he suddenly went rigid, all his muscles straining tightly against his skin. His body exploded in a violent shudder as his jaw clenched. His head fell forward, dark hair veiling his extraordinary face.

Heart hammering, Livvie shuddered as something foreign yet intensely wonderful tore through her body. Her hips bucked against her hand. The muscles inside her throbbed with a deep rhythm, clenching and releasing to the beat of her heart. Uncontrollable shivers racked her spine and every muscle in her body seemed to tense and contract at the same time. Her eyes fluttered closed as she panted. Her head dropped forward and she bit her lip to control the noise that tried to force itself past her lips. She relished each sensation as the feeling began to wane into tiny aftershocks. She smiled as she opened her eyes.

"Holy moly. That was something."

Her jaw dropped.

The man stood at the window. She couldn't see his face. The glowing lamp behind him bathed him in shadow but outlined his big tall body in a glimmering aura of spun gold. He looked like an expelled dark angel standing outside the gates of heaven. For one moment, she couldn't breathe. Her glance darted to her own lamp, sitting innocently beside her on the dressing table. She would not be a stark black silhouette to him. The glow bathed at least half her body in light. Hot, sizzling heat burst into her face. Her nipples hardened. She wanted to hide her face, but Olivia Raines was no coward.

She tugged her ruined wrap of idiocy across her breasts, clutching it closed.

His hand rose then moved from side to side in a friendly wave. Livvie swallowed hard and lifted hers in a return gesture. When his laughter swept across the courtyard and slammed into her, she jerked the drapes closed, yanking so hard the rod bent.

Livvie slumped to the floor. She rubbed her hands over her face and her fingers touched the rim of her spectacles. "Oh, charming, Liv. Really charming."

Chapter 3

"The First Lady will see you now, Miss Raines."

Martin squeezed her hand and gave her a smile. "Good luck, Miss Raines. I'll wait for you in my office."

Livvie smiled back then stood up, tugging the short navy jacket of her day suit. She patted the back of her head and felt a few tendrils of hair had slipped from her knot but she couldn't worry about it now. She took a deep breath and followed Mrs. Harrison's secretary through the double doors.

Caroline Harrison stood on the far side of a bright, airy room. Sunlight streamed through the tall open windows throwing wide splashes of light on several easels spread throughout the room. One held the most beautiful landscape Livvie had ever seen. Caroline laid down her palette and brush on a nearby table, turned and immediately took off the smock she wore, tossing it casually on a nearby stool. She rushed toward Livvie and enveloped her in warm arms and the soft scent of vanilla.

Livvie's eyes burned with sudden tears as her mother's image flickered through her thoughts. The inviting scent of vanilla often surrounded Jessie Raines, but Jessie had never been a good cook. The stench of something burning often quickly followed the pleasant aromas. The vanilla smell caused a wave of homesickness just the same. She blinked back the tears as the First Lady kissed her cheek.

"Livvie, it's wonderful to see you again. You look positively stunning, so much like your mother."

Livvie smiled her thanks and swept her arm toward the paintings. "I can't believe how talented you are. Look at these gorgeous paintings."

Caroline wrapped an arm around Livvie's waist and led her toward the easels. "Which one do you like best?"

"Oh, this landscape." She stood in front of the painting that depicted a lazily rolling river, a tidy little bay, and an expanse of green grass. A large willow tree bent toward the water casting its huge shadow and creating a dark sanctuary that inspired tranquility. "It reminds me of an area near Riverbend, my mother's favorite place. She said it's where she positively fell in love with my fathers."

"I painted that one from memory after my last visit with your parents. Jessie and I spent a delightful afternoon there and she told me the story of how she met your fathers. What an amazing family you have. I thought I'd send it to your parents as a thank you gift. Would they like it, do you think?"

"They'd love it," Livvie said quietly. "All three of them."

"Good then. I'll have it sent out tomorrow. You know I can never quite decide which of your fathers is more charming."

Livvie snorted. "Mother always says it's impossible to choose."

Caroline cocked her head. "You don't believe that?"

Livvie pursed her lips as she thought. "Well, I imagine it's a bit like saying you couldn't possibly choose between your children. But there always has to be a favorite, doesn't there?"

"You think your mother has a favorite? Either child or husband?"

"Well…I don't know," Livvie said. "She's not like other people. My mother is pretty special."

"So are you, Livvie, which is why you're here today."

Caroline took her hand and led her to a cozy corner where Miss Browning had set up a tea tray. Livvie sat on the sofa and Caroline in a chair. While the First Lady fixed two cups of tea, Livvie tried to keep her hands still in her lap though she flicked at her nails. A soft smile played around Caroline's mouth.

"You can't fool me, Livvie Raines."

Oops. Livvie dug her nails into her palms. "About what?"

She glanced downward to Livvie's high heeled boot tapping haphazardly against the carpet. "You're dying for me to talk about the mission."

She heaved a sigh. "Yes. Yes, I'm dying here." She clenched her hands in her lap, pushing down on her thigh to stop the tapping. "I'm just so excited and so very grateful for this opportunity, for the faith you have in me. I won't let you down, Caroline. I'll do my absolute best."

"I know you will, dear. I have it on the highest authority."

Livvie's brows rose, but Caroline did not explain who the highest authority might be. She pressed her lips together to keep her mouth shut. She certainly couldn't question the First Lady, particularly when at this point Caroline was her employer.

"Let me tell you a little about what's been going on. You've heard of the orphan trains?"

Livvie tilted her face and nodded. Of course she had. Her mother talked incessantly about the orphan trains. When she really got on a tangent, it took both Cutter and Billy to talk her down. Unwanted and orphaned children were loaded on trains and sent halfway across the country. Alone, impoverished and scared, they were practically auctioned off at stops throughout the west. There had been successes and failures. Some had been fortunate to find decent homes and had been adopted into the family. Others served more as indentured servants, providing labor in exchange for room and board. For others it was far worse and the runaway rate had become very high.

"My mother told me about several instances where children have been mistreated in their new homes, and others who've never really been given homes at all, but are used more as unskilled, unpaid labor. She suspects some have actually been sold to organizations as slave labor."

"Exactly, Livvie. These are the claims I'd like you to investigate for me. Benjamin is very busy right now, particularly with affairs involving the native tribes. Since I am involved in several charitable endeavors here in the city concerning abandoned children, Ben asked me to conduct this investigation and make the arrangements personally. So I have done so."

Livvie picked up her cup and took a sip as the door opened. Two men walked into the room. She choked and the tea exploded from her mouth. The liquid sprayed all over the polished silver tea set just as the cup handle slipped in her finger. She dumped tea all over her lap, ruining her navy skirt, and promptly entered into a fit of coughing. Mrs. Harrison lurched to her feet and patted her back, dropping a napkin into her wet lap. Livvie continued to cough, staring toward the door.

Her dark, dangerous man from last night stood in the open doorway, his hard muscled body encased in a neat black suit and gold toned vest. The fashionable string tie tucked around the snowy white band collar appeared to be silk. The outfit looked entirely suitable for a visit to the White House but his hat looked like something a cowboy might wear. She wondered if he'd even combed his hair. Long strands curled across his tanned throat. His deep midnight eyes immediately focused on her and a sultry smile lifted the corner of his perfect, utterly seductive and talented mouth. His handsome face had been shaved to smooth perfection and she had a sudden desire to feel his skin. She couldn't seem to tug her gaze away from him and images of what he'd been doing last night flooded her mind.

She couldn't begin to wonder at the impossibility or incongruity of his appearance because only one thought filled her head: *There are two of him.*

Only one difference existed between them. The duplicate wore a silver tone vest.

Oh, my God, which one—?

"Good morning, gentlemen. Please come in," Caroline said. "We had a slight accident here. Just give us a moment."

As her choking fit subsided, Livvie glanced between them from beneath her lashes—mirror images of one another from the size of their big bodies and the intensity of their gazes to the nonchalant cock of their hips and the luscious lips smiling with the same charming ease. Caroline continued to mop her skirt like a mother would for a clumsy child.

"Connor and Desmond McBride, please meet Miss Olivia Raines."

The two men took off their hats, releasing strands of hair to fall across their foreheads, and strode across the room. Each offered a slight bow then they settled in the chairs Caroline indicated. In identical fashion, each man leaned back, raised a leg and planted his ankle on a knee. Caroline grabbed another napkin from the tray and went back to mopping up Livvie's mess.

"Miss Raines will be holding primary charge for the operation."

The two men glanced at one another and two dark brows rose simultaneously. Livvie's face burst into flame.

"Raines, is it?" one of the men asked.

"Yes," Livvie squeaked. She cleared her throat and lifted her face to the First Lady. "We're to work together on this operation? In what capacity? I mean, I don't see how these…men can be of any value to me and I'd thought—"

"They're for your protection, Livvie," Caroline said. "It's not an option."

"But I can't possibly…not after…well, I'm not sure I'm comfortable with this."

One of the men pursed his wonderful lips. Connor? Desmond? She had no idea which one was which. And she had no idea which one she had watched having incredible sex the night before. What a nightmare.

"What happened to your chin, Miss Raines?" the left twin asked.

Livvie ran the backs of her fingers over her jaw, wincing as she grazed the cut. "I had a little accident. Nothing to worry about."

"You have to be careful when you're spying, Miss Raines," the man said. "You never know what you might see or hear. Best to be prepared for anything."

A trickle of sweat swelled between her breasts. She blushed to the roots of her hair. It spiraled up from her neck, over her face and practically set her hair on fire. She was so glad she'd decided to wear a hat. She suddenly couldn't remember. Had she worn a hat? Her hands fluttered upward, helplessly and stupidly. Yes, the pretty blue hat with the feathers. Good.

"I learned a valuable lesson," she said. "It won't happen again."

The man wearing the gold vest smiled. "I'm not so sure about that. You seem like the curious type."

"Curiosity killed the cat," she said curtly. "I assure you it won't happen again."

She plucked at her wet skirt, wishing she could dissolve into the chair like a sugar cube. She couldn't possibly be assigned to a mission with these…Wild West Adonises. She wouldn't survive.

Caroline dropped a pile of soggy napkins onto the table and took her seat. Livvie sank farther into her chair as Caroline began.

"I've already spoken to the McBrides about the nature of the mission and what their duties will be. They have come highly recommended from a third party I know very well. Your safety is of primary importance here, Livvie. Though I want the information, and I feel we can stop what is happening in Kansas, I cannot allow you to put yourself in danger. Connor and Desmond will make sure you don't. And they'll keep danger away from *you*." She pulled a portfolio toward her and handed it to Livvie. "Although you are the primary contact on this operation, in questions of safety, the purview falls to them. Do you understand that?"

"Yes, ma'am. I understand perfectly." Her gaze fluttered quickly between the Terrible Twins. They both watched her like a hawk surveying its next meal as it scampers through the field, alive, happy and oblivious one minute, dead and eaten the next. She'd just have to prove to them she wasn't a skipping little bunny that would fall prey to their charms.

Good luck with that, Liv.

Pulling what was left of her dignity together as well as she could after her near-drowning, Livvie sat up straighter and opened the portfolio. She perused the documents inside, flipping through them with a sinking feeling. A train ticket. An envelope of cash. A bank draft. Letters of recommendation. A diploma and certificate from a ladies academy in Philadelphia. A deed to a piece of property located in Fort Cloud, Kansas. The name and location of a woman named Anna Glaser. She raised her eyes and met Caroline's.

"What are these documents? They all have my name on them."

"They are your cover, Livvie. As an agent of the government, we need to ensure you have all the proper documentation in the event there are questions. I have a contact in Fort Cloud, who you will report to and update on occasion. Her name—"

Livvie nodded. "Anna."

"Yes. She is well acquainted with some of the orphans and has been concerned as well. She is aware of your status, but no one else in the area will be. These documents are just a precaution."

Livvie glanced at the portfolio again and gulped. "This is a teaching certificate."

"Yes, you will be working as a school teacher in the town of Fort Cloud. I hear it's a rather nice school for the area though needs some repair and maintenance. Most of the students come from the town, but a smattering come from the outlying farms. A great many of the children in this town have arrived by the train. This is the perfect cover. Anna Glaser has arranged it and told the town council you have impressive credentials."

"But I know next to nothing about teaching and less about children."

"That happens with any new teacher. You'll learn on the job, as do most."

Oh, no, it's not possible. Abigail will laugh her head off.

Livvie's mind whirled. She found herself shaking her head and barely heard Caroline as she continued, giving her smaller details about the town. One thought stuck in her mind. She stuttered and could barely get the words out of her mouth.

"I-I'm to be a schoolmarm?"

"Yes, dear, a schoolmarm."

The man wearing the silver vest glanced toward his twin. "She's much better looking than any schoolmarm we ever had."

His brother laughed. "We never stuck around long enough to find out."

Caroline gave them an indulgent smile. "Teasing her already, gentlemen?"

The left twin said, "Just trying to lighten the mood, ma'am. She seems a little bit…spooked."

"This is all new information to her," Caroline said. "She didn't have the luxury of sleeping on it overnight like the two of you had."

The right twin stared her up and down and said, "She doesn't look like she did much sleeping last night at all, ma'am. Are you sure she has the endurance needed for an assignment of this nature?"

Livvie's jaw clenched. She slid forward on her seat then jerked as the cold skirt hit a warm spot on her leg. She found the strength to return the stare. "I have more endurance than both of you put together."

"Really?" The right twin propped his hand on his chin. "I think you'd be surprised."

"Keep your surprises to yourself," she muttered.

"That's enough for now, gentlemen. You have an entire train ride to monopolize Miss Raines' time. For now it belongs to me."

"Sorry, ma'am," they said simultaneously.

Caroline turned back to Livvie. "The house you will reside in is located outside of town several miles, on a small ranch. We thought that best since it wouldn't be wise for them to be seen simultaneously. That might cause additional complications we don't need. Fortunately for us, the McBrides have extensive experience in ranching, farming, construction and many other occupations that may come in handy on the property. They're also excellent trackers, have knowledge of firearms, and are familiar with the Kansas terrain. I think you'll find them more than adequate to meet all your needs."

The twin wearing the silver vest said, "Any need at all." If their voices got any more seductive Livvie planned to throw herself out a window and escape from this nightmare.

She blushed again. Her glance darted once again to the brothers. She would be eternally grateful to someone if she got out of this room without bursting into flame. Was that an identical smirk on their faces?

"Is there a way I can tell you apart?" she snapped.

The twin wearing the gold vest leaned forward. "Our names." He hooked a thumb in his brother's direction. "And he snores. I don't."

Livvie sniffed. "That is of no concern to me."

Caroline laughed. "Well, Livvie, you might find it somewhat of a concern."

Livvie's eyes widened. "How could it possibly concern me?"

"The McBride brothers will be posing as your husband."

"My *what*?" Livvie shook her head and whispered, "Oh, no."

Caroline winked. "One at a time of course." Caroline stood and held out her hand. Each McBride brother gave her a hearty shake and a dazzling smile. "Thank you for coming today, gentlemen. Olivia will meet you tomorrow at the train station about a half-hour before the scheduled departure time."

As Livvie sat stock-still on the sofa, feeling the wet dress steal every ounce of warmth she had, a hot whisper of breath touched her face and a soft voice filled her ear.

"You've really no need for that corset, Miss Raines. You're quite a beauty."

She was too horrified to turn her face. She sincerely hoped Martin had a headache powder back at his office.

Chapter 4

"I'm really not sure I can do this, Marty. The men are beastly. They're cowboys, for God's sake, or something like that. I don't know what they are."

Martin dropped a coin into the porter's hand when he finished loading Livvie's trunks onto the cart. He handed her the train case and picked up a small overnight bag. They strolled through the station leading to the platform. Preoccupied, Livvie smashed into three people as they walked and stepped on two sets of feet.

"A schoolmarm of all things, Marty," she muttered. "I know nothing about children."

"Think of them as a roomful of Billys. You adore Billy."

"I do, but I'll never survive this. Billy has the attention of a gnat, always flitting from one thing to another."

"You have a lot in common with Billy."

She rolled her eyes. "I can focus. I can finish a task." She stopped dead. "I should have gone into theater. They don't have children in theater. Is it too late? Can I get a train to New York?" She glanced around the station.

"Stop worrying, Liv. You'll be fine. You're perfect for this assignment."

"But the *cowboys*, Marty. How am I going to get through this with my dignity intact?"

"You'll manage. I'm not sure what the problem is. You wrap men around your finger faster than my sister." Martin waggled his brows. "So which one is the lucky bridegroom?"

She slapped his arm. "You're enjoying this far too much. They hadn't finished that paperwork yet. Caroline said the McBrides would have it with them when they arrive today. She was having it delivered to whatever hole they slept in last night."

"Hoping for one or another?" Martin paused and tapped his lips. "Let's try it out, shall we? Mrs. Connor McBride? Mrs. Desmond McBride? Which do you prefer?"

"They're both equally detestable."

"I was talking about the name, Liv."

She pressed the bridge of her nose. Of course. The name. Why should she be thinking of which brother she preferred? That was utterly ridiculous. And impossible to decide. They were identical for crying out loud. She didn't even know which was which.

Oh, stop thinking about them at all.

She shook her head. "Does it matter? It's in name only."

"What's really bothering you, Liv? Having a set of male nannies, or the men themselves?"

"They're just different than I am, that's all."

"I can't imagine Caroline would put you in an uncomfortable position. Seems to me she'd have selected men who are young, attractive, bright, responsible, reliable—Liv?"

She blinked but couldn't tear her gaze away from the Terrible Twins as they moved down the platform in long strides. They each had a rifle carrier and a leather bag flung over their shoulder. Both bags looked like they weighed a ton and yet neither man seemed to notice the weight. Today they wore the frontier outfit she'd seen in what Livvie would forever call "the night I lost my mind." Soft leather shirts stretched across wide chests. Pants hugged their hips and outlined every line and ripple in their bodies, including the rather large bulges between their legs. Livvie gulped. Each step bought them impossibly nearer and pushed her closer to the edge.

They wore the same cowboy hat they'd worn the day before. Every woman's head turned in their direction, gawking as they strolled by. Even a prune-faced woman smiled as they tipped their hats.

They looked totally out of place in the station. They should have been riding the plains beneath a cloudless sky on wild stallions, their hair blowing out behind them as their long muscled thighs gripped—

"Liv!" Martin snapped his fingers in front of her face then followed her gaze with his. "Are those your beastly cowboys? You've got to be kidding me. No wonder you're scared to death." He burst into laughter.

He held out his hand as the men stopped several paces before them and dropped their possessions to the platform. "Martin Travers. I'm Livvie's uncle, or brother, depending on who you talk to."

Both twins said their names simultaneously then shook his hand in turn.

Livvie swayed from one foot to another, her gaze ripping across the train, the other passengers, the track, a bit of orange peel on the ground.

"Here's my sweet bride!"

Large arms encircled her waist and swung her up, lifting her as easily as a child. The offending twin twirled her around until her head spun. All three men laughed as she fell forward, clutching the pair of shoulders within reach.

He dropped her feet to the ground and she staggered until the other brother grabbed her elbow. When he released her, she had no idea which one had picked her up.

"I think I'm going to puke," she muttered.

"Too much excitement for one day," the twin on the left said.

"It's not every day a pretty lady gets married," the twin on the right said.

She held up her hand. "Stop. You're giving me a headache. And it's worse than the one you gave me yesterday."

The twin on the left shook his head. A sad look settled on his face as that perfect bow mouth drew down in a pout. "A headache? Already? There hasn't even been a honeymoon yet."

"Got a couple hat pins in your woman's box of magic, sweetheart?" the twin on the right asked.

Her mouth dropped down. "My what?"

Martin nodded toward her hand. "The train case, Liv. What the hell did you think he meant?"

She sat the case on a bench and flipped the catches. "I don't know, Marty. I've been so confused lately." She ransacked the interior and plucked out two hat pins.

Each of the twins held out a hand and she deposited a pin into each palm. They then reached into their pockets and pulled out a hard sheet of small paper, pinning it to their shirts. One read *Connor.* One read *Desmond.*

"No excuses now," Desmond said. "And no headaches either."

"Today's your lucky day, Mrs. McBride," Connor said. "Come give your new husband a kiss."

He yanked her toward him and before she could think, react, move or otherwise repel him, his mouth swooped onto hers. He bent her over his arm and kissed her until she couldn't breathe. The touch of his mouth caused an ache in the lower part of her body and she swore she felt wetness pool there. Suddenly he flipped her up—causing that puking feeling again—and another pair of arms grabbed her. Desmond's mouth took hers in a searing kiss and his hand curled around the back of her neck, holding her close. When he released her, she stumbled again. She vaguely wondered when she'd gotten so graceless.

"I thought I was married to only one of you."

Desmond shrugged. "Seemed only fair. Why should Connor get all the fun?"

"Why indeed?" Livvie muttered.

The train whistle blew. Livvie hurtled herself into Marty's arms and dotted kisses along his face. She whispered in his ear. "Please write to me, Marty."

"Every week. I promise." He turned to the men, his arm tight around her. "Don't let her get away with anything. She's a handful."

"We'll manage," Desmond said.

"There's two of us and one of her," Connor said.

The men gathered their belongings. Desmond picked up her train case and overnight bag while she gave Marty another hug. Connor took her arm and led her to the stairs. A tear slipped down her cheek as she settled into her seat next to Connor. He wiped it away with a smile.

* * * *

The next days went by quickly in a blur of ever-changing landscape, stops in cities of all sizes and descriptions, and the attentions of two men. No sooner had one left her sight then another took his place. Other than when she slept, one of the brothers remained vigilant at her side, and she often suspected if she peeked out the curtain of her berth, she'd find her husband-of-the-hour sleeping in the narrow corridor. She never found the nerve to draw the curtain because she feared what she might do. She couldn't get the images from her night at the Willard Hotel out of her mind.

Over the course of the journey, however, Livvie began to see the subtle differences between them.

Though Desmond's eyes were as dark as she'd imagined, Connor's were a lighter shade of blue. She likened them to the sea at midnight and the sea at twilight and both colors held equal beauty and fascination. Though the brothers stayed in a perpetual good humor, Connor had a tiny dimple that appeared in his cheek when he laughed and he laughed a little more than his brother. Connor found everything amusing. Though she obviously perplexed them both at times, Desmond's brows rose slightly higher when confused. And she confused Desmond far more than Connor. She thought maybe Desmond took her more seriously.

But the touch of their hands held the biggest difference between them. As her new bridegroom, they delighted in touching her at every presentable opportunity. A hand often grazed her back or cupped her elbow. A sheltering arm slid around her shoulder and gentle fingertips touched her face. Those perfect lips brushed her cheek and forehead. Neither of them made her feel uncomfortable or embarrassed her by their behavior and she found herself walking closer than necessary and leaning into both as she laughed. She shamelessly encouraged their attention and touch.

Yet they touched her in different ways. Connor's touch was comforting, affectionate, and sweetly endearing. Desmond's hand felt protective, supportive, and slightly possessive. She began to crave both and that worried her a little, but not enough to discourage either.

When she lay down at night, she found herself wishing for morning. When morning arrived, she found herself dreading the setting of the sun. The men entertained her with stories of their lives as they'd traveled from one place to another and held every occupation imaginable. They'd journeyed to almost every state, and several territories, lived with several native tribes and had even been to Europe. But they never talked about their childhood, and though her curiosity rose higher and higher, she never pressed. That surprised her. She always pressed.

That didn't stop Livvie from talking though. Never one to sit quiet for long, the moment they ran out of steam, she regaled them with every adventure she'd had since she could remember. And Livvie Raines had a great memory. She told them stories of her parents and Martin, Jake, and Abbie, and all the important people that populated her life. Connor said it sounded as though she collected people and she laughed, realizing she'd probably done just that. She couldn't begin to imagine her life without even one of the souls she knew. They'd all contributed in one way or another.

Though she was having the time of her life, she missed Riverbend and Stardust, her mother's hugs and laughter, and the very different looks her fathers gave her throughout the day—the slight confusion perpetually settled on Cutter's face and the delight and adoration in Billy's eyes. She missed Jake's quiet presence and, much to her surprise, she even missed Abbie's perfection.

She settled more comfortably in her seat and let her gaze wander over the magnificent vista out the window. Livvie'd been east, north and south of Kentucky but had never been west of Chicago. She loved watching the scenes change and looked forward each day to a new view and numerous delightful surprises.

A cup and saucer appeared magically on the table before her.

"Your tea, Mrs. McBride."

Desmond slid into the seat next to her, his hip bumping against hers. A delicious little thrill went through her. She wiggled slightly and it wasn't in the opposite direction.

"Would you like about a hundred napkins with that or will one suffice?"

"Ha, ha, very funny."

"You've done well on this trip. You haven't had an accident since we boarded."

"You're making me less jumpy," Livvie said.

"The jumpy Olivia is kind of cute. She's probably expensive to keep with ruining so many clothes, but I have a feeling you can afford them. I think that's the fourth dress I've seen." He cast a quick glance at her rose-colored traveling suit.

"Afford them or not, Cutter still wouldn't like it. He's very generous but he takes wastefulness personally. He's a big pussycat generally, but you don't want Cutter on your bad side."

Desmond stretched out his legs. "I've been wondering something." His hooded gaze roamed the car seeking out hidden danger, as though any moment someone might try to abscond with her. Desmond never stopped working but she admired that. "Why do you call your fathers by their given names?"

Livvie laughed. "I don't to their faces. They're both Daddy to me. But it gets confusing in a house when you're discussing two different fathers so unless I'm kissing them goodnight, they've always been Cutter and Billy. We all speak of them that way. I miss them both." She sighed.

"Sounds like you have a lot to miss, Liv. You've been lucky in life."

"I have, haven't I?" She studied his profile, at least what she could see of it in the sweep of his hair. He chewed thoughtfully on his lower lip. She wanted so much to cup his face and taste those lips, but of all the kisses she'd received on the trip, none of them had been on her mouth. "I've gotten the impression you and Connor haven't always been so lucky, Des."

He glanced at her. "Not always."

"Would you—?"

"No, I wouldn't. Maybe some day, but not today."

She patted his hand. "Okay, Des, but sometimes it feels better if you open up."

Desmond laughed. "That coming from the expert. If you were any more open, Liv, I swear we'd see clear through you."

He gripped her hand in a tight squeeze then stood. His gaze once again roamed the car, and her gaze focused on the bulge in his pants. Heat seemed to waft toward her and envelop her body in a musky scent she'd learned days ago to associate with the McBride brothers. Inside the soft leather of his pants, she swore she saw a slow pulsing like the beat of a heart. Some day she'd figure out which one of the brothers she'd watched. And on that day, she would do something with that knowledge. She had no idea what, but definitely something.

"I'm off to fetch Connor. He'll be here in a minute. You'll be alright?"

She craned her neck to peer into his face. "Of course, Des. I'll be fine. See you later?"

He winked. "I'll tuck you in."

"I dare ya."

A flash of color swiped Desmond's cheeks. She leaned around the edge of the seat to watch him walk down the row. He appeared to saunter but Livvie already knew Des better than that. There was purpose in every movement he made. At the door, he paused, turned, and flashed her a smile.

Chapter 5

Livvie almost wished the journey could go on forever because she loved sharing space and swapping stories with the McBride brothers, but engaging them in a more intimate environment filled her with a fluttering anxiety she couldn't understand. She trusted them. They'd given her no reason not to. But she didn't quite trust herself. Without the chaperonage of scores of other passengers and the limits placed on her behavior by the confines of the train, she had no idea how she'd react to them in close, private proximity. Livvie doubted her ability to stay away from them and that could throw a real wrench into her mission.

The reality of the situation set in hard as the conductor made his final evening round through their car and announced they'd be arriving in Concordia, Kansas the next day with several stops following immediately, including Fort Cloud, their destination. Her new life stared her in the face and she had a hard time meeting that stare.

The next afternoon they disembarked from the safety of the train. She stopped dead on the first step. Her hands shook and sweat greased her palms. She stupidly stared at the hand Connor stretched toward her.

"Livvie," he said quietly. "There are people behind you."

She tightened her grip on the train case, then slid her other hand down the side of her dress. She reminded herself she'd grown up under the guidance of William Marlowe, a consummate actor and true professional. Following his example, she'd enmesh herself in the mission and become Mrs. Connor McBride. She could do this. She put her hand in Connor's, descended the stairs, and stepped into Kansas.

The first thing she noticed about Kansas was Desmond had vanished.

She glanced left and right, stood on tiptoes to peek into the train windows, twisted her body to see around workers and passengers, peered at the station and finally, turned to Connor. "Where's Des?"

"He's around."

Her shoulders slumped. She suddenly felt bereft with only Connor at her side. But Connor seemed unconcerned, so Livvie followed him as he arranged to have their baggage held in the station and headed inside to get information on transportation to their new home. They discovered that Anna Glaser had left them instructions to go to the livery where she'd arranged for a horse and buckboard. She'd also left a detailed map of how to find the property. Her accompanying note read:

Olivia, please settle in and come see me in the next few days. School starts in one week and we have much to discuss. The house has been filled with basic foodstuffs and it should get you through until your next trip into Fort Cloud. You will find the stock has been tended and the barn holds all the supplies you need for the next few months.

Welcome to Kansas.

Anna Glaser.

Livvie stared at the note in shock. "Stock? The next few months?"

"It's a working ranch. Your husband needs a visible occupation."

"Hmm. That's a surprise. I knew we'd be living outside of town, but I don't know much about tending animals, other than horses. And even then—"

"Des and I will handle it."

Her usual chatty Connor seemed preoccupied and incredibly taciturn. Kansas had stolen the smile from his face. Livvie didn't like it one bit. She pursed her lips and tucked the note into her reticule.

Connor arranged to have their luggage delivered to the livery—and seemed to take his blessed time doing it—while Livvie waited on a hot bench in the wilting heat, tapping her foot and snapping her fan in front of her face. With the stationmaster in possession of their luggage, Connor finally took her arm and they began the two-block walk to the livery which also served as the smithy. Livvie gazed at her new surroundings, eagerly reading signs, peeking in windows, and hoping for a glimpse of anything unusual. She had no idea what to expect in Kansas, but she thought of animal stampedes, bucking broncos, cowboys with clattering spurs. She didn't see a one. Kansas seemed to offer nothing her overactive imagination had conjured.

The train station stood at the end of Main Street on the south edge of town and appeared to be the most prominent and active building. Livvie thought without the railroad, Fort Cloud would have sunk into oblivion because it seemed to offer nothing beyond basic survival. Where were the opera houses, the restaurants, the post office, the banks, the shops, the markets?

Fort Cloud boasted only the necessary businesses. Two rows of closely spaced buildings paralleled the wide, dusty avenue. From where they currently stood, she had a view of the livery, a drug store, a hardware purveyor, a dry goods store, and a rather large lumberyard. A small hotel, a grocery, two saloons, and a granary flanked the opposite side. A small square stood in the center of Main Street several blocks up holding a band shell and several park benches. Livvie glimpsed a church steeple and what could be the school. The street seemed to go quite a bit farther, but she couldn't see much without her spectacles. Those were not an option if she hoped to maintain her dignity in this paradise. She'd investigate the rest of the town later.

Two residential streets ran perpendicular to Main, boasting homes of all sizes, some as large as three stories. All had front yards clinging desperately to their last strands of parched grass. Several other streets intersected but Livvie couldn't tell how far they went. She shaded her eyes against the afternoon sun and continued to peer around Fort Cloud. Finally she sighed.

"Not exactly what I expected. You're the only cowboy in sight."

"I'm not a cowboy, Liv." Connor glanced at her. "Besides, I haven't been on a cattle drive in years."

She studied him from head to toe. "But you're wearing the outfit."

Connor sighed wearily. "Ladies wear outfits. Cowboys wear clothes. They don't wear outfits. And even if they did, it wouldn't be like this."

"I've seen clothes like yours before. What's it called again?"

"Buckskin."

Livvie nodded. "Yes, buckskin. I saw it in a Wild West show several years ago. The Fathers took us to Chicago. They had a personal invitation from William Cody and—"

"Your fathers know Buffalo Bill?"

Livvie laughed. "Oh, yes, my parents seem to know everyone. William Cody is a very talented performer."

"Jesus, Liv, Cody's not a performer. He's Buffalo Bill for Christ's sake, a real honest to goodness—"

Livvie waved her hand. "Yes, I heard he had some history in the west, but he's a performer now. The show was very exciting— Indians, stagecoaches, gunfire, target shooting, pony tricks. I got to meet Wild Bill Hickok too." She studied his clothing again. "A lot of the players wore clothing like yours. I thought everyone in the west dressed like that, so I'm rather disappointed to see they wear the same old boring clothing everyone else wears. Except for you. Have you been in a Wild West show?"

"No, Livvie, I've never been in a Wild West show. These clothes are good for traveling, especially on horseback. Des and I don't always have the luxury of traveling by train."

"Hmm, I suppose not."

"And what do you call that outfit you're wearing?" He fingered the collar of her jacket.

"My traveling suit? It's the latest design. The fabric is silk brocade. Do you like it?"

"It's soft and silky…kind of like you, and it feels expensive."

Livvie laughed. "Oh, it was. Cutter almost had a heart attack when he saw the bill. I like to look nice, even if I don't always feel comfortable." She glanced up and down the street. "I'm sorry to say though I feel woefully over-dressed…and incredibly warm."

Connor gave her a wink. "But fashionable."

"I'm going to have to learn to fit in here. At least we have a few days to adjust to Kansas life before I'm teaching the tots of this town. This place is a lot smaller than Maysville, and slightly more primitive, but it has potential. Except for the streets." She waved her hand as a cloud of dust moved toward them, stirred up by several horses being led from the train to the livery.

The train station had been busy. Several other passengers had disembarked and the platform rang with the clatter of sliding doors and the bump of crates as the railroad workers unloaded the train to the waiting suppliers. Once they crossed the street, it had become practically deserted.

"How many people live here do you think?" Livvie asked.

"From the looks of things, a shopkeeper and a couple of kids."

He nodded toward three children—two boys and a girl—who tossed a ball back and forth in the street in front of the dry goods store, where a middle-aged man swept the dusty sidewalk. Livvie pulled down the collar of her dress as sweat dripped down her neck.

Connor laughed suddenly and it was music to her ears. "Oh, and don't forget the drunks."

The doors of the Prairie Schooner had swung open with a bang and two men staggered into the sunlight, shielding their eyes against the sudden glare. They swayed slightly then began the tortuous twenty paces down the wooden walk to the Grasslands Saloon. They disappeared inside, leaving more dust in their wake.

"Which do you think you'll like best?" Livvie asked. "The Schooner or the Grasslands?"

Connor tweaked her chin. "Wouldn't be much of a husband if I frequented either one. Desmond and I don't drink much, Liv, so there's no need to worry."

Despite the heat, Livvie tucked her arm through his and cuddled for a minute. "I wasn't worried." Her gaze strayed down the street to a larger three-story clapboard building. A wide awning, its bright green color a shadow of its former dust-free self, shaded the front door. "Do you think the hotel serves meals this time of day? I know we just had lunch, but I'm starving. I'd love some pie."

After arranging for the wagon to be harnessed and the baggage to be loaded, Connor and Livvie headed toward the Brandywine Hotel, hoping for a big slice of peach pie.

Chapter 6

Livvie's heart sank deeper and deeper as they traveled across several miles of dusty prairie, struggling to find landmarks in the blazing sun. She began to feel as though her eyelids had melted off her face because even closing her eyes brought no relief. Connor glanced at her several times and finally said, "You're going to burn alive out here with that hat. Take it off."

She struggled with the pins then tossed her hat into the wagon behind her. The hat was stylish and pretty but she hated it anyway and other than a couple cows they'd passed, there was no one to impress in the seemingly empty landscape that called itself Kansas. Connor pulled his hat off his head and slammed it onto hers where it slipped down to her nose. For one moment, she felt a blessed relief. Unfortunately, she realized she couldn't see a damned thing but her own lap when he said, "Let me know if you see any kind of boulder. That's where the path to the ranch is."

"The path?" Livvie asked. "This entire state seems to be one giant path. Don't they have any roads out here?"

"We're *on* the road," Connor said.

As a windmill came into view, they began to search for the boulder. When Livvie saw a small rock sitting next to a fence post Connor turned the wagon onto another expanse of nothingness. How he thought the rutted overgrown patch of brush offered a pathway was beyond her comprehension. The wagon clamored over rubble and rocks, and dipped and swayed unsteadily into holes and over prairie dog mounds. Livvie's teeth clacked together and her spine felt like it had twisted into a spiral.

Gradually the property came into view. Though everything was neat, tidy, and looked relatively prosperous in this expanse of ever-loving Kansas, it also looked parched, grizzled and in desperate need of a good rainstorm. A two-story clapboard house stood in a rather parched looking patch of grass surrounded by various outbuildings—a small barn, an icehouse, a small dugout which was probably a root cellar and off in the distance another larger barn. The windmill circled lazily in the back yard.

But Livvie loved the house. It had a wide shady porch that stretched around two sides and a small kitchen addition tucked off to the side. A smaller porch off the kitchen opened to a fenced area housing a garden plot, filled with an array of ready-to-harvest vegetables. Livvie felt sticky, sweaty, and dust-ridden and couldn't wait to get into the shade of the house. She practically flew up the porch stairs and waited impatiently while Connor moved like a snail behind her. But when Connor opened the door he swept her up in his arms like a bride, letting out a joyous whoop, and carried her over the threshold. She giggled and decided to enjoy their little play-acting though she doubted the prairie dogs at Old Man Carpenter's homestead would care one way or another.

He swung her in a circle and the parlor flew by her tired eyes in a blur, and the hat sailed to the floor. Before he put her down, he kissed her softly and deeply. His tongue played with her lips, explored the inside of her mouth, and stole what little breath she had left. Her arms wound around his neck, tugging him closer, as her fingers slid into the hair at the nape of his neck. Reluctant to release her, he pressed gentle kisses across her cheeks, then her mouth again before he set her back on the floor. But his arms stayed locked around her. She lifted her face, and Livvie thought she might truly hate Kansas. The smile had left Connor McBride's face.

"I shouldn't have done that," he said.

"Why not?"

He dropped his arms and took a step back, shaking his head. "You're not my wife, Liv. After the last few days, I kind of forgot that. I'll get the luggage and see to the horse. You look around."

He retrieved his hat from the floor and left her standing in the middle of the parlor staring at his back as he strode through the open door. Livvie brushed her hair back from her sweaty face and frowned.

"I want that smile back and I'm going to get it. In the meantime…"

She whirled around, inspected her surroundings, and found everything cozy and comfortable. Clean rag rugs dotted the hardwood floor and a narrow staircase led to the upper floor. A small piano, its top littered with music books, sat tucked beneath the stairs. An archway led into a bright airy dining room and a swinging door opened into the kitchen where she found a large stocked pantry. A pie safe stood in the corner holding freshly baked apple and cherry pies.

"Yum." She owed Anna a very large thank you. Everything in the house was clean, dust-free, and seemed to offer everything they could need or want.

Upstairs were three bedrooms. One had a dressing table so she selected that one. It faced the front of the house and when she swept aside the gauzy linen curtains, she saw Connor unloading the trunks and bags. She carried her train case and overnight bag upstairs to start unpacking. She also planned to see how much Kansas dust she could scrape from her skin.

* * * *

"You're cooking?" Livvie asked.

Connor chuckled but continued to slice the potatoes, his hand guiding the knife smoothly over the wooden cutting board. A large pile of potato chunks and diced onion lay beside him. Livvie knew she would have cut off three fingers by now. He glanced at her as he scooped the vegetables up and dumped them into a pot.

Livvie's hand fluttered over the table. "You don't want *me* to cook dinner?"

His brow rose. "Do you know how?"

She grabbed a towel and swiped it across the clean side of the worktable, refusing to look at him. "No, not really."

"Didn't think so."

She slammed a hand on her hip. "What does that mean exactly?"

He reached for a carrot and began to chop. "It means I listened to all your stories on the train. You're upper class, Livvie. I'm not sure how much money your family has but obviously, it's a *lot*. A girl like you, well, let's just say it's doubtful you've learned to cook."

She leaned across the table and ducked her head to peer into his face. A smirk sat there, waiting to turn into a laugh. "Are you saying I've been spoiled?"

The knife hit the cutting board with a clunk and stopped. Livvie watched a piece of carrot roll to the edge of the table where it whirled then fell flat.

"I guess I am," Connor said.

He continued to chop.

"Fine." She spun on her heels, went to the pantry and manhandled a sack of flour into the kitchen. She dropped it on the table and a cloud of white powder enveloped her. Connor waved his hand in front of his face, making exaggerated choking noises.

"You don't need to prove anything here, Liv."

"Oh yes. I really do."

"Don't do us any favors," Connor muttered.

"Just make the stew," Livvie snapped. "I'll do the biscuits."

Some kind of look settled on his face. It seemed the kind of look you'd give to someone who'd just proclaimed they intended to swim the entire length of the Ohio. Livvie didn't like it one bit.

She stood undecided for a moment, trying to remember what Glory had done when she'd made biscuits. Livvie'd sat in the kitchen often enough, her body perched on a stool kept there just for her, leaning over the table as Glory worked. Livvie chatted about her day, her lessons, her interests, her fights with her brother and sister, keeping the old woman company while she whipped up wonderful meals.

Glory's husband Rob often lingered nearby, shucking peas or chopping vegetables, listening in his quiet way as they talked. Livvie had always enjoyed the old woman's company as much as she'd loved the smells and tastes in the kitchen at Riverbend. She wished Glory was here with her now.

She went through the motions she remembered. Connor glanced at her from time to time but finished the stew preparations quietly and finally set the pot on the stove to cook. With one final, almost condemning, look at her floured hands and the mess she'd made on the table, he shook his head and stepped toward the kitchen door.

"Give it a stir every now and then. I'll be busy for awhile."

She nodded curtly and pushed tendrils of hair away from her forehead with the back of her hand.

"You'll be sorry you said I'm spoiled, Connor McBride."

* * * *

Dusk had begun to settle over their new homestead. She knew that because she'd been forced to light a few of the lamps and had looked out the window a hundred times. She'd watched the sky darken from shades of blue and lavender to indigo. Finally the door in the kitchen opened, and she heard the sound of boots clomping on the hardwood floor.

In the parlor, Livvie leapt to her feet and quickly tucked the book she'd been holding back onto the shelf. She hadn't read a word and had no idea of the title. She'd simply flipped through the pages, watched the clock and wondered where Connor had gone and where Desmond had been. It seemed important for her peace of mind that she occupy herself in a more constructive way than pacing. She'd spent a good twenty minutes doing that after her biscuits were ready for the oven.

She careened through the dining room and shoved open the swinging door, catching herself on the doorjamb. The men stood at the sink, pumping water. They both glanced toward her. She straightened up, adjusted her apron, and darted forward when the swinging door nearly clipped her shoulder.

"I'll get the biscuits in the oven," she said.

Desmond gave Connor a funny look. Connor returned it with one of his own then went to the stove. He lifted the lid and peeked into the pot. A cloud of steam and smoke filled the corner of the kitchen. He jerked back and grabbed a wooden spoon from a nearby Mason jar. He began to scrape the inside of the pot.

"Um, Liv, how often did you stir this?"

She whirled around with the tray of biscuits in her hand. "Oops."

Desmond filled a jar with water and poured into the pot. Connor stirred the concoction like a witch at a cauldron and Livvie wondered if they had some kind of psychic connection. Desmond tossed himself into one of the chairs, stretching out his long legs, blocking her path. She stood there for a moment but Desmond didn't move.

"Excuse me." She stepped over his legs and moved toward the stove where Connor blocked the oven door. "Excuse me."

When he didn't move, she nudged her hip against him. Connor lurched backward like he'd been scalded. Juices from the spoon splattered on the floor.

"Damn it!" Connor said.

While he grabbed a towel to clean up the mess Livvie slid her tray of biscuits into the oven. After slamming the oven door, she plopped into a chair and folded her hands on the table. Desmond nodded toward the stove.

"Aren't you going to adjust the heat?"

"Do what?" Livvie slowly rose her feet. "Of course I'm going to adjust the heat." She swished her skirts around the other edge of the table, avoiding his legs entirely, and marched to the stove. Then she just stood there, staring at the oven door. Desmond burst out laughing.

"I'll do it," Connor said, putting the lid on his pot. "Sit down."

Heat enveloped her face, and though the stove gave off plenty of heat, it certainly wasn't the cause of the blush she knew stained her face. She shoved her hands into the apron pockets and watched as Connor did something with the stove. She'd never remember it.

She turned to Desmond with a smile. "There's pie for dessert. Apple or cherry. I'm not sure where it came from but it's in the pie safe. Connor and I had peach pie this afternoon at the hotel and some of the most delicious coffee I've ever had. Glory makes excellent coffee but there was something really tasty about the coffee at the Brandywine and—"

Desmond stared at her as though all of her words had been in a foreign language. He drummed his fingers on the table.

She tilted her head and stood still, though her hands clenched inside the pockets. "What?"

Desmond cast a quick glance toward Connor, who leaned against the sink. "So...you and Connor had fun today?"

"Well, of course, we did." Her face pivoted toward Connor. She felt like she'd been pushed through the looking glass like Alice in a story she'd once read. Everything seemed like it had turned upside down. "We *did* have fun, didn't we?"

Connor nodded. "Sure."

Her heart started to hammer. She did not understand any of this. Neither man had smiled since they walked through the door. She knew she lacked domestic skills. And, okay, maybe she'd been spoiled, but it certainly wasn't her fault, and she hadn't asked to be spoiled. And she was *trying*, damn it. She thought she should at least get some credit for that.

She wanted a drink of water but Connor blocked her way to the sink. Damn these men. They seemed to be everywhere. She'd never felt so trapped in her entire life. And they wouldn't even smile at her.

"The Brandywine has a nice restaurant." She busied herself walking back and forth to the pantry to collect bowls, plates, and spoons, talking to anyone who wanted to listen. "I looked at their daily menu and they had some very appealing items—beef roast, ham steaks, chops, all kinds of things. They even have ice cream on occasion though the owner, Mr. Mercer, couldn't guarantee when that would be. I thought maybe when we go into town for my meeting with Anna we could spend the afternoon, do some shopping, and have dinner there. My treat, of course. And—"

"We both won't be going with you," Connor said.

She put the spoons on the table and fiddled with them for a moment, laying them out in a straight line. "Oh. I forgot." She scooped them back up in her hand and dropped them into an untidy pile.

"You and Des can go though," Connor said. "Since I've been and all."

She sighed and said softly, "It wouldn't really be fair. I mean it's *dinner*." She grabbed some napkins from the pantry and placed them on the table. Earlier today, the napkins would have made her laugh but for some reason she didn't feel like laughing at all now. She sniffed and smelled something burning. She glanced around and Desmond nodded toward the stove.

"Damn it!"

She scurried across the room and yanked open the oven door. As she reached toward it, both men screamed, "Don't touch it!"

The sound of a chair screeching against wood filled the room and, combined with the shouts, made her wince. She snatched her hand back, her heart hammering with her own stupidity. Connor reached around her with a towel and pulled the burned biscuits from the oven. Desmond was at her side in an instant, grabbing her wrists and inspecting her palms.

"I didn't touch it," she murmured. "I'm fine."

Connor set the hot tray on top of the stove and the oven door slammed closed. She pulled her wrists out of Desmond's hands and backed away. Connor lifted a burned hunk of hard dough and hit it against the stove. It made the sound of a rock striking metal.

"They wouldn't have been very good anyway," Livvie murmured.

"We can try them," Connor said. "Maybe after a good soak in the stew..."

Livvie backed toward the swinging door. "No, don't bother."

As she pushed on the door, Desmond said, "Where are you going, Liv?"

She shook her head. "I'm not very hungry. I-I'll see you in the morning."

She turned and fled.

Chapter 7

Connor dumped the bowls into the soapy water while Desmond poured them coffee. Des wasn't too worried about drinking coffee this late at night. He doubted he'd sleep much anyway.

"She seems jumpy again," Desmond said. "What happened today?"

"No more than I've already told you."

"You neglected to tell me about the peach pie."

Connor waved his soapy hand. "It didn't seem all that important."

"So what else didn't seem important?"

Connor glanced over his shoulder. "Nothing else happened, Des. I'm not sure what all she did while I was outside, but I'm sure as hell no one was here."

"This could get bad, Connor. After talking with Anna today, I realized we've got to play this exactly right. They sure as fuck didn't do Livvie any favors here. This town's in the middle of a hornet's nest and they've shoved her into godforsaken fucking nowhere."

"We've been in godforsaken fucking nowhere before, Des. Plenty of times. Piece of cake."

"Jesus, Connor, I'm not thinking of us. This is practically paradise for us. But that little woman hasn't gone much beyond her beloved Riverbend without the watchful eyes of those fathers of hers. What the hell is that about anyway? That whole thing had me confused."

"Apparently she has two fathers."

Des put the coffee mugs on the table. "She talks about it like it's the most normal thing in the world. How she'd get so fucking lucky? We couldn't even manage to get *one* between us."

Connor wiped a bowl and laid it on the table. "Our pa didn't ask to die. You need to stop blaming him."

"Well, he sure as hell wasn't using his brain on the day he joined up, leaving Ma alone with two newborn babes. Who does that to a woman?"

"Most men did at the time, Des. It was a war."

"Stop being so goddamn logical. You know it annoys the hell out of me."

"It's the subject that annoys the hell out of you, not the logic. You run circles around my logic." Connor finished with the dishes and wiped down the table. He picked up his mug and peered over the edge. "So what exactly did Anna tell you?"

"Sit down and have some coffee first. You're going to need it." He glanced around the room. "Where's the pie? What the hell is a pie safe anyway? That girl speaks a foreign language sometimes."

"I'll get it," Connor said.

Connor moved to a small cabinet near the washroom door. Desmond stared into his coffee mug for a minute, allowing his brother a few more moments of precious sanity before unleashing the panic he knew would follow. Desmond wondered what decision they would have made had they known the entire situation going in.

Connor slapped forks and two plates on the table. One held apple, one cherry. "Take your pick."

Desmond pulled the cherry pie toward him while Connor slid into a chair on the other side of the table. He shoveled a forkful of apple pie into his mouth, talking while he chewed.

"How'd you manage to stay in a good mood the entire time on that train? I swear it was like being with a different man."

Desmond dissected his pie, pulling out bits of cherry and smashing them. He ground the crust into powder with the edge of his fork.

"You going to eat that or mangle it?"

Desmond picked up a plump, dripping cherry and flung it at his brother. Connor laughed, scooping it off his shirt and licking his finger.

"Tasty, but not quite as tasty as Ma's," Connor said. "Livvie's good for you, you know. She's good for me, too. But she's especially good for you. Isn't she the most adorable thing you've ever seen?"

Desmond grunted. "Hmph. That's a bit of a problem, too."

"I don't see where there's much of a problem. Livvie's bound to like one of us more than the other...eventually. It's entirely her decision. If she wants to fuck me, I'm certainly more than willing."

"Nobody's fucking anybody," Desmond said.

"Hasn't truly been decided yet, now has it?" Connor pushed his plate away. "Anyway, she might like you best."

"Doubtful."

"Don't be so glum, little brother. With any luck, she'll like us both the same."

Desmond fell back into his chair. "Now how would that benefit either of us?"

Connor winked. "She has two dads, Des. There has to be some sort of reason for that."

Desmond scratched at the growth of beard on his jaw. It definitely had to go soon. It itched like crazy. "Maybe, but there's not going to be a lot of time to think of fucking, or anything else for that matter."

Connor folded his arms on the table. "So tell me."

"There was another man here before us, name of Skylar."

"And?"

Desmond ran his finger over the edge of his fork then stuck his finger in his mouth. The pie was pretty tasty. He took a bite of mashed cherry. "Skylar was sent out to investigate claims concerning runaways. Apparently a lot of boys had been running away—more so than in any other area—and all between the ages of twelve and sixteen."

"So? It happens. Kids get it in their heads things are better down the road and usually they are. We ran away. For damn good reasons."

"These boys all came from the same ranch here in the Fort Cloud area."

"Oh, well, that's not so good."

"No, it isn't," Desmond said. "Skylar came to Fort Cloud earlier this year, settled in downtown at the hotel and began to ask his questions. Anna wasn't involved at that point. He was to report back to a man in Concordia, where the orphan train makes its first stop in Kansas. Anna didn't even know he was investigating until he showed up on her doorstep one afternoon asking questions. He knew she kept in touch with most of the townsfolk in one way or another. Skylar'd been here several weeks by then and had already spoken with half the town."

"I take it he stirred something up?"

"Stirred things up enough to get himself killed."

"Christ." Connor ran his hand over his mouth, rubbing hard. "How did it happen?"

"It wasn't as simple as your basic shot to the head. That would have aroused suspicion. They found him in back of one of the saloons beaten to a bloody pulp. He lasted a couple hours, but never regained consciousness. Witnesses said nothing unusual had happened that night. Just a regular night of card playing and carousing. Of course some of the witnesses knew some of the people he'd been questioning."

"So, what's Anna's take on all this?"

"She's positive the killer was either an Anthony Pack or a Robinson Booker. They own a ranch north of town. Apparently Pack does most of the day-to-day operation because Booker is rarely around. They've indentured boys throughout the last year to work with their herds. The majority of them have eventually gone missing and the magic number comes to eleven. Want to guess what their ages are?"

Connor heaved a sigh.

"There's been one other runaway in this district recently that Anna knows of but she doesn't know if he's part of this. After speaking with some people in town, she feels it was abuse and was sorry she hadn't known of it sooner."

"The world could use a lot more people like her," Connor said.

"Sure could. It might have saved us a world of hurt."

"I don't like it," Connor said. "They send an actual investigator who manages to get himself killed. That didn't work. So they're apparently trying another tactic now."

"Gotta give them credit for originality. Who'd suspect the new school teacher of being an agent for child welfare?"

"I hope no one," Connor said, "but they've put her in a world of danger, and we don't know if we can keep her safe. Skylar could have been killed by anyone. And it's going to take some time to get enough evidence to bring either or both of these men in. That means anyone who approaches her is a danger. How are we going—?"

Desmond sighed. "I know, Connor. I've been thinking of that all afternoon. Skylar told Anna he planned to send a telegram to his contact in Concordia but when he turned up dead that night she checked with the operator and he remembered nothing concerning Skylar. Apparently he never got the chance to send the message. That's when Anna stepped in and contacted Concordia herself. Livvie has no idea what she's signed up for and neither did we. Mrs. Harrison sure as hell should have told us this."

"She told us Livvie could be in danger, Des. She was very firm about that which is why they wanted two agents with her."

Desmond spread his hands. "I know, but a man died here. Anyone who'd kill a government agent doing an investigation isn't going to think twice about making a young woman disappear permanently. No matter what her connections are. We have no idea what Skylar discovered, how close he was, nothing."

"How did Concordia react when Anna approached them?"

"Very concerned," Desmond said. "The head of the agency contacted their Washington bureau immediately, and that's how Mrs. Harrison became involved and why Anna was chosen as our contact."

"So what do we do now?" Connor said.

"Anna was very clear she didn't want Livvie to know about the murder. She feels it might cause Livvie to falter, make a mistake. I'm not sure I agree with that line of thinking, but I said I'd keep it quiet for now. But we do need to ask Livvie some questions, find out what she can do and what she can't."

Connor shook his head slowly. "We already know she can't cook or anything like that. And she can't teach and knows nothing about kids. I know she can ride a horse." He rolled his eyes. "I heard enough Stardust stories to know that, but I think that's about it. She's going to stick out like a sore thumb in this town in her pretty little silk brocade dresses and feathery hats. She doesn't seem to have any of the skills necessary to survive in a place like this or for an assignment of this magnitude."

"That might have been part of the reasoning behind all this."

"To put her out in plain sight? Helpless, hopeless?"

"Does she look like she'd be a threat to *you*?"

"Hell no. And that mouth of hers—"

"Could work to our advantage. She's a little butterfly, Connor, flitting around, spreading joy and happiness. People adore her. You saw her on the train. She made friends with everyone by the end of the first day. I don't know about you but she was running me ragged. She's a rare thing, Connor. She looks like she hasn't had a bad day in her life."

"Until today."

"Yeah," Desmond said. "Until today. I hated that look on her face. We'll make it up to her."

"You can take her out to dinner at the hotel. She'd like that."

"Oh, no, I—"

Connor shrugged. "It's only fair, Des. I got her today." He smiled slightly and Des let it go. He knew what an afternoon in Livvie's presence could do to a man. "So I guess tomorrow we'll be playing inquisition with Little Miss Butterfly. Got some questions on your mind?"

"Yes, I do. But I also want to know about these fathers she keeps talking about."

* * * *

Desmond plodded up the stairs. He needed to sleep and he needed to do it bad. *Good luck with that, Des.*

He glanced inside the two open bedroom doors and saw both beds had leather bags thrown onto them, neither of them unpacked. He had no idea which room was his. He'd wait to see which one Connor went into.

He tapped on the closed bedroom door. "Liv?"

"Come in."

He opened the door and peeked inside. She glanced up, those green eyes boring into him as her brows rose. She sat at the dressing table in a dark green silky robe, holding a pen poised over a sheet of pink stationery.

"Did you want something, Des?"

He couldn't think of a thing to say. He'd forgotten why he'd even knocked in the first place. She continued to gaze at him. Her hair tumbled over her shoulders in curly disarray. Though she'd worn quite a collection of traveling clothes, all in the latest fashion, and her hair was always done in the current style, she'd never looked prettier. Well, except maybe for that night he'd watched her in the window of the Willard Hotel. That had been something else.

She looked beautiful in green. It made her eyes bright and shining. They sparkled in the glow of the flickering lamp on her dressing table. But he also knew what lay under that robe. He'd never forget that. It had been on his mind ever since the Willard. She had apparently put it far from her own and forgotten all about it.

His cock twitched as he peeked in the couple of inches of open space and stood there like a dunce. His cock worked far better than his brain sometimes.

"I just came up to see if you're settled in, how you're feeling. If you're hungry, there's plenty of food left in—"

"No, I'm fine, but thanks." She glanced down at the piece of paper on the dressing table, touched it gently as though trying to decide what to say then laid down her pen. She looked back at him and smiled. "Come in for a minute, Des."

He heard Connor coming up the stairs so he stepped inside. He wasn't sure why. But it seemed important. He nodded toward the piece of paper. "I didn't mean to disturb you."

"You're not disturbing me at all. I'm just writing to my mother, trying to explain an almost impossible situation." Livvie laughed and shook her head. Desmond couldn't take his eyes off the dark curls bouncing on her shoulder. "Mother will think I've positively lost my mind—in more ways than one."

She studied him for a minute and stood up. The robe gaped a little bit in the front. For the first time in nearly a week, he saw the valley between her breasts. He wanted to plunge his face in that soft warm haven and surround himself in the lure of her flesh. He wanted to breathe in her warmth and the sweet heady scent that came from her. He'd wanted her from his first glance. When did he ever gotten anything he wanted?

"But you, Des… I don't think you've ever come close to losing your mind, have you? You're always in control."

"Not always."

"You're in control right now, aren't you?"

He didn't know how to answer that so he kept his mouth closed. His cock sure didn't think he was in control. It wanted the girl. He heard a door down the hall close with a soft click. Livvie continued to glide toward him, and if she came much closer, he'd have to bolt. But when she got close enough to touch him he just stood there, anchored to the ground like a tree waiting for the sun to rise.

She placed her hands on his chest. The shock of it caused his heart to lurch. She leaned toward him, straining on tiptoes. He angled his head downward and her lips pressed against his ear.

"I know it was you, Des."

Her words almost made him jump away, but he stood his ground because this was the only chance he'd get. He knew that. If he botched this up, it was over for him. Connor would get the girl. Not that he minded Connor being happy because he didn't. But fuck, he deserved something every now and then, didn't he?

His lip twitched. "What did I supposedly do now?"

"You watched me."

"You watched me first." He smiled. "What makes you think it was me?"

She laughed softly. "Who else would know I watched you first, Des?"

He closed his eyes for a moment at his own stupidity. He needed to get focused. He couldn't afford to lose it now. "So how did you figure it out?"

"It took a few days. But ultimately it was in the way you move, the way you kissed me at the train station, the way you look at me when you think I'm not watching. Everything about you."

"And?"

"And I've decided you'll never make the first move. Maybe because of Connor, maybe because of something inside you. I don't know. But it doesn't matter." His heart stuttered as her arms moved up his chest and her fingers curled into his shoulders. "Kiss me like you kissed that woman, Des. I want to feel the heat, the fire I saw that night."

He crushed her against him. His mouth found hers faster than any target he'd ever aimed for in his life. Another woman's lips had never felt as silky or as tasty as hers. Her mouth scorched him, burning with the same hunger he felt for her. He tasted every inch of her lips, the soft flesh inside her mouth. He slid his tongue over her teeth, pressed hot searing kisses into the corners of her lips. When his mouth returned to hers, her tongue swept into his mouth and she did the same to him, consuming him.

His cock grew, pressing into her body, and his balls ached. Heat poured through their clothing and the musky scene of her arousal enveloped him in an intoxicating aura. It filled his head and nearly stole his reason. She made a small noise and he dipped his head, sucking on the flesh of her neck, dropping more kisses over her throat. He nosed away the fabric of her robe and took small nips at the flesh of her shoulder. Her head fell back and he pressed kisses along her jaw. Her hips angled toward him, shoving against him, burning him with her heat.

Her nipples swelled between them. Even through his shirt, he felt the hard peaks nudge against him. His hand swept up from her waist and cupped the underside of her breast, feeling the tight fullness of it in his hand. It wasn't enough. He needed to feel her bare skin. He tugged at her robe and it slipped farther, allowing his hand contact with her skin. He held in a groan as his hand curled around her breast, kneading, rolling her nipples, causing her to arch against him, but still it wasn't enough. He wanted to taste her.

He lowered his head, determined to suck on her. His lips locked on her breast and she sighed, a sound of quiet ecstasy. He sucked harder, drawing more of her breast into his mouth, tasting the perfection of her skin.

He pushed his hand between her thighs. Without hesitation, she opened them wider, leaning against him, so close. She was so wet. He could have slipped his finger into her, but there was something he wanted more. He dropped to his knees and her hands tightened on his shoulders.

"I want to put my mouth on you, Liv. Taste your pussy, lick your clit."

"Oh, Des…yes, please…"

He touched her clit with his tongue and she lurched forward, her body shuddering. She clutched at his hair. He dipped his face lower, his tongue tracing her pussy lips and sliding between them for a taste. She tasted wonderful. The cream of her body burst onto his tongue and he ached to push farther inside but she needed time to adjust to the new sensation. The way her body shook and the fierce grip she had on his hair told him she'd never been tasted before. He forced himself to take it slow even as his cock insisted on burying itself in that wet warmth.

He cast a quick glance toward her face. She gazed down at him, her eyes half-closed but glimmering with curiosity and a dreamy lust-filled glaze. Her lips parted. He lapped at her pussy, his tongue stroking hard and tight, licking every drop from her damp skin. Her clit swelled and pulsed under his tongue, and he wrapped his mouth around it and began to suck, enjoying the shivers racing through her pelvis and the small startled gasp that escaped her lips.

"Oh God, Des, don't stop," she whispered.

He sucked harder and her body stiffened for a moment. He slid his hands around her, grabbing her ass and pulling her tighter. She sagged against him and her head dropped downward. A curtain of hair fell around his face.

"For fuck's sake, Des, say goodnight and get to bed!"

Livvie's body tensed under his hands and she jerked upright. She uttered some kind of strangled cry.

Connor's voice trailed down the hall punctuated by the stomping of feet. "All I did was fucking kiss her. Bastard." A door slammed.

Livvie's hands curled into his hair, making fists. Her voice was a croaking whisper. "Was he watching us?"

Desmond glanced toward the open door. "I don't know." He turned back toward her, dropping his forehead against the warmth of her hip. He felt like shit. "Probably."

Livvie combed his hair away from his face then cupped his cheeks. She bent down and ran her nails lightly across his whiskers, then dropped a kiss on his lips. She took a step backward and pulled her robe together.

"We should say goodnight."

He stood up and looked down at her. Her flushed face said more than she could ever say in words. He cupped her face and leaned down, kissing her mouth, a soft, thorough, gentle kiss. Livvie swayed closer, but he released her.

"Goodnight, Liv."

"Goodnight, Des." A smile flickered on her lips and those sparkling eyes held a dreamy quality. "That was better than I ever hoped it would be."

"Yes, it was." His gaze dropped down her body as he remembered her face in the window of the Willard. It couldn't compare to the one he saw before him now. "You plan to finish what we started here?"

"You can count on it."

"Damn. How will I sleep with that image in my head?" He tweaked the collar of her robe and smiled. "The pink one was pretty, but I think I like this one better."

Desmond walked into the hallway and shut the door behind him. He closed his eyes, leaning back against it for a moment then strode down the hall to the only open door.

Chapter 8

"Thanks for leaving me breakfast."

Desmond's voice infiltrated Connor's wayward thoughts. When he turned, Desmond held two hunks of bread filled with eggs and bacon and had taken a huge bite. He sat two coffee mugs down on the railing.

"You're welcome." Connor jammed the pitchfork into the bale of hay and tossed it into the stall. "Someone has to feed your sorry ass. But the offer's off. If you think I'm going to stand aside and let you spend an evening with Livvie *and* get a beef roast in a hotel dining room, you're crazy. Now get the hell out of my barn."

He glanced over his shoulder to see his brother lean against the center post of the barn. He rolled his eyes with a grumpy noise. It looked like Desmond wasn't going to leave any time soon. Des waved his sandwich in the air.

"Your barn, your animals, your kitchen. Anything else you want to claim?"

"Nope. That just about covers it. Seems to me you've claimed the rest." Connor rammed the pitchfork harder, tossing the bale. It thumped against the back wall of the stall.

"I haven't claimed anything."

"The fuck you haven't." He speared the fork into a bale and leaned against it, turning to glare at his brother. "I will never get that sight out of my head."

"You shouldn't have been watching."

"Fuck you, Des." He strode across the barn, the sound of his boots punctuating the feelings roiling in his gut. He knew there'd be a chance Livvie would choose Desmond, but it still rankled his ass. He'd never thought it would happen so soon. Or really at all. He wondered at the incongruity of it at all. Desmond rarely made a move toward a woman. Connor always got the girl. Always. He flung open the double doors, swinging them wide. Hot sunlight flooded the interior. He hung his head for a moment, scratching the stubble across his jaw. "So how'd you do it?"

He turned to find Desmond standing behind him. Connor took the coffee mug he held out.

"I didn't do anything," Desmond said. "She did."

"You can't blame this on her. I saw you down on your knees with your mouth on her pussy. She was just standing there…standing there with such a look on her face. As though she'd died and stood at the pearly gates. I swear, Des, I think I could have killed you last night out of sheer envy." Connor shook his head. "I've never seen a look like that on a woman's face before. I went to bed with a rock hard cock. I couldn't even bring myself to touch it after what I saw."

Desmond took another bite of his sandwich and shrugged. "Not my problem you can't touch your own dick. You could have—"

"I can touch my own dick, you bastard. I can touch it plenty. But it's not the same and you damn well know it. So. You got a taste of that delicious pussy, and I'm apparently shit out of luck. What did she supposedly do?"

Desmond sat down on a bale of hay and told the story of the Willard Hotel. Connor listened, his jaw dropping at various points in Desmond's tale.

"You mean if I'd have chosen the blonde in Washington it could have been me last night?"

"Probably," Desmond said.

"Christ, how'd you get so lucky?"

"You insisted on the redhead, Connor. Maybe next time I should get first dibs."

"Fuck that. I'm older than you are." Connor's gaze shot toward the house. With any luck their future might not include fighting over whores. Man, that look on Livvie's face—dreamy, filled with pleasure. Her sighs had filled his ears and he'd have given anything to be the one to feel her body tremble. She'd liked it. She'd liked it a lot. But she had a wonderful innocence about her. He'd love to teach her all he knew.

"How long are you going to hold that five minute jump over my head?"

Connor shook off Livvie-thoughts and chuckled. "I'll always be older, Des."

"I tried to kick you out of my way but you wouldn't move your stubborn infantile ass. Must be some flaw inside that causes this incredible need to be first in everything."

Connor dropped down on a nest of hay and laughed. "Nope. Nothing wrong with me, Des. I just like to be first. Less messes to clean up that way."

Desmond didn't laugh. He sat, dangling the empty coffee cup between his thighs. "You're good at cleaning up messes, Connor. Right good."

Connor knew his brother's thoughts like the back of his own hand because they almost always mirrored his own. "Stop thinking of that, Des. It's been nearly twenty years."

Des glanced up, his eyes shadowed by a fall of hair. "It still hurts."

"Well, hell yes, it hurts. It's going to hurt forever."

"I wouldn't be here if—"

"Stop that, Des."

"If it weren't for you."

Connor fell back on the hay and twined his hands beneath his head. Jesus. He didn't want Desmond to be thinking of that night again. For one thing, they couldn't afford to be preoccupied with personal shit right now. The mission was too important and they had to concentrate and be focused on Livvie's safety. For another thing, he hated to watch those gruesome stories suck the life out of his brother.

Desmond's quiet voice fell over him. "If you hadn't found me that night I would be dead."

Connor felt the hay shift as Desmond lay down beside him. When he glanced over, Desmond had his hands behind his head and stared at the rafters above, squinting his eyes against the bands of light that filtered through the cracks.

"Lucas Price had just about beaten me dead," Desmond said. "I can still feel the pain sometimes in my bones. But somehow you managed to bring me back to life. You were fucking ten years old, Connor. Where did you find the strength to do that?"

Connor closed his eyes. "From you, Des. I got it from you."

It was the absolute worst night of Connor's life in a seemingly endless series of worst nights. They'd been separated for almost a year and that separation caused an ache in Connor's gut that never disappeared. He knew Des had felt the same. He didn't care how hard he had to work—he was used to that—and he didn't care how nasty or ill-tempered his foster parents were—he was used to that too—but the lack of Desmond's presence hurt something inside he could never explain to anyone. Not that he'd had anyone to really listen.

But they'd managed to see each other once a month, sneaking out and rendezvousing at a predetermined place, a small creek that held some sheltering trees and a tiny cave. There they'd start a small fire, share a bit of stolen food and just talk. They shared the horror stories of their beatings, the grueling labor, the constant hunger and planned for the day they could run away. The thought of true freedom never entered their heads. They just knew they had to be together because without the other they seemed only half a person. They needed to be whole.

But one night Desmond didn't come. Connor waited until the sun peaked over the horizon then hurried back to his cold pallet in that disgusting soddy on the plain. For four nights Connor made the trip to the cave, waiting and praying in his own way that Des was okay. On the fifth night, he couldn't take it any more. He followed the county road for miles and miles, trying desperately to remember what the Price house had looked like and hoping he'd be able to find it in the dark.

He found Desmond in the decaying barn, lying broken and battered on a bed of dirty hay. Dried blood covered every inch of his body. His eyes were swollen shut and Connor knew he had some broken bones. Hard bruised swellings covered several parts of his arm, stretching his skin tight. His body was so thin he looked like a strawboy covered in blood. Tears running down his cheeks, Connor had wrapped him in a ratty horse blanket and carried him away from that horrible barn miles and miles back to the cave. He spent the next several weeks stealing food from gardens and a bucket from a farmer's porch. He carried water from the stream and bathed his brother several times a day to bring down the fever that had settled in him.

During the third week, Desmond finally started to come back to life and after several more days they took off on their own, never looking back.

"Tell me a story about Ma, Connor."

"Sure. Which one do you want to hear?"

"The flower one," Desmond said.

Connor settled more comfortably in the straw. "I think we were about four, almost five maybe. We'd been out in the fields, catching frogs and hunting for bugs. We'd already caught a big fish for supper and knew Ma would be happy. But you wanted to make Ma's day even more special. Might have been 'cause we'd had such a special day ourselves."

"Wish I could remember that day," Desmond said.

"It was a great day. And that's why you wanted to take Ma some flowers. You picked a bunch of dandelions, tall ones with firm stems, really bright yellow. You held them in your hand like a king's treasure and right before we walked inside you hid them behind your back. When we walked into the house I handed Ma the fish and she smiled and thanked us, telling us what good fishermen we were. She plopped it down on the table and was getting ready to scale it when you pulled out your arm and held out the flowers."

"I wish I could remember that."

"Me, too, Des. 'Cause Ma laughed like those dandelions were the greatest present anyone could get. Then she started to cry and she pulled you to her in the biggest hug I've ever seen. She got a Mason jar, and put your flowers in the middle of the table. They sat there for days, and after that Ma called you her 'little bit of sunshine.' She always said it with a wink and smile."

"She was pretty special, wasn't she?" Desmond asked.

"Yes, Des, she was." Connor was quiet for a moment then turned his head and stared at his brother. "Why do you think you can't remember her, Des?"

Desmond blinked several times. Connor had to strain to hear his quiet voice though he could have reached out and touched him. "Not sure. Sometimes I think I had to let her go to make room for the hate."

Connor nodded. "I wish I could do something about that."

"You've done what you can," Desmond said, "more than you know. But I'm trying to push out the hate to make room for new memories."

"That's a start, Des." Connor sat up. "Let's go check on your latest. From what I heard that's one memory you'll want to keep for a lifetime."

Des joined Connor in a rare laugh on the way to the house and Connor thought that was an excellent start.

* * * *

By the time they got to the kitchen, they practically stumbled up the porch steps they laughed so hard. Connor could envision every move Livvie had made that night and wished to hell he'd been there. He envied Des all to hell and back. Lucky bastard.

Livvie was bent over the stove door, shoving in bits of twigs and sticks, barely enough to start a tiny spark let alone keep a stove fire going, but it was an excellent start too. She turned with a bright smile when they clomped inside.

"The fire was getting low. I added more wood."

Desmond said something about an old dog learning new tricks and Connor smiled, taking in her flushed face and the beautiful smile that adorned it, but his gaze was drawn to the table. A Mason jar stood in the center, filled to overflow with tall, bright yellow dandelions. Desmond hadn't noticed them yet. His brother's attention focused on the other bright object in the room—the ever bubbling Livvie Raines. Connor doubted anything could steal the happiness from her. Even now, she practically danced around the kitchen, moving to music he couldn't hear, as she washed up her breakfast plate, emptied her coffee cup, and delivered everything clean to the pantry. Her dress swayed with her movements, the curls on her back swinging. Damn he envied his brother. If he could just get a taste of this woman, he'd die a happy man.

"Thank you for leaving me breakfast," Livvie said.

As Livvie wiped down the sink, Connor's gaze lifted from her ass to meet the eyes peeking at him over her shoulder. "Sure thing." He glanced toward the table. "I see you've been exploring this morning."

"Oh, yes." She swung around to face them, her back to the sink. "I couldn't resist the sunshine. I didn't go far. I knew you'd worry. I just walked through the fields a little ways. I saw a couple bunnies, and I think I saw a fox, so we'll have to make sure the chickens stay safe. We have chickens, right? I thought I heard some. I'm hoping maybe this afternoon we can take out the horses, because I'd love to explore a little farther. I went as far as the creek off that way."

She gestured to the right then paused and glanced at the table.

"And there I found the funniest thing—a whole field of dandelions. Usually you can't find dandelions blooming this time of year. They've most often seeded by now and with this heat," she waved her hand in front of her face, "not to mention the blazing sun, they should really all be dead. But, I walked right into an entire field of them, like they'd been put there just for me. So I picked a bunch to bring home."

Connor pursed his lips and studied the dandelions, nodding. "You know dandelions are really just weeds, right?"

Livvie laughed and waved her hand. "Weeds. Flowers. What's the difference as long as they're colorful and pretty and make me happy? The only difference between a weed and a flower is the time you put in caring for it." She gazed at her vase of weeds, a soft smile on her face. "These flowers grow entirely on their own, without care of any kind. They don't seem to need anyone to grow tall and strong. That's very special. I think they're beautiful. A little bit of sunshine."

Desmond turned and left the room without a word.

"What's wrong with Des?" Livvie asked.

Connor stared at Desmond's back as he angled toward the barn. "Nothing a few more memories won't cure. Got a kiss for me this morning, Liv?"

Livvie flew across the room and Connor got the best kiss of his life.

* * * *

Desmond had the horses saddled when he and Livvie got outside. It seemed they were going for a ride. Connor didn't say anything about all the work they had to do. He'd already taken care of the animals, but he knew a thousand other chores waited. Connor shrugged. If Des needed a ride, then Des needed a ride.

"I assume Stardust taught you everything you need to know about riding a horse?" Desmond asked.

Livvie nodded, her head bobbing enthusiastically. "Oh, yes, I went riding every day, even in winter. I can handle myself. Don't worry about me. Just try to keep up."

She laughed then strode to her horse. She vaulted into her saddle while they pushed their rifles into carriers. Before they'd had a chance to mount, she'd dug her heels into the horse's flanks and shot off across the field without a backward glance.

"Damn," Connor said. "What a sight. She looks like she was born to it."

Desmond tightened the straps then swung into the saddle. "She was born to just about everything else too. Wealth, privilege, political connections, social status. She has good roots, family history, and obviously great parents. She's like a Kentucky princess or something. She's nothing like us, Connor."

"Really?" Connor stuck his foot in the stirrup and climbed into his saddle. He tilted his face and studied his brother. "Then why do you think she seems to like our miserable asses?"

"Not sure," Desmond said. "Could be she's a little too adventurous for her own good. She's bound to get hurt one day."

"It's not going to be by me, little brother." He shoved his finger toward Desmond's face. "And it better not be by you."

Desmond glanced toward the field and Connor followed his gaze. Livvie's body seemed a dark spot in the bright sun. "I'm trying, Connor."

"I know you are, Des. Keep up the good work. Now let's catch up with her before she ends up in Colorado. I have a feeling a state border wouldn't stop Princess Olivia."

Chapter 9

When Livvie reached the little creek and could see her field of dandelions, she slid off her horse and tethered it to a sapling. She knew they wouldn't want her getting too far ahead. But, she'd also been determined they know she could certainly handle herself—at least with a horse. The rest seemed to still be up in the air. She had no idea what kinds of things she might have to face on this mission. She thought the McBride brothers might be the most dangerous part.

Last night had confused her. This morning had confused her more.

After taking care of the little "problem" Desmond had created in the most enjoyable way she could imagine without a man beside her, she'd lain awake for several hours. She couldn't get the feel of Desmond's lips off her mind, couldn't forget the fire that had flowed through her, the way it had burned her skin. New words flickered through her thoughts—pussy, clit. She'd no idea words like that existed. What kind of life had she led? Sheltered to say the least.

Desmond's mouth and hands had proven she desperately needed the touch of a man. The problem was...well, Connor's kiss this morning had been just as thrilling in an entirely different way. Had they been truly alone she'd have begged Connor to fall to his knees and put his mouth on her pussy. She shivered even thinking of that word. It felt so...right.

She wanted it again. And, she wanted both the McBride brothers. The idea should have shocked her. Instead she laughed. She threw herself down in a shady refuge of tall grass and stared into the bright blue expanse overhead.

"Mother will understand. The Fathers will have a fit, but Mother will understand."

The horse nickered. Clearly the horse understood as well.

"Now what to do about it…"

She rose on her elbows at the sound of hoof beats. The McBride brothers galloped toward her, seated identically in the saddles, their hats at the same angle, the same expression on their faces. She loved looking at them—their beautiful faces, the dark hair falling over their collars, the hard muscled bodies encased in that soft leather, buckskin. But inside they had differences, and it was those differences that Livvie loved most. She refused to give up any of it and she refused to come between the adoration they felt for each other.

She just had to nestle herself between them and make them agree to her terms. Livvie Raines knew she could wrap just about any man around her finger. It might be a little harder with two, but she liked a challenge.

"Took you long enough," she said as they slid from their saddles.

"Would have been here sooner," Desmond said, "but we couldn't see through the dust."

"Ha!" Livvie said. "And you doubted I could ride."

"We'll not underestimate you again, sunshine." Connor looped his reins around a branch and squatted down beside her. "But your safety is still our primary concern. Desmond has some things he'd like to ask you, so we're more prepared going into this mission."

"I understand." Livvie sat up. "What do you need to know?"

Desmond scratched his chin. "First off, have you ever been in real danger before?"

She pulled back slightly. That question caught her off-guard. Oh, she'd heard of dangerous things happening in their area of Kentucky from time to time, and she'd actually crossed paths with a bobcat once, but Stardust could outrun a bobcat any day. But real danger? The idea seemed preposterous when she considered how hard Cutter and Billy worked to keep Riverbend a safe haven for all of them. She finally laughed.

"Well, no, probably not. Unless you count being on a strip of nowhere Kansas with men who look like you."

Connor smirked. "We'll thank you for the compliment, but not what we had in mind. Would you even recognize real danger?"

"Hard to say until I see it I guess."

"That's the problem." Desmond stared at her hard. "Generally you don't really see danger until it's smacked you on the ass."

Okay, so neither one of them smiled. They took this conversation seriously. She had a hard time taking anything seriously today. The sun was shining, baking the land in an incredible heat, but the warmth spread around her and made her think of good things, not things that might ruin the day. And she'd really wanted to concentrate on getting their mouths on her again.

"What do you know about the spying business, Liv?" Desmond asked.

So much for a fun day.

"Not much. I listened to my parents' stories. I found them fascinating. They went to so many places in the early days, working on assignments for President Lincoln. Of course, once Jake was born they settled down a little more. But they continued to work for President Grant until Cutter put his foot down. He wanted to retire and—"

"And what did you learn from those stories?" Connor asked.

"Learn?" Livvie chewed on her lip. "To get the job done?"

Desmond blew out a breath, shaking his head. She was glad he didn't question her further on that particular topic. Mostly she'd just loved the stories and knew she wanted to do the same thing. It seemed fun and exciting and—

"Do you know how to lie?" Desmond asked.

"I would never lie."

Connor nodded. "That was pretty damn good. So, what—"

Heat welled in her face and she waved her hands. "Wait. What does that mean?"

"You're a natural liar," Connor said. "Must have had a lot of practice. Desmond's question came out of nowhere and yet you answered it with a straight face. Your body never changed position or reacted in any way. It was very believable."

Livvie's brows drew down as she peered at Connor. "What makes you think I've had a lot of practice?"

"Let's just say you seem like that kind of girl. Bet you worked your way around these parents of yours more than once. Probably had them running in circles."

"No, they're actually very hard to get around," Livvie said. "It took a lot of effort."

"Good," Desmond said. "That's great experience."

"But what did you mean by it was damn good?"

Connor leaned forward. "Lying's an art form. Most people can't do it for shit. Their faces shift. Their gazes dart around. Their body posture changes. You learn to watch for these signals. When a normal person lies—"

"I'm perfectly normal."

"You see?" Desmond said. "You just told us another lie. And you never made a move."

"I *am* normal," Livvie said.

Connor laughed. "Not by a long shot and you know it. But we like that in a girl."

Desmond didn't laugh, and it was obvious he wasn't done with her lesson. "Lying is something you'll learn to recognize in others and do without thought. At least we hope that's the case. I'm a little concerned with what your expectations are for this mission."

"I haven't figured that out yet," Livvie murmured. "I thought maybe you'd help me."

"We can," Desmond said. "But most of it will fall to you. We want to make sure you don't talk yourself into a corner or put yourself at risk. Do you know how to shoot?"

Livvie glanced toward the rifle in the carrier. "I know the basic idea behind it."

"Have you ever shot a gun?" Connor asked.

She nodded. "Cutter caught me touching his precious rifle. He pitched a holy fit and told me never to touch a firearm unless I knew how to use it. I think he was more upset I'd touched his treasured Henry. I remember rolling my eyes—which never fails to please him—and saying the Henry was such an antique, I doubted it even worked. That did it. He took me to the back of the property to prove me wrong."

"And did he prove you wrong?"

"Oh, yes. The Henry's a good rifle, ancient though it is. Cutter's also an excellent shot, even at his age, but he practices a lot. Cutter's a great believer in being prepared. Kind of like Desmond."

She smiled and Desmond blushed a little. She liked that.

"The next time I had a lesson was when we'd heard of some renegades near the Ohio. Since we live on the Ohio, Cutter wanted us all to practice shooting a couple times just in case. Abbie is a miserable shot I'm happy to say. Jake is good at everything so I wasn't surprised when he hit all the targets. Mother's actually a pretty good shot too."

Desmond glanced at Connor. "It's never a simple yes or no with her, is it?"

"Nope," Connor said, "but it's always entertaining. How did Stardust do?"

Connor's serious expression caused Livvie to burst out laughing. She fell back on the grass. Even Desmond chuckled. When she'd recovered, they resumed their inquisition.

"Are you a good shot?" Connor asked.

"Compared to whom?"

"Did you hit the target?"

"Well, yes, but…"

"Then you're a good shot," Connor said.

"This all happened a couple years ago and—"

"She needs eyeglasses for distance," Desmond said.

Livvie pressed her lips together and folded her arms across her chest. "I don't like people knowing that, Des. It's embarrassing."

"No need to be embarrassed about it, Liv," Desmond said. "You look cute as hell in those spectacles."

Connor's head dropped back. "Damn. I missed eyeglasses too?"

Livvie's jaw dropped. "You *told* him about the hotel? Desmond, how could you do that?"

"I don't keep secrets from Connor."

Livvie jumped to her feet and paced. "That was the most embarrassing night of my life. It was bad enough that one of you witnessed it and now you *both* know?" She stopped and spun around, her gaze darting between them. "How am I going to look either of you in the face again?"

Connor burst out laughing. "You just did, sunshine. After the afternoon in Mrs. Harrison's parlor, nothing should embarrass you. Now get your pretty ass over here." When she dropped down beside him, he whispered, "I really want to see you in those eyeglasses."

Livvie pouted. "I feel kind of funny in them, but I guess seeing them won't be a problem if I have to prove I can shoot. I doubt you'll put the target right in front of me."

"If you can hit a small target with your eyeglasses," Desmond said, "then I can rest assured you can probably shoot a man without them."

"Shoot a man? Why would I want to do that?" Her face swung between them.

"It's just a precaution," Connor said. "We're trying to plan for anything."

Livvie stared at them each in turn. "Well, I'm certainly not going to shoot a man, no matter what. That's just not something I could ever do. Really. I'm not lying about that."

Connor took her chin and twisted her face toward him. "We believe you, but sometimes things happen, Livvie. Horrible things. And to prevent more horrible things you have to make choices. Sometimes killing is a necessary thing."

"Have you ever killed anyone?" Livvie whispered.

Connor's eyelids dropped for a moment. When he looked back up he stared straight into her soul, his dark eyes filled with knowledge, pain, and anger, but it wasn't directed at her. She took a deep breath, waiting for his answer. "Yes, Livvie, I killed a man once. A long time ago. He deserved it for what he did."

Desmond rose and stared down at his brother. "I thought we didn't have secrets, Connor."

"It wouldn't have made things any better for you to know, Des."

"You should have told me."

"Yeah, I probably should have."

Livvie watched them stare each other down. As much pain as she'd seen in Connor's eyes, that pain was tripled in Desmond's. She didn't know what they talked about but whatever secrets they held between them needed to be exorcised, and she'd had enough lessons for one day. The mission could wait a little while longer.

She hopped to her feet and grabbed her reins. They lurched to their feet, their gazes immediately roaming their surroundings. Livvie pointed across the field of dandelions.

"See that tree over there? If you two can catch me before I reach it, I'll give you a surprise."

She vaulted into the saddle and kicked her horse. When their laughter reached her ears, she pulled back slowly on the reins, hoping they'd catch her. Pretty Girl was no Stardust, but she took instructions well. They made a good team, and with any luck, Livvie would get what she wanted.

* * * *

When Connor's arm wrapped around her waist, he grabbed her from the saddle and yanked her into his lap. Livvie's heart burst with excitement. She cuddled against him as he slowed his mount and when they stopped, Desmond held out his arms. She slid into them without hesitation.

Both men looked at her with expectation but Connor threw out the question. "So what do we get?"

She walked away from them for a few paces then turned to them with an excited bounce. "I'm going to have sex with you. Which of you wants to go first?"

The look on their faces made her want to laugh, but she stood silently, her hands clasped behind her back.

"First?" Desmond's voice sounded strained. "Like right now?"

"Yes," Livvie said. "Right now."

"Livvie…" Desmond glanced around the field, rubbing the back of his neck, his gaze darting anywhere but toward her. "That's not something—"

Connor took a step forward. "I will."

"Like hell you will," Desmond snapped. "What the fuck is wrong with you?"

"She's offering, Des. And it's a mighty tasty offer." Connor took another step toward her and Desmond shoved him in the chest. Connor flew backwards, sprawling in the grass. He immediately leapt to his feet and took a swing.

Livvie jumped between them, her eyes squinched closed as she waited for a fist to hit her somewhere. She wasn't sure where it would hit, but the inevitably of it made her want to puke. A burst of wind swept near her face then vanished.

Desmond grabbed her waist and pulled her backward. "Are you out of your fucking mind, Liv?"

Connor rubbed his forehead. "I almost hit you for Christ's sake."

Livvie lifted her chin. "Go ahead. I'd rather you hit me than him. It's all my idea. I should take the punishment."

Connor's mouth dropped. "I'm not going to hit you!"

"But you'd hit him?" Livvie jerked her chin in Desmond's direction.

"Well, no, but—"

Livvie put her hands on her hips. "That was clearly a punch, Connor, directed toward your brother." She threw up her hands. "I knew this would happen. I could see it coming without a pair of spectacles."

"What did you expect?" Desmond asked. "That I'd just let him fuck you? Right in front of me?"

"It's bound to happen sooner or later," Livvie murmured. "We might as well get it over with."

"*What?*" they both shouted.

Livvie held out her hands. "Look. Let's just be adults about this. You both seem attracted to me. Is that right?" They nodded. "And I want both of you. It's as simple as that. Don't ask me to choose because I can't. I won't. The solution to that problem is to have you both."

"It's amazing how logical she makes it all sound," Connor said.

"In a twisted, perverse sort of way," Desmond said.

"I learned that sort of logic from Billy." She shrugged. "It's the best of all possible worlds."

A red stain burst into Desmond's face. He clenched his fist. "What kind of world do you live in?"

Livvie whirled around, her arms spread. "My own world! I make my own rules and do what I want. I don't care what anyone thinks." She ran to Desmond and wrapped her arms around his waist. "Please don't be shocked, Des. I'm sure both of you have been wondering where all this would lead. Sure, we can ignore one another, squash the feelings we have, go to our lonely bedrooms at night and think of each other, but how's that going to help any of us?"

Connor nodded as though she'd just solved the mystery of God. "She's right, Des."

Desmond's hands tightened on her shoulders, but he glared at his brother. "And you're okay with this idea?"

Connor took a deep breath. "More than okay. I think it sounds like a great idea. She's brighter than I would have imagined. A real problem-solver."

"I think you've both lost your fucking minds. How could any of this be a good idea?"

"For starters," Connor said. "We both get *her*. She seems to want both of us, and this is a way to do it. Let's face it, Des. Separately we have flaws. Between us we make one pretty goddamn good man."

"So we've decided then?" Livvie asked.

Desmond shook his head. "I can't do this," he murmured.

Connor slammed his hat to the ground. "Jesus Christ, Des! You're a fucking pussy! What? Are you embarrassed? I've seen your dick before. We're practically identical. And I'm not going to judge your technique for Christ's sake, though I'm pretty damn sure I'm going to outlast and outperform you." He glanced at Livvie. "I don't think the lady will have any regrets. She'll be entirely satisfied. I can guarantee I'll make her come."

Livvie laughed. Desmond turned a brighter shade of red.

Livvie studied Connor. "You can outperform Desmond? Well, I have to tell you, I've seen his work and felt a small sampling." She fanned her face, pretending to swoon. "It's pretty impressive."

"Fuck that," Connor said. "You have anything to compare it to?"

Livvie made a face. "Well, only Jeremy Hicks, and I can tell you there's no comparison there."

"You're not a virgin?" Desmond said.

"No," Livvie said bluntly. "Is that a problem?"

Connor smiled. "Not to me. Not at all. Des?"

"No," Des said softly. He scratched at his cheek. "Not a problem. Though I'm rather surprised. How'd you manage that?"

"With a *lot* of effort," Livvie said. "Now…if we've made our decision, I—"

"We haven't," Desmond said. "We're still talking."

"Oh, I think I can make you decide faster." Livvie started to unbutton her blouse.

Chapter 10

Desmond gulped and Connor's mouth curved into a smile. When the buttons opened and exposed her camisole, both men's eyes widened. She knew her breasts peeked above the low neckline, offering an enticing glimpse of creamy skin and even a hint of a rose-colored nipple. She'd picked out the most seductive underthings she owned.

"You're not wearing a corset," Desmond said.

"No, I'm not. It's entirely too hot here. Besides, no one's around to see me, and, well, you told me I didn't need one. Have you changed your mind?"

"No," Desmond said. "I haven't changed my mind. You're perfect."

"Hardly perfect," Livvie said with a smile.

"Pretty perfect," Desmond said.

"Will you shut the hell up, Des? I want to see this perfect body. I only got a tiny look last night." Connor nodded toward her as though she needed encouragement. "Keep going, Liv."

Livvie unbuttoned her skirt and let it drift to the ground. She stood in her camisole and petticoat. She shuffled her boots in the grass. She knew this was the right thing to do, knew she'd been right in getting it out in the open, but suddenly she felt a little nervous. She didn't want to disappoint them.

Desmond ran his hands down his thighs. It didn't surprise her when Connor took the more direct approach. He put his hand on her shoulder and slid one of the straps down her arm. His warm mouth pressed against her skin as his fingers trailed down her arm to clasp her fingers. She wound hers tight around his.

His lips touched her ear lobe and he whispered. "You don't need to be nervous, Liv. This is going to be the easiest and best thing you've ever done. I promise."

She nodded, staring over Connor's shoulder into Desmond's unreadable eyes. He could have been looking at anything, not her half-naked body being kissed by another man. He stood stock still, hands at his sides. She tried to smile but didn't think she'd succeeded because he didn't smile back.

Connor's mouth moved down her neck, so warm, so gentle, so loving. Her body, already hot with the sun, grew warmer, and her breathing deepened as she swayed against him. He was right. No need to be nervous at all. If there was something she didn't know—and she was almost positive there'd be plenty—she knew they'd be willing and patient enough to teach her.

Connor's hand touched her breast, engulfing it in his palm and squeezing gently. She tilted her face upwards just as his mouth sought hers. His lips settled hard over hers, his arms sweeping around her waist to draw her closer and she forgot about everything but Connor McBride.

Lost in his kiss she sucked in a breath when his big hands grabbed the hem of her camisole and tugged upward. He released her mouth long enough for the fabric to pass over her face then his lips fell on hers again, hungry, almost brutally, as both hands covered her breasts, pulling her closer. The slight pain on her breasts rippled down her abdomen and settled in her hips. Her pussy clenched as his grip tightened and when his fingers pinched her nipples a sharp ache stabbed her lower body, grinding through her pelvis and spiraling to center deep inside.

Her hands clutched his lower arms, kneading, pulling, anchoring herself before she sank to the ground. But Connor did sink to the ground, pulling her down with him. He took her shoulders and gently lowered her until she stared at the beautiful sky overhead and held her breath in anticipation. He unlaced her boots, tugging them off and tossing them over his shoulders with a laugh. His arms braced on either side of her body, he moved toward her face slowly, growling. He leapt at her and pushed his face into her neck, his mouth locking on her skin. He shook his head like a big cat with prey, his growling noises and warm breath tickling her. She burst into a fit of giggles, squirming beneath him.

Connor finally lifted his head and gave her a cheeky wink. "Now that I've captured my prey, I'm going to eat it."

His fingers gripped her petticoat and slowly raised it up her legs. He stared into her eyes for a moment, giving her time to change her mind, allowing her control. She appreciated that, but she had no intention of stopping him. His gaze followed the line of the fabric as it unveiled her calves, her knees, her thighs and finally reached her hip bones.

"I swear, Liv, I think I've died and gone to heaven."

He slid his hands all the way up her legs until he reached the tops of her thighs. His thumbs lightly stroked the sensitive flesh there and she shivered as he stretched them out to touch between her legs. His thumbs dipped between her pussy lips, pressing then tugging them open. He slid his index finger across her clit and down the slit, prodding gently. Her pussy clenched around the tip of his finger.

He shook his head then closed his eyes.

"What's wrong, Connor?" she whispered.

"Absolutely nothing, sunshine. Look at you. Pink, perfect, swollen. So fucking beautiful."

He scooped his hands under her ass and lifted the lower half of her body. Surprised, Livvie laughed and rose up on her elbows but thumped back to the ground when he tugged her closer and flung her legs over his shoulders.

"Connor! What are you doing?"

"We're going to have a little fun."

He lowered his head and his mouth latched onto her pussy. Livvie's hand clutched at a handful of grass, pulling it out by the roots.

"Oh God...yes, let's have...a little fun."

She arched her back and her legs tightened on his shoulders, her heels pressing into his back. After a moment, she realized she wanted more. She lifted her feet and braced them against his shoulders. Her thighs fell open, granting him better access. She pushed her pussy tighter against his mouth and his tongue speared inside. She bit her lip, tugging, as new sensations poured through her. Her body shivered in both anticipation and delight as Connor's tongue touched the soft recesses of her body. He pulled back slightly and dragged his tongue up her slit, pressing the tip against her clit.

Her body spasmed in his hands, and she burst out laughing. Connor pulled his mouth away and glanced over his shoulder.

"I'm licking her pussy and she's laughing. Did she do that to you?"

Desmond took a step closer and he frowned. "I didn't get very far before we were interrupted."

Connor's tongue swiped her clit again. "That's right. I forgot. Too bad."

Livvie reached up and grabbed Connor's face, twisting it toward her. "Concentrate, will you?"

"He distracts me."

"I didn't say a fucking word," Desmond said. "If you can't treat the lady right, back away."

"I wondered when you'd come to your senses, little brother." Connor snuggled closer to Livvie. "But there's not a chance in hell I'm moving right now."

Desmond dropped to the ground and rested his arms across his knees. "Then I'll just sit here and wait 'til you're done. If you think I'm—"

"Stop your bitching and get undressed, Des," Connor muttered.

His words became lost in her skin, but she felt their vibration deep inside. Her clit tingled and her pussy spasmed. She was positive she leaked again. Connor didn't seem to mind. He lapped at her, catching every bit of moisture he could find. The tingling increased and so did the ache. Her muscles tensed, as though waiting for something. Now that they'd stopped bickering, Connor put his total effort into eating her alive.

He drew her pussy lips into his mouth, sucking gently on each one then laving it with his tongue. He blew tiny breaths onto her skin, causing a shiver and even more anticipation. His tongue dipped into her body, lapping and licking as though he ate the most fabulous dessert, then flicked across her clit, tiny little movements that drove her insane. Her leg muscles tightened as her hips lifted closer.

Desmond watched. Her glance darted to him time and again. She sensed he watched every movement she made, each expression on her face. When Connor's mouth latched onto her clit and sucked rhythmically, she closed her eyes and forgot about Desmond. Her hands gripped more grass and in a shattering moment of bliss, her hips bucked against Connor's mouth. Waves of pressure and sensation flooded through her body, moving so fast she couldn't stop the soft cry that burst from her. She'd known this experience would be wonderful, but she'd no idea *how* wonderful it would be.

Her body trembled and Connor showed her no mercy. His sucking motions slowed, but even as he stopped, his tongue pressed against her clit, sending more ripples of delight through her. Finally, he lapped the length of her pussy and dropped a kiss on her mound. Her eyes fluttered when she heard his voice, but she didn't have the strength to open them.

"Well, Des? What are you waiting for? You met her first. It's only fair you fuck her first. I'm certainly willing to share. I just wanted a taste, but if you don't want her, I'd be—"

A shadow fell across her face. She opened her eyes when she heard, "Quit talking and move out of the god-damn way." Desmond towered above her, a completely and gloriously naked Desmond. Her gaze traveled across the broad shoulders, across the wide chest full of dark hair and over lean hips to settle on the hard cock that jutted from his body. He looked so much more *vivid* close up. She held up her arms and Connor moved from between her thighs, sitting back on his legs.

"She's more than ready," Connor said.

"Shut the hell up, Connor," Desmond said. "I can see that."

She caught her lip between her teeth as Desmond dropped to his knees. He stared at her a moment and suddenly her whole body became enveloped in the heat and scent of this man who'd filled her head for days. He cupped her face in his big hands and his mouth stole hers in a kiss that also stole her breath. Her tongue pressed between his lips wanting to taste him. One hand tightened around her head, the other slid down her body, seemingly memorizing the curves along the way. When his hand slipped beneath her ass, she opened her legs and he drove inside with a groan.

"Fucking jealous here," Connor muttered.

Desmond kissed his way down her throat. "Get over it."

"Oh I will," Connor said lightly. "In fact, I—"

"Shut the hell up, Connor," Livvie murmured.

She buried her face in Desmond's shoulder as she wrapped her legs around him, pulling him tighter against her. He moved in hard, slow thrusts, lifting her body as he moved, as though reluctant to pull out of her for even a second. Her pussy clenched tight around his cock, refusing to be separated. With each downstroke he pressed against her clit, causing flutters to pulse deep inside her and his cock drove deep, hitting something inside that made her pelvis ache with an unbearable needy tension. The ache ground through her and she pressed against him, trying to find a way to make it end.

Skin to skin, Desmond's strokes became tighter, more controlled, a small movement that drove her crazy and gave her pleasure at the same time. That spot inside burned, threatened to tear her apart but Desmond held the key. She knew it, could feel it.

"Stop," she said. "Right there. Stay still for a minute."

Desmond stilled, his cock lodged in her body, staring at her with concern.

"Just let me..." She pushed up slightly. Oh God, that was it. She clenched her muscles and rocked against him gently, clutching his ass to keep him still. She moved just a fraction, her legs tense, her fingers digging into his skin. One more movement and...

"Oh my God," she whispered.

Every muscle contracted at the same time and that burning ache exploded into a wave of sensation that ground through her pelvis and her pussy, clutching Desmond's cock so violently he groaned. Her body throbbed with such a wonderful feeling she thought she might laugh. It was better than anything that had come before and overwhelmed her completely. She threw her arms over her head and lifted both of them off the ground as her back arched.

Desmond ground his hips against hers to bring her back to reality. She was limp, exhausted, every inch of her body pulsing.

"She's a goner, Des," Connor said. "Might as well get yours."

Desmond rose up on his arms and withdrew slightly. Her pussy contracted and clamped down, trying to keep him inside. He plunged inside and she gasped as her back arched again. She clutched his shoulders as he pumped in and out, his cock sliding easily into the damp folds of her body. Flutters stirred inside her once again, excruciating little pulses that made her tremble, but her body felt so tired. She rode the waves of pleasure with a smile and watched Desmond as he stared into her eyes, her hands skimming downward to curl in the hair on his chest and feel the droplets of sweat that dotted his skin.

With one final plunge, Desmond fell against her, wrapping her in his arms. She wound her arms around his neck and held him as he shuddered. His heart thundered against her breast. Warm pulses of fluid shot deep inside her, spurt after spurt as he filled her with his cum.

He pressed a long kiss against her neck then threw himself into the grass, shielding his eyes with his arm. His hand reached out and took hers, squeezing lightly. Livvie lifted up on her elbows and her mouth dropped open.

Connor stood a few yards away, his back against a tree. His pants were open and he stroked his cock, a hard long length in his hand.

* * * *

Her hair cascaded around her flushed face when she rose up on her elbows. No one could have mistaken that look on her face. Her eyes were dreamy and unfocused, a soft smile on her lips. She looked like a woman who'd just been fucked and fucked well. Desmond hadn't disappointed her.

He wasn't too worried. Desmond was good but he knew damn well he could be better. His cock was more than hard enough to satisfy her.

Her gaze finally found him. Her pretty little mouth dropped open and those green eyes widened as they dropped to his cock.

"I have a little unfinished business."

"I-I see that," she stammered.

Her eyes tentatively moved back to his face as though suddenly shy. He considered for a minute this might be too much for her too fast. He sure as hell knew it might be too much for his brother and there could be consequences from that. But Connor'd been willing to risk that. He wasn't normally so selfish but the last thing he wanted to do was hand Livvie to Desmond on a silver platter and give up all hope of having her. He'd done the right thing: he'd let Desmond have her first. Now all bets were off. Livvie might ultimately choose Des, but Connor had already figured one thing about Livvie Raines. She'd made a bargain and she'd stick to it. She'd fuck him. If it turned out to be only once, he'd live with that. But he sure hoped it was more than once.

"I can take care of it myself if you like."

Desmond sat up, squinting against the sun. "Please do."

"That wouldn't be fair," Livvie said. "He's the one who actually caught me. What kind of person would I be to hold back his surprise?"

Connor smiled, grabbed his cock and wiggled it. Desmond fell back to the grass with a sound of disgust. Livvie didn't look disgusted at all. She licked her lips and her eyes filled with a heated lust.

She scooted onto her knees then stood. Her breasts, flushed and rosy from kisses and caresses, bounced with her movement, their nipples still hard. Her petticoat fluttered down around her legs, hiding that glorious glimpse of pussy. She started toward him, her hips swaying beneath the soft fabric.

As she neared an intoxicating scent enveloped him—the aroma of a truly satisfied woman. He'd been happy to do his part, but he was ready for more.

She stood in front of him for a minute, quiet and unusually still. Then her hand reached out and the tip of her finger grazed the head of his cock, wiping at the small bead of moisture on the tip. She lifted her finger to her mouth and her tongue peeked out to swipe across it. Her gaze rose to meet his eyes.

"Can I taste you?"

Connor swallowed thickly. "You just did."

"No, I mean, can I take your cock in my mouth? Suck on it? Is that something I can do?"

He nodded because he couldn't seem to get any words past his lips.

She lowered to her knees in front of him. He braced himself against the tree because he had a feeling he'd fall over. He stared at the top of her dark head until she lifted her beautiful face.

"You'll let me know if it hurts?"

"It's not going to hurt, Liv. Trust me."

He was aware that Desmond had sat up and stared at them. Livvie took his cock in her hand, her small fingers stretching to try to wrap around him. He watched her mouth open, stretch wider, and close over the head. He nearly jumped out of his skin when her tongue touched his skin. She made a little mewing noise in her throat right before she began to suck.

"You lucky son of a bitch," Desmond whispered.

Connor found he couldn't say a word.

Livvie's hands settled against his thighs, rubbing him with soft caressing strokes, then they slid upward and into his pants, pushing the fabric aside and down over his hips. Her fingers cupped his ass, tugging him closer and she swallowed his entire dick. It slid to the back of her throat. She pumped her mouth over his cock, sliding in and out, her lips tight around him, creating such friction he pressed his back tighter against the tree to maintain control.

Her hands slid back over his hips, her thumbs stroking the skin stretched over his bones, the soft nest of curls, the muscles of his abdomen. He pulled in a huge gasp of air. His head slammed back and hit the rough bark of the tree. He barely felt it. The only sensation in his body seemed to be the mouth that tugged on his cock, the soft lips that enveloped his flesh, the warmth of the tongue that swept up and down his length, the fingers that trailed over every inch of visible flesh. But when she reached between his legs and cupped his balls, he thought he'd come in her mouth. As much as he wanted to, he really wanted to come in her pussy. It seemed only fair.

He cupped her face and reluctantly pulled his cock from her mouth. It jutted upward and bounced against his body in protest. When she lifted her face, he bent down and tugged her up, struggling to get the petticoat out of the way.

"Next time we do this completely naked," he said.

She smiled and reached down to help, sweeping it up and bunching it at her waist. When he lifted her under the ass, she wrapped her arms around his neck and her legs around his waist. He lifted her higher then slammed his cock into her, driving into her soft, wet pussy in one hard stroke. Her muscles clenched around him like a hot glove. He'd never felt anything like it. Pulsing, perfect, warm, soft, wet. Her head fell back, exposing the smooth column of her throat and his mouth pressed against it, feeling the fast beat of her heart and the warmth of her skin. Her soft hair enveloped him in a dark web.

He was glad she'd already come several times because he'd just about run out of time. He pulled her tight, hoping to stimulate her clit against his body. Instinctively she angled her body. He pumped her up and down in sure hard strokes, his cock sliding in and out in a steady rhythm, deeper and rougher with each stroke. Her breath came in tiny pants and her small body tightened in his arms. He waited, holding back until he felt her tremble in his arms and her pussy clamped down hard on his cock then beat against it in a warm pulse of heaven.

Her sigh filled his ears and her forehead fell against the top of his head. He lifted her and yanked her down. He let himself go with a shudder, his cock thundering with a beat to match his heart. He poured into her, his cock pulsing in tiny waves to fill her with his cum. He slid down the tree, holding her in his arms until his ass hit the ground. She lay against him, a soft warm bundle of the most enticing woman he'd ever known. Desmond looked jealous as hell.

Connor smiled.

Nope. He didn't plan to lose this battle without a fight.

Chapter 11

Early that evening Connor and Desmond headed to the barn to feed and water the animals. Livvie didn't even know yet what kinds of animals they might have other than the horses. She'd seen the cattle of course, a small herd off in the distance. She assumed there were cows because they had milk and the loud clucking she'd heard several times signaled they had chickens. She wondered how Desmond and Connor would be able to handle the ranch on their own, particularly when one of them seemed determined to be with her when she left the house.

Trying to be of some value around their new homestead, Livvie decided she'd attempt to cook dinner. When they returned from their extremely pleasurable exploration, she set to work starting a fire in the stove. The stove reminded her of a blowing, puffing locomotive, powerful, terrifying and far beyond her limited capability of controlling it. She wondered how Glory managed to do everything back at Riverbend, even with Rob's help. She realized the men had been right. She was incredibly spoiled. She'd eaten great meals, lived in an impeccable house and had never considered how much work it had taken to make that happen. She'd managed to make her bed this morning, but her mind spun with all the tasks they'd need to accomplish—cooking, cleaning, laundry, tending the animals, teaching, maintaining the school, not to mention the mission. Sometimes the mission actually slipped her mind.

Tomorrow she and Desmond planned to go into Fort Cloud for her meeting with Anna. She hoped Anna had information for her. She had no idea exactly where to start the investigation, who to speak with or how to go about it. As usual, she'd taken on a commitment without a thought to the consequences. She dropped into a chair and pushed the sweaty hair back from her face.

It had taken all her time and energy to simply keep the stove supplied with wood and making sure nothing burned became a herculean task. Either the fire seemed too hot or the fire began to dwindle. Each time she opened the vent, waves of smoke engulfed her. Soot dotted her apron.

The potatoes she'd sliced and put in a pan to fry had blackened into something that vaguely resembled charcoal. The ham steaks bordered on the texture of shoe leather. Everything smelled like it had been rescued from a burning building at the point of disintegration. Sweat dotted every inch of her body and her hair stuck out in wild strands. She feared walking past a mirror. More so, she feared the look on the men's faces when they saw what they'd be forced to eat for supper. In a matter of days, she suspected Connor would take over the cooking duties and she'd be relegated to the barn. Heaven help the animals.

She heard footsteps on the porch and the sound of boots scraping on the mat. She jumped to her feet and ran to the stove, stirring the potatoes and quickly flipping the ham steaks. Another wave of smoke billowed toward her.

Connor came through the door, waving his hand through a dark cloud and choking. "Damn, girl, how are you not asphyxiated?"

"I've gotten used to it," she muttered.

She slapped the ham steaks onto a platter then scooped the potatoes from the frying pan into a large bowl. As she placed the food on the table, she noticed even the dandelions seemed a little droopy from their afternoon in the heat of the kitchen. She went to the ice box and took out the garden greens she'd prepared earlier then slid into a chair. She waited for them while they washed up, rubbing her hands across smoke-weary eyes.

They sat at the table without a comment, struggling to keep the grimaces off their faces. She finally dropped her forehead into her hands.

"I know. I'm entirely hopeless. How can I expect you to eat this after you've worked so hard all day?" She spread her hands, gesturing to the lumps of food sitting on the table. "I tried. I really did. And do you know the saddest part? This is probably the most I'm capable of. This is probably the best of my work. Everything else will be worse."

They glanced at one another. Connor speared hunks of ham onto each plate and Desmond spooned out potatoes around the table. Connor forked some greens into their bowls. She wasn't even sure what half of it was but it looked edible. When they began to eat without a word, she hesitantly took a bite of potatoes, groaning inwardly, and choked it down. After several more bites, she pushed her plate away and stared at them.

"Are you really going to try to eat it?"

"It's food," Desmond said. "We've had worse."

"How could you possibly have had *worse*?"

"Believe me we have. In fact, we had your biscuits last night."

Livvie wrinkled her nose. "None of our dogs would have touched this."

Connor sliced his ham. "Your dogs must be spoiled too."

Desmond sprinkled some salt on his potatoes. "Don't worry about it, Livvie. If it keeps us alive, we appreciate the help. We don't care how it tastes." He nodded to her plate. "Go ahead. Finish up. It's a hard life out here and you'll need the energy."

"Especially if we're going to be fucking," Connor said with a wink.

Livvie peeled her blouse away from her damp skin. "How can you even think of fucking when I look like this?"

Connor smiled. "It's surprisingly easy. Now, come on. Listen to Desmond. Eat up."

Feeling a little better, she managed to eat the rest of her supper. Sure, it was barely edible and Glory would have scraped it into the trash, but she'd made it herself and felt a little bit of pride at that. She determined though that she might discuss the possibility of getting some help with Anna—both in the house and on the ranch. The three of them might be doomed otherwise. They'd never have time to investigate let alone have a satisfactory conclusion to their mission.

When Livvie pushed her plate back again, it was empty. She brought the pies over to the table and poured the men each a glass of milk. She hated milk but she did like apple pie.

"Can I ask you something?" She toyed with her fork, tapping it against her plate.

"Shoot," Connor said.

"You say very little about your childhood. How old were you when you struck out on your own?"

"Ten." Desmond lowered his head, suddenly interested in the crumbs on his plate.

"What happened to your parents?"

Connor cleared his throat and Desmond glanced up and gave a slight nod.

"Pa died in the war," Connor said.

"Oh," Livvie said. "I've heard that was a terrible experience. Cutter was in the war."

"That would be one of your fathers," Desmond said.

"Yes, Cutter was a surgeon, *is* a surgeon actually."

"Which army?" Connor asked.

She glanced between them, her mouth dropping. "What kind of question is that? The Union Army of course! Your father was a Confederate? He fought *against* this country?"

Desmond leaned back in his chair. "No, Liv. He fought for the south. There's a difference. A Virginian is a Virginian first and everything else second."

Livvie shook her head. "An American is an American. First and foremost." Her face pivoted between them, not really believing she'd heard them right. "So you'd take up arms against your country now?"

"We haven't been Virginians in a damn long time," Connor said. "No one owns us. No ties, no loyalties, no commitments."

"How do you live that way? I can't imagine not having my home, my family, my friends. Where do you live?"

"Here," Desmond said.

She smiled and slid her hand across his. "No, Des, I mean before you came here."

"Here and there."

"That's not a home!" She leaned back in her chair.

Connor took another slice of pie. "No, it's not. But there's nothing to lose either."

"But what kind of life is that?" Livvie asked.

"A pretty good one." Connor shrugged. "We have each other. We've had women from time to time. We know people in every state and territory in this country, and a couple elsewhere. Lots of places we can shelter for the night. What more could we want?"

Livvie shook her head. The life Connor described sounded adventurous, exciting but it also sounded lonely. Seeing the world, meeting new people, having new experiences seemed a wonderful way to spend a small amount of time, but she wasn't sure she could imagine living that life without something to ground her—without parents, a home, siblings.

"What happened to your mother?"

"She died," Desmond said.

"How old were you?" Livvie asked.

He held up his hand. "I have a question for you."

She nodded and smiled at Connor. "Shoot."

"We were kind of surprised to hear your last name," Desmond said.

"Raines? Well, it's Cutter's name. What name did you think I'd have?"

"Marlowe," Connor said. "We heard the assignment would be led by Billy Marlow's daughter. But, you don't look anything like Billy, so I assume this Raines fellow is your real father. Billy is your step-father?"

"Oh, no." She laughed and waved her hand. "They're both my real fathers."

"You do understand the whole fatherhood thing, right?" Desmond asked.

"Yes, I do."

"So Raines is your real father? You look like him?" Connor asked.

Livvie hesitated, unsure exactly where this led and how much she'd need to explain. "I look like my mother."

"That doesn't really answer my question," Connor said.

Livvie straightened. "I don't...well, I kind of look like Cutter, but I'm my mother's daughter. Everyone says so. They shake their heads and say 'There goes Jessie McGee's daughter' like it's a bad thing." She laughed. "What difference does it make who I look like?"

"Well," Desmond said, "since Billy's the one who recommended you for this mission, we were kind of hoping your parents were behind it. I'd hate like hell to get in trouble with this Cutter Raines. He sounds like—"

Livvie held up her hand. "Stop. What do you mean Billy recommended me for this mission? Billy has nothing to with missions any more. That was long ago."

"What do you think Billy does?" Desmond asked.

"Billy teaches a little in Maysville, invents things out in his barn—he has some of the most beautiful stage props you've ever seen—but mostly he acts. He travels a lot, sometimes for months at a time, with a performance. It's hell on the rest of us 'cause we miss him something fierce. How in the world could Billy possibly recommend me for something like this?"

The men glanced at one another and Connor shook his head. "So you don't have any idea what Billy *really* does?"

"He acts," Livvie said. "Plus about a hundred other things. He can't seem to focus on any one thing because he loves so many things. I don't know what the hell you're talking about. You're making me crazy."

She stood up and began to pace around the room. Her boots stomped hard against the floor. She snatched up bowls and plates from the table and stacked them in the sink, mumbling to herself. Billy? Involved in missions? That was crazy talk. Okay, so maybe they had met Billy somewhere on one of their escapades. After a performance. Or on a train. Or… She whirled around.

"Where did you meet Billy?"

"Cincinnati," Desmond said.

"That explains that then. Billy goes to Cincinnati all the time. He plays in the opera houses there. So you saw one of his performances?"

"Sit down, Livvie," Connor said. When she slid into her seat, she had an ominous feeling, as though she might not want to hear what Connor had to say. She pushed her hands into the apron pockets and squeezed her fists. "Do you know a man named Cyrus Sheffield?"

"Of course. He's married to my mother's best friend and he's been a friend of Cutter and Billy's for years. Cyrus spends a lot of time at Riverbend with us and… So you met Billy through Cyrus?"

"Sure," Desmond said. "At Cyrus's office."

"Oh, well that explains that. Everyone knows I've always wanted to be an agent. It's all I talked about as a child. I'm sure Billy just told Cyrus and—" She started to stand and Connor took her arm. He stared until her she sank back into her chair.

"Billy Marlowe's been running an espionage network out of Cincinnati for almost twenty years."

What they said wasn't possible because her parents had been out of the spy business for quite a while. In fact, her mother said as their family grew, the decision to be involved became harder with each mission. They simply had no inclination to risk their lives for a 'little bit of fun and adventure'.

"Oh, no, that isn't possible." Livvie laughed. "Cutter and Mother would never stand for that, and Billy would never be able to keep his mind on something that long. He certainly doesn't have the time. He's far too busy with all his Billy-projects. Cutter used to say that if Billy would just settle down for a minute he might actually accomplish something."

"It's true, Livvie," Desmond said. "He and Cyrus. They answer directly to the president."

Livvie pressed her lips together. "Hmm…well, even if it's true, why would he keep something like that from me?"

"He does dangerous things. He probably didn't want you to worry. And tell Cutter Billy's accomplished more than anyone will ever know."

"Oh that's not necessary." She threw back her head and laughed. "Cutter knows. He'd have to. This is not something Billy would keep from either of them." She jumped to her feet and whirled around the room then pressed a kiss to the top of each dark head. She continued to dance around the room. She couldn't believe her good fortune.

Connor twisted in his chair, his brow furrowed. "Am I missing something here?"

She looped her arms around his neck. "If Billy recommended me for this assignment, then I'm not in trouble! Mother and Cutter already know and they had no objections. They all agreed. Believe me, that's the way they are. I've got to write to Martin and tell him. He's probably waiting for Cutter to arrive in Washington and kick his ass. Can one of you do the dishes?"

"Sure," Desmond said, grabbing her wrist as she skipped to the door. "But first, explain about Billy."

"I already told you. Billy Marlowe. Cutter Raines. They're both my fathers."

"But your name is Raines and one of them has to be your *real* father."

Livvie tilted her head. "My mother had to marry *someone*. I guess Cutter volunteered. Look, I don't give a damn which is my real father. I love them both. I'm not sure I can be any plainer. Why should anyone else care?"

"But surely there's a bigger connection with one of them. You must love one of them more than the other, feel something more…kinship or something?"

"I love them both the same. Why can't I?"

"It's not exactly—" Desmond began.

"Normal?"

He nodded.

"Is there a reason I have to be normal?" Livvie asked.

Desmond glanced at his brother. "I don't know. Connor, is there a reason?"

"Not to my way of thinking," Connor said. "I kind of like her the way she is."

Desmond shook his head. "But how is it possible to love two men in the same way? How does your mother do it?"

"I don't know exactly," Livvie said. "But that's the way it works in my family. I love them both the same. She loves them both the same."

"But how can you *know*?" Desmond asked.

Livvie smiled. "Because I know my own feelings and my mother told me hers. She's never lied to me. I've got to finish my letters for our trip into town tomorrow. Any more questions?"

"Not right now," Connor said. "Go write your letters."

After finishing the letter to her mother and one to Martin, she took a semi-warm bath and settled into bed with a lighter heart and better spirits. To know that her parents loved her enough to want to grant her greatest wish filled her with contentment. She'd worried that they might be concerned about her disappearance. That fear had been settled. When Connor and Desmond joined her, she gave each of them a bit of attention until she had two eager cocks ready to please her.

They spent a good hour teasing and fucking, laughing and talking. As they settled down each of the men gave her a loving kiss and fell asleep lying on either side of her. Relaxed from coming at least four times—she'd lost count—she stared out the window at the moonlight. After all their questions tonight, she felt a little more hope for their future together in this place. She fell asleep listening as Connor's light snore filled the room. Her life in Kansas seemed full of promise.

Chapter 12

"Planning to shred that into a rag rug?"

Livvie's face swung toward him, her brows raised. "Did you say something?"

Desmond nodded to her lap where her hands twisted nervously, plucking at the folds of her silky striped skirt. The little ball of fire had been unusually quiet most of the trip. Now as they neared the town limits, Livvie's hands tightened in her lap. She glanced down then unclenched her fists and slid her hands along her thighs.

"Anything you want to talk about?" Desmond asked.

"No."

She'd woken up in a good mood, her usual talkative overactive self. She'd helped Connor make breakfast when he came in from the barn then dressed in one of her Livvie outfits. That little green and white striped skirt and dark green jacket probably fit right into an afternoon of shopping in downtown Maysville, but here she'd soon keel over from the relentless sun. The cute hat perched on top of a pile of dark curls was probably straight from a lady's fashion book, but it did nothing to shield her face. Already she had a swipe of sunburn across her cheeks. When they finished their meeting with Anna, he planned to take her to the mercantile and get her some proper clothes before she died from the heat.

He stole a glance at her from the corner of his eye. Her hands had settled quietly on her thighs, but her lips remained pressed tight and she sat ramrod straight against the seat. He'd wait until she was ready to talk.

Desmond's gaze swept the dusty road then darted to the surrounding prairie. Just another ordinary day on the Kansas plains— dry, dust-choked and hot— but he wasn't taking any chances. To the majority of the citizens of Fort Cloud they were strangers and an unknown quantity, therefore suspect. Any one of those citizens could have killed Frederick Skylar, and that citizen could be watching them now.

"I'm in over my head here," Livvie whispered. She licked her dry lips.

"Why do you say that?"

"You know I am."

"Maybe I do."

She twisted toward him. "So what am I supposed to do about that?"

He tilted his hat back and studied her. "What do you think you should do?"

She huffed, the movement bouncing the seat which protested with a squeak. He waited for the eye roll. She didn't disappoint him. "If I knew what to do I wouldn't have to ask."

He squinted, straining to see who lingered at the train station in the distance. "You need to learn to think these things through on your own. But if you have a question, you should ask. Everyone has a first assignment. Everyone needs guidance. You're not the first person to be tossed into a situation with very little preparation. Most of those people actually survive to have another."

Her jaw clenched. "That's not funny." The sunburn got lost in the heated flush that rose over her face.

"Probably not, but it's true."

"Do you know how hard this is for me? I hate admitting I don't know something. I *always* know. That's just the way I am."

Desmond's brow rose. "And which father do you get that from?"

When she ignored his question, it didn't surprise him at all. Livvie cocooned herself in her thoughts at times.

"I haven't felt in control since I saw you through that window. My world has shifted upside down. I can't even think for all the doubts and anxiety filling my head. I took one look at you and knew, positively knew, there were things in this world I haven't begun to comprehend. I've been sheltered, coddled, adored, and practically handed a perfect life. Now I'm not prepared for anything that might happen here. I don't have the skills, the temperament, or the patience. I'm hopeless."

Her shoulders slumped and she ran her hands over her face. He let her have a few moments of misery then cupped her chin in his hand, lifting her face.

"So you'll learn."

"Can I?" she asked miserably.

"Guess that remains to be seen."

She nodded and he drove the wagon across the railroad tracks. They stopped at the station where he delivered Livvie's letters to the postmaster then headed down Main Street and turned right on one of the side streets. He stopped in front of an elegant, three-story home and dismounted. Livvie took a deep breath as he helped her from the wagon.

"You look nice today," she said.

He glanced down at his dark suit and gold tone vest. "Just trying to be a good husband. Wouldn't want to embarrass you too much." He winked at her then leaned down and pressed a kiss on her mouth. It seemed the husbandly thing to do.

* * * *

The sound of the door opening pulled Livvie out of the kiss. She jerked backwards and smashed into the edge of the wagon.

Wonderful, Livvie. So professional.

She reached behind her to dislodge her skirt from a bit of slivery wood then took Desmond's arm. He led her up a pristine sidewalk, through a white garden gate and up the three stairs to the porch where Anna Glaser waited.

Livvie struggled to keep the shock from her face. She'd no idea what she truly expected—a grandmother type perhaps, a woman with a matronly figure, a smiling face and kind, gentle eyes. Failing that, perhaps she'd find a spinster or widow—a plain woman with a pensive, rugged face—who'd found a purpose in the life she tried to carve alone on the Kansas plains.

The tall, slender woman who held out her hand was probably slightly over thirty. Her blond hair had been pulled back at the nape of her neck, but the length hung in soft waves over her shoulder. Her face held a classical beauty that would have been lauded and admired on the stages of any city or the canvas of any artist. Tiny pink flowers dotted her pretty white calico dress and hugged her perfect figure tightly until it flared out at the hips. She'd opened several of the buttons in deference to the heat and her breasts swelled through the opening. She looked cool, breezy, and entirely comfortable. Anna didn't have a drop of sweat on her and Livvie caught the aroma of face powder. Her gaze dropped for a moment and saw that Anna had dotted powder over every visible surface of her body.

Livvie felt like a child playing dress-up in her mother's clothes. As she moved closer to take Anna's hand, she had to tilt her head up to meet Anna's dark brown eyes. Anna's hand closed around her own sweaty one in a sure grip, drawing her closer.

"Olivia. I'm so pleased to meet you." Sultry, deep, her voice would make men sigh.

"Thank you. I'm happy to be here." Livvie tried to smile but every nerve in her body flared in heat. Anna was the kind of woman who knew everything, who never had doubts, who never questioned any decision she'd made. She also knew how to dress for the Kansas heat. Livvie wilted more with each passing moment.

Livvie wanted to suddenly hide behind Desmond's big body and let him handle the meeting. She could abandon this crazy idea, abdicate the responsibility, get on a train and find the nearest theater that might be willing to take a shot on an unknown woman with no talent, no experience, just a father who happened to be a very good actor and—

She straightened her spine and took a deep breath. "I'm sorry, Anna. I'm a little overwhelmed by the heat." She snapped open her fan and swished it across her sweaty face. "I've decided I need an entire new wardrobe. As you can probably guess, I've never been to Kansas before."

Anna laughed. "The heat does take people by surprise. "Please come in. It's not much cooler inside but at least it's out of the sun. You're going to need some different dresses." She swept her hand over her breast. "Even this is often too warm, but it's the best we have here. Don't go to the mercantile. You'll end up looking like a farm hand. Bradley's—that's up before the band shell on Main—has some lovely fabrics but…" Her gaze slid over Livvie's body and a perfectly shaped brow rose. "Do you sew?"

"No, I-I've never had to."

"Of course not." Anna smiled. "That's not a worry. You probably won't have time for it anyway. Luckily, Bradley's also has ready-made dresses, and Freda has a wonderful selection. I hope they have something that fits. You're a tiny little thing, aren't you?"

Anna's gaze ran the length of Livvie's body again and Livvie resisted the childish impulse to squirm under the inspection. When Anna finished she turned to Desmond with an appraising look. "Desmond, you look positively yummy. You clean up very well."

Livvie nearly choked. "You know each other?"

"Oh, yes. We're well acquainted." Anna swept her hand toward the open door.

Livvie took a step toward the door as Anna stood back. When Desmond lingered on the porch, Livvie paused and lifted her chin toward the door. Luckily, Desmond took her hint, and she didn't have to kick him in the shin to get him moving. He followed behind her.

Mercifully the cooler interior of the house seemed like a soothing balm. She'd had enough heat. She unbuttoned her jacket. As she slid it off her shoulders, Desmond pulled it down her arms. She opened the top buttons of her blouse. She'd about decided she could handle this just fine. Finding out Anna and Desmond knew each other had been just the push she'd needed. She would now become Olivia Raines, investigator, if only to figure out their history.

Anna took the jacket from Desmond and waited while Livvie pulled the pins from her hat. She handed that to Anna who hung everything on hooks around a mirrored foyer bench. Livvie glanced around the immaculate interior while she thanked Anna for all the work she'd done to prepare for their arrival. Not a speck of dust anywhere on the polished surfaces, not a mark on the sparkling wood floor and the heavenly aroma of baking cinnamon bread came from an area down the hallway. Livvie wondered how Anna managed to stay so cool and pretty while maintaining a house this size. When she glanced into the parlor, she saw a maid in a starched black uniform setting a silver tray down on a beautiful mahogany tea table.

Livvie rolled up the sleeves of her blouse and blew out a breath. "Now I can think."

"Let's go have some refreshment." Anna looped her arm through Desmond's and turned to him with a bright smile. "How is Connor? I thought he'd be here today. Isn't he the blushing groom?"

"Connor's back at the ranch. We decided…"

Livvie narrowed her eyes at Anna's back as she followed the chatting couple into the parlor. Desmond settled into a chair, stretching out his long legs. Livvie sat next to Anna on a couch and took the glass of lemonade from Anna's hand. After she let the sweet delicious taste slide down her throat, she swept her gaze between them. Curiosity might kill the cat but it sure as hell wasn't going to stop her.

"So, how do you two know one another?"

Anna leaned back on the sofa, her wrist trailing over the armrest. "Oh, we've known one another for years. I lost track of the fabulous McBride brothers some time around... When was that, Des? I think you were around fifteen or so. They just vanished and left a hole in my young girl's heart let me tell you. I missed them terribly. But lo and behold they turned up in Tulsa about eight years ago when I was there with my husband."

"Oh, you're married then?" Livvie asked.

Anna laughed. "Good lord, no! Gregory's dead." She leaned forward conspiratorially. "A bit of advice, Olivia. Never run with a pack that's crazier than you are. That gets you into trouble every time. Sometimes it even kills you." She winked.

"I'll try to remember that," Livvie murmured. She offered Anna a smile. "So...then you haven't seen Connor and Desmond in eight years?"

"Oh no," Anna said. "We've caught up with one another several times. Kansas City, Tombstone, St. Louis, and dozens of smaller towns. As government contractors, they move around a lot out of necessity. I move around a lot because I like different places. I like doing different things. Sometimes *very* different things."

Desmond laughed. Livvie chose to ignore it. She didn't think she wanted to know what kinds of things Anna liked to do, particularly with Desmond and Connor.

Anna gave Desmond an intimate, almost loving, look that made Livvie's hand clench on her glass. "I've been here in Fort Cloud about four years now. I just decided to settle down for a while and I've made a great many friends here. You'd be surprised how easy it is to make friends when you have money. Or perhaps it wouldn't surprise you at all." She laughed and glanced at Livvie's outfit. "But I've certainly missed my boys, and much to my delight, Desmond showed up the other afternoon."

What?

"He just seemingly dropped out of the sky. I was told you'd have agents with you, but had no idea I'd get so lucky."

Trying to keep herself from blurting out the curse on her lips, Livvie took a gulp of lemonade and dumped too much into her mouth. The acidy taste burned going down and a lump of sugar caught in her throat. She choked, nearly spitting it into her lap. She grabbed a napkin from the table and pressed it to her mouth. She slid the glass back onto the tray and when Anna leaned toward her, Desmond waved his hand.

"She's fine."

Fine, my ass.

"How many of those napkins do you have, Anna?" Desmond asked. Anna laughed as though they shared an inside joke.

Oh, Desmond, you are dead.

Her face twisted toward Desmond. She struggled to find her voice, lost in the back of her scratchy throat. She cleared her throat several times, massaging her voice box with the tip of her finger while giving Desmond her deadliest look. "You were here the other day?"

He scratched his chin. "Yep. Thought I'd better check in, tell Anna we were here, see if—"

"You shouldn't have come without me," Livvie snapped.

"Well, Liv, I didn't think—"

"No, you didn't. May I remind you who's in charge of this mission?"

"You taking charge all of a sudden?"

"I don't have to," Livvie said. "I *am* in charge. Caroline said so."

Desmond held up his hands and drew back in his chair. "Oh, well, if *Caroline* said so, then I guess I better just back down and let you handle it, boss."

"Damn right," Livvie muttered.

"Should I leave you two alone for a moment?"

Livvie had almost forgotten Anna was there. She brushed a strand of hair from her forehead and met the concerned look on Anna's face.

She tried to smile. "No, Anna, we're fine. I just wish he would have told me he'd already been here." She shot Desmond another dirty look. He looked unperturbed. She obviously needed to practice her dirty looks. "You apparently have to go over the details twice as he neglected to tell me anything that you discussed."

Anna shook her head. "Well, I didn't tell him much. I'm sorry to say I have very few details. Eleven boys have disappeared in the last year, all between the ages of twelve and sixteen. We've had runaways in this area before. Just last week a boy named Wesley Grimes disappeared, but his foster father, Charlie Stoker, is a bit of a drunk and known for his temper. But, other than Wes, these other boys had all been indentured off the train by two local ranchers—Anthony Pack and Robinson Booker." Anna leaned forward slightly. "Pack operates the ranch. I've never seen Booker. He appears to be involved in only the financial end of it. His name is attached to all of the paperwork I've discovered. I believe the boys furnish labor on the ranch until Booker comes to collect them. The town has become very concerned and the authorities have become extremely suspicious. And that's really all I can tell you, Olivia."

"Has anyone spoken to Anthony Pack or visited the ranch?" Livvie asked.

Anna's gaze fluttered to Desmond then down to her lap where her hands clenched together. "Not to my knowledge, unless the agency in Concordia sent someone I'm not aware of."

Livvie sighed. "Anna, I'd appreciate a bit of honesty here."

Desmond choked on his lemonade and lunged for a napkin. Anna's eyes widened as a blush crept into her creamy skin. Her mouth opened and she began to sputter. "Well, Olivia, I...I'm not sure...I've told—"

Livvie twisted and faced the woman. "You're lying to me about something. I'm not sure why exactly but I know you are. This is a desperate situation and there could be lives on the line. These boys are depending on us and time might be of the essence. If someone has already investigated these incidents I need to know what they've done and how I can contact them."

"You might as well tell her, Anna," Desmond said.

"Oh, Des, that's not a good idea." Anna got to her feet and paced back and forth between the sofa and the window.

"Tell me what?" Livvie's jaw tightened. "If someone doesn't tell me soon I'm going to get in the wagon and find Pack's ranch by myself. It's my damn mission and you're treating me like a child. I'm going to succeed at this, and I'm not letting either of you stand in my way. I'll bypass you entirely if I have to."

"That won't be necessary." Anna dropped back to the sofa. "Concordia sent a man named Frederick Skylar. He spoke with everyone in town and visited Pack out at the ranch. At the time, there were several boys there. One has since vanished."

"And what did Skylar discover?"

"I don't know, Olivia. I spoke with him very briefly. The ranch is a successful, legitimate business and Pack runs it well. Skylar implied he could find nothing to implicate him in the disappearances though he suspected the man was hard on the boys. That, in itself, is not unusual in some of these cases. Skylar planned to send a message to his contact but that message never arrived. Skylar died that evening."

Livvie's brow furrowed. Her heart rhythm increased. She didn't know if it resulted from the shock at realizing just how high the stakes were or from the fact that no surprise or concern registered on Desmond's face at all. She stared at him for a moment and one thought slammed into her. The son of a bitch knew about this and hadn't told her.

"He died? How?"

"Beaten to death," Anna said.

"Did anyone see Pack that night?"

"No, no one would admit he'd been in town. I assume you know why I wanted to keep this from you."

"I can see why you may have thought it best, but I'm not grateful for your presumption. I'm not a scared child, Anna. I sure as hell can't make progress without all the information and my safety may depend on knowing everything. But that's over now. I assume I can count on you to be entirely honest with me from here on in?"

Anna nodded. "Absolutely."

"So a few questions and his appearance at Pack's ranch signed Skylar's death warrant. That means Pack knew Skylar's suspicions and doesn't bode well for us. It's still not a hell of a lot to go on."

"No, it's not. And I suspect that you'll meet with some resistance from the locals. We have a good community here and many of these people are good parents and foster parents. Most of the children that arrived here have found decent, caring homes and are on their way to a bright future. These parents will resent your intrusion into their lives and will ward off questions in fear that their children may be taken from them. They're truly concerned, but they don't want someone poking into their affairs. Which is why I've come up with the alternative." She waved her hand and laughed. "I know it's a little out of the ordinary. I'm sure Mrs. Harrison thought I was crazy, but I think it will work."

"You *are* crazy, Anna," Desmond said.

"Crazy like a fox," Anna said, tapping her temple.

Livvie reached for her glass. "Yes, of course. The alternative." She had no idea what the hell Anna talked about. She glanced at Desmond for any kind of sign or help but after Anna's response he turned his gaze toward the window and stared through the lacy curtains like he had no interest in anything they discussed. He'd already gotten on her last nerve. She needed more information and she wanted it now.

"Desmond, what do you think of the alternative plan?"

He shrugged and lazily turned his head toward her. "It's worth a shot."

Damn you.

She tried again. She planned to torture him later for this. "Do you think it will work?"

"Sure. It could." Desmond's eyes sparkled in the light that fell across his face but his serious face offered no help of any kind. He was determined she figure it out herself. She wanted to leap across the table and choke the life out of him. "It'll take a light touch but hopefully you can pull it off."

"I'm glad you think I'm capable of making it work."

"I said *hopefully* you can pull it off, Liv."

Her hand clenched around her glass, and she closed her eyes for a moment. After taking a deep breath, she opened them and turned to Anna. "So when do we start?"

Anna smoothed the hair over her shoulder as she thought. "Probably not the first week. You'll want to acclimate yourself and get to know them. And then of course you'll have to gauge their abilities because a few of the parents may want to know the lesson plans before the week is out. Some of them are notorious for interference. I know they probably just want the best. But after that, I'd say they'll be comfortable and receptive."

Livvie's brow furrowed. "The parents?"

Anna burst into laughter then shook her head. "No, Olivia. The children."

"Receptive to your questions, Liv," Desmond said softly.

"My questions?" Livvie swung her face between the two.

Anna rose and went to a desk in the corner. As she unlocked and opened a drawer, sorting through some things, Livvie mouthed, "What the hell is she talking about?" to Desmond. Livvie straightened when Anna held out a leather folder.

"That's everything I know."

Livvie flipped through the dozens of sheets of paper. Children. Each sheet was about a child and not every child was an adoptee. She quickly read through some of the notes. *Randall Gerber: age 13, natural child of Harvey and Mary Gerber—father owns butchery;*

Lisa, 8, George, 10, and David Mercer, 14: natural and adopted children of Stanley and Iris Mercer—owners of the Brandywine. Under each entry, a log indicated names, ages, home circumstances, the child's regular activities, interests, strengths, vulnerabilities, and information about the parents, their occupations and personal pursuits. She ruffled the pages in her hands. "What is all this?"

"Information about your students," Anna said.

Livvie continued to scan the pages. "Well, it will certainly help but… Well, I'm not sure why you haven't taken the teaching position at the school. You seem to know so much about the children and—" She paused as a note caught her eye.

"I'm not exactly the teaching type," Anna said softly.

Livvie quickly scanned the note. *Stanley Mercer is in debt to Anthony Pack, who holds a second mortgage on the hotel. Stanley is petrified Iris will find out, as the original lien is held by Iris's father Ike Murdock. Stanley has an affinity for card games and drinking and can often be found at the Prairie Schooner any time after sundown except on Friday when the hotel has a special supper.*

Livvie re-read the note then glanced up. "How did you get this information, Anna?"

"Oh, well…" A blush rose over the soft skin of Anna's throat. She gestured toward the folder and smiled. "Some of that is from the things the children say. A child to my mind is not something to ignore unless they act up. I like to listen to them, hear their stories. I actually adore children. I'd have liked to have some of my own some day but of course..."

She frowned and glanced at Desmond.

"Don't think about that," he said softly. "Go on, Anna."

"You're right." She brightened for a moment as a soft smile skimmed her face then she began to pace in front of the window. Livvie squinted as the light flickered across her eyes. "Anyway, I'm friendly with the children. I let some of the girls sit in my garden to have iced tea in the afternoons, and I'll toss the boys a candy at the grocery from time to time. And the older boys..." She shrugged then laughed. "They just seem to like me."

"No surprise there," Livvie murmured. Desmond's brows drew downward.

"Most of what I've collected is from the mouths of babes. Other things were obtained from...well, from conversations I've had, observations I've made."

She glanced at Desmond. Livvie saw a look pass between them she didn't understand. A headache flared between her eyes.

"I see," Livvie said quietly.

Anna returned to her desk and locked it. Desmond leaned forward, clasping his hands between his knees and said quietly, "*Do* you see, Liv?"

She sighed and pressed her fingers against her forehead. "No. I don't."

Anna's voice nipped at the edge of her headache and tugged for her attention. Between the cryptic notes she'd seen and her inability to see where this mission headed, she'd just about reached the end of her rope.

"I'm sorry, Anna. What did you say?"

"I'd love to hear about your acting experience, Olivia."

Livvie's heart lurched. "My acting experience?"

Anna glided onto the sofa in the most graceful move Livvie had ever seen. "It's not every day I meet the daughter of a famous performer. I saw William Marlowe on stage in St. Louis once. He's a wonderful actor. If you have half the talent he does, I know this situation is in good hands. We'll have the answers we need in no time."

It had gotten hotter in the room. Sweat beaded her brow. "Well, I—"

"Olivia performed in some local theater in the Kentucky area, under the auspices of her father's direction," Desmond said. "I've never seen her perform but I have it on the highest authority she's very good. The children will never know they're being interrogated. Olivia is a true professional. She will *become* the teacher."

Livvie clutched the folder in her hands. *Desmond, you're not entirely forgiven, but I could jump up and kiss you right now.* The pieces fell into place, snapping into her brain like the most complicated jigsaw puzzle finally completed. *Become the teacher. Interrogate the children. Yes, that's perfect. No one will know the school teacher is analyzing each word the children say, each story they tell, each movement they make. No witnesses. No questions. No suspicion.*

"Yes," Livvie said. "I'm Billy Marlowe's daughter and I can do this."

* * * *

"I don't know if I can do this."

Desmond patted her knee then gathered the reins. "Of course you can. You're Billy Marlowe's daughter."

"You realize I helped Billy behind the scenes a few times and never actually did any acting, right?"

"Yes. I know that." He pushed the hat lower on his head to block out the sun. "I didn't see any reason for Anna to know. No need to worry her after everything she's done. You failed in there, Liv."

"In what way?"

"When Anna asked about your acting experience, you froze. The stammering and blushing didn't help either. You really need to be able to come up with a story off the top of your head. Sometimes adapting to a situation quickly without getting ruffled will keep you alive. You can't let anyone see your confusion and never let them call your bluff. It's part of the game. You need to learn it."

"You're right. I'll do better next time."

"But you were spot on with that lie. I knew you had a gift for reading people."

"Good thing too since no one planned to tell me about something as inconsequential as murder." She tilted her face toward him and peered at him, those green eyes sliding across his face with accusation.

"I wanted to tell you," he said, "but it wasn't my call."

"Next time make it your call. No secrets, Des. I need complete honesty." She glanced at him with a smile. "You had fun in there, didn't you?"

"Partly. The other half gave me a headache. I swear, Liv, sometimes you're dense." He turned to her. "Did you really not know where this was headed?"

She flounced the seat and seemed to develop an interest in a young hound meandering along the fence line. Desmond waited for her answer, watching as the dog sniffed along the path, stopping often to inspect closer, burrowing its nose into the yellowing grass and shrubs. Finally the dog lifted its leg and shot a stream of urine onto a scraggly rose bush and shot into the yard, a bundle of quivering muscles. Once the dog was out of sight, Livvie darted a quick glance toward him. "Of course I knew where it was headed. I just wanted to see if you knew."

He grabbed her chin and twisted her face. "We have an honesty deal now, remember?"

She lowered her eyes. He tightened his grip and finally her lashes fluttered up. The sunburn on her cheeks blazed as she blushed. "I didn't know. I kept trying to figure it out. I listened to every word, read those notes, kept wondering what I had missed. Sometimes I don't know where my head is."

"Your head floats around sometime in its own little world. We have to work on that." He cupped her face and gave her a long, leisurely, new-husband kiss. "You can do this, Liv. I know you can. You've got the heart and mind to do this job. And you've had good mentors. We've just got to get you the proper tools." He slapped the reins and the buggy lurched, nearly tipping Livvie out of her seat. He grabbed her arm and pulled her against him. "Next stop Bradley's."

Chapter 13

Livvie paused on the wooden walk, cupped her hands around her eyes, and peered into the window of Bradley Clothiers. When she backed away dust smudged the tip of her nose. Desmond wiped his finger across it and opened the door. A tiny bell tinkled a greeting as he hauled Livvie through the doorway. Her reluctance confused him at first, as Livvie had touted herself as a world-class shopper. But as Desmond's eyes roamed the displays and the shelves he realized why Livvie hesitated. This place would be nothing like the shops she had frequented. Not a gown or day suit anywhere in sight. She looked petrified.

A long L-shaped counter ran the length of the left wall and halfway around the back of the store. It had been divided into several distinct areas—one for dealing with customer purchases, one for holding bolts of fabric, taffeta and organza, silk and satin, and another for measuring. Behind the counter, wooden shelves rose to the ceiling, holding garments and footwear of all description. The glass case under the back counter held a nice variety of accessories. The pegs along the right wall held dresses. Livvie's face grew more sullen as she glanced around the dark interior.

Several wire mannequins held a silent vigil behind the counter, and behind a half-closed door a sewing machine whirred in a mechanical frenzy, the sound drilling into Desmond's teeth.

A young girl of about fourteen suddenly popped up from behind the counter. Livvie practically jumped out of her skin and uttered a tiny squeak. The girl's mouth dropped open and she rushed around the counter. The faint streaks of sunlight coming through the dusty window glanced off a metallic object and Desmond saw the folding knife just as she stuck out her hand. He backed up quickly, hauling Livvie with him.

"Whoa, girl! Slow down before someone gets hurts."

The girl skidded to a stop, her wide-eyed gaze darting quickly between them. She glanced at her hand and burst out laughing. She dropped the knife onto a bolt of shiny black material. The sewing machine clatter died.

She offered them a smile then flipped a lock of dark brown hair off her shoulder. "Sorry. I'm supposed to be listening for the door but I got all involved in opening the crates that came off the train. I love when we get new things in the store. We got the prettiest little dresses in and—"

"Alice, as usual, you've past the point."

A heavy set woman whirled out of the back room like a short, squat cyclone, holding her skirts as she sashayed around the counter, her hips moving up and down rhythmically. She swatted her daughter on the butt and, with her hands on the girl's shoulders, swung her toward the counter. The girl wagged her head as she plodded back behind the counter, her shoes pounding on the wooden floor with her heavy steps.

"Ah, Ma, I want to talk. They're the new people."

"Yes, and I will handle the new people. Finish up with those crates then we'll talk about that dress."

Desmond caught a smile on Alice's face as the woman turned to them with a bright smile and held out her hand. Desmond shook it, said "Connor McBride" and the woman launched a verbal assault. Words gushed from her like water from a fountain and the smell of peppermint wafted around them.

"I'm Freda Bradley. Welcome to Fort Cloud. If you're looking for clothing, then you've come to the right place." Her bird-like gaze swept across Livvie, perusing her with a practiced eye. "Though you seemed extremely well dressed and, I must say, extremely fashionable. You're also a tiny little thing. What can I do for you?"

Desmond gave Livvie's back a tiny shove. She lurched forward. "Hello, Mrs. Bradley, I—"

"Freda, dear. Everyone calls me Freda. Mrs. Bradley is my husband's mother." She heaved a sigh. "She lives with us, you know. Not that I'm opposed to that, mind you, but it does get a little tiresome at times."

"I imagine it might," Livvie said cautiously. Desmond moved away, pretending to look into the display case. Alice studied him from beneath lowered lashes, her lower lip caught between her teeth. He made a concerted effort to stay away from Alice. When he glanced over his shoulder, Livvie gave him a *thanks for nothing* look. "Well, Mrs...Freda, my name is—"

"Olivia McBride, yes, I know." Freda reached out and gripped Livvie's hand, folding it in a tight grasp. "The new teacher. We've been looking forward to your arrival for a week now. My Alice will be in your class. She's a bright girl, but you'll have to watch her. She gets easily distracted."

She tossed a look at her daughter. Alice groaned, the sound rolling from her with all the disgust her adolescent body could muster.

Freda shook her head. "It's boys, you see. She likes them. No two ways about that."

Alice mouthed *Shut up, Mother* and blushed furiously. Desmond pulled his hat down lower on his head, hunkered down and stared into the glass case, trying to keep his shoulders from shaking.

"We have a few strapping young bucks around here. She's also become—Alice, hang up that dress before you get your paw prints all over it—addicted to clothing, as you can see. She wants to wear something different every day, all to catch the eye of these new boys who roll in on the trains. " Freda tossed her hands up. "I don't know what she'll be like once school starts."

Alice reluctantly put the dress on a hanger and walked across the shop to hang it on a peg, her shoes once again clomping sullenly on the wooden floor.

Freda leaned closer to Livvie. "She wants that dress. It's one of the prettiest of the arrivals. And she'll get it, but not before I make her suffer for it." She winked. "I probably have one that will fit you as well."

Livvie flickered her fan in front of her flushed face. She took a deep breath, seemingly determined to get her conversation finished.

Good luck with that, Liv.

"Your outfit is lovely." Freda gripped her shoulders and spun Livvie around. Livvie blanched and began to sputter. "New York designer, I'd say. I get all the ladies' books here. They arrive late, of course, but it does help to keep us reasonably up-to-date. This suit is simply beautiful. I'd love to study it to make a pattern. I love that color on you and the material…" She ran her hand down Livvie's sleeve, pinching the fabric between her fingers. "It's so soft. Satin brocade simply invites touch, doesn't it?"

"I guess so," Livvie muttered.

"But!" Freda clapped her hands together. "It's also a bit warm, isn't it? You've come to me because your clothing is uncomfortable here, is that right? Had I known your size I would simply have sent clothing out to the old Carpenter place. I can imagine you've been dying in this heat." She bustled across the floor and began to pull dresses from the pegs. "How is the Carpenter place by the way? You know when Abel Carpenter died I was so afraid that place would fall into ruin. The last I'd heard…"

Desmond tuned Freda out and wandered over to where Livvie stood, her hand gripping her fan in a fist, her mouth opening and closing as she stared at the woman's back.

Livvie leaned toward him and whispered, "I've never seen anything like her." Freda continued to talk about the Carpenter ranch, asking random questions but never waiting for an answer.

"You'll get used to the way people are here in Kansas." He leaned down and kissed her cheek. "I'm going to sit outside on the bench. Keep an eye on the wagon."

Livvie spun around, her jaw dropping. She clutched his hand. She ground the words through clenched teeth. "You can't leave me here alone."

"You'll be fine. Get to know the denizens of your new town. Take your time."

When the bell tinkled over the door, he turned and gave her a wave. She gave him a murderous glare as Freda whirled around, her arms filled with frocks and dresses, and said, "See you later, Mr. McBride! Now, let's go try some of these things on, shall we?"

"Come back soon, Mr. McBride!" Alice called.

He burst into laughter when he hit the wooden walkway. "God help her. That was worse than a pit of vipers." He shook his head as he stretched out on the bench, angling his hat over his face to cover his inspection of the street.

* * * *

Bathed in sweat and fuming like a volcano, Livvie battled her armful of clothing, shoving it onto a bench and holding back a screech that would wake the dead. She struggled with the buttons of her blouse, losing one in the process, and peeled the sticky clothes from her body. She let them drop into a heap on the floor. She didn't care because she didn't intend to wear them again in Kansas. When she stood in her slip, she felt considerably less irritable and a lot cooler. Beyond the closed door, Freda kept up a constant string of one-sided conversation. Livvie tried her best to keep up as she pulled and tugged clothing over her head. She hoped her muffled responses were enough and they seemed to be because Freda continued on unabated.

"Oh, do let me take a look, dear. I want to see if I've chosen the correct size."

Reluctantly Livvie cracked open the door and peeked around it. Freda stood in the small hallway, waving her forward. Alice hovered nearby, straining to see beyond her mother. Livvie walked out in stocking feet and stood for inspection. Freda once again whirled her in a circle, making tiny noises before finally nodded her approval.

"You look lovely. I knew it would fit." She clapped her hands together. "Now let's see the rest."

Livvie's heart sank, but she nodded and returned to the tiny changing room. When she got her hands on Desmond, he was a dead man.

Two hours later, Livvie wore a sky blue cotton dress printed with white flowers. She also wore a straw bonnet that shaded her face from the sun and a pair of lightweight boots. Alice and Freda helped Livvie carry the purchases out to the walkway. Desmond, who looked like he'd fallen asleep, unfurled his long body from the bench and stretched. His gaze raked over the mountains of packages in their arms.

"You buy everything in the store?"

"Everything that fit," Livvie muttered. "And I didn't stop there."

She'd bought new clothing for the McBride brothers as well— trousers and shirts in several varieties, two of each kind. Freda had given her a questioning glance on the duplicates but for once hadn't commented.

When everything was loaded into the wagon, and the thank yous and farewells were said, the Bradleys returned to their store. Livvie heaved a sigh of relief, casting a glance at the closed door.

"I thought Anna said the people here would be reluctant to talk."

"Not all of them. Prairie people either never shut up or never open their mouths."

"Just out of curiosity, were you sleeping when I came out?"

"I'm under cover, Liv. I'd look a little suspicious watching people's every move. A *real* husband would fall asleep if his wife made him go shopping." He flicked his fingers across her bonnet, tipping it down over her eyes. "Cute hat. Not quite—"

She held up her hand. "Isn't it enough that I look like a country bumpkin? Do you need to make it worse?" She ran her hands down her thighs, her fingers tracing the light cotton fabric. She didn't really care how it looked. She loved the way the warm breeze seemed to flow through it, not quite naked, but as close as she could get. But if her friends could see her, they'd wonder if the heat had stolen more than her fashion sense.

"I like it," Desmond said.

She pursed her lips and lifted her face, peering at him suspiciously. There had to be some kind of ridicule in there somewhere. She knew she must look like she'd stepped out of a dime novel. But his gaze traveled down the length of her body and back up to linger on the tops of her breasts and that look in his eye said he might be telling the truth.

"I like it too," Livvie said. "And I can finally breathe. Wait 'til you see what I got for you."

He took her arm and she cast a glance back to the window of Bradley's Clothiers. Shadows moved inside. Apparently Freda and Alice hadn't gotten enough entertainment for one afternoon. Livvie suspected they hadn't gotten enough of looking at Desmond.

"I meant to ask Anna about getting us some help at the ranch," Livvie said. "But Freda Bradley seems to know everything about this town. Do you think I should ask her who might be available for hire?"

Desmond shook his head as he led her across the street. "We can't get help, Liv."

"Why ever not? We can't possibly do all the work around the ranch, cook the meals, clean the house, teach school and—"

"How are you going to explain two husbands?"

Livvie's shoulders slumped. "Oh."

"We'll manage." He cast a glance up and down the street. "As long as we can keep people away from the ranch."

He escorted her to the Brandywine Hotel for a late lunch. They ate thick ham sandwiches on crusty white bread and iced tea, followed by a slice of chocolate cake. Over lunch they quietly discussed Livvie's assignment, perusing the portfolio Anna had given her. She'd be teaching the entire spectrum of ages from a little boy of six to a boy of fifteen. Her heart sank deeper and deeper as she read, knowing she had no idea what she'd be doing.

She shuffled the pages back into the folder. "I never thought I'd say this, but I wish Abbie was here."

Desmond laughed, pushing his plate away. "You *are* desperate."

She stared out the window, her chin cupped in her hand. Her gaze lingered on a child skipping down the street, rolling a hoop—one of her potential students no doubt. He was a tiny thing, possibly her six-year-old, Tyler Talbot. She wished she could be out there playing with him instead of dealing with a churning stomach and aching head. She should have listened to her parents' stories with a more critical ear. She'd heard only glamour, excitement, danger. She'd heard nothing about the day-to-day grind of fulfilling an assignment with no guarantee of success and no idea where to start. She'd learned one thing in the last couple weeks since she'd gotten Martin's letter about the mission—she needed to stop leaping into things with both feet before she thought things through. She had only herself to blame for this dilemma.

Her little student looked carefree and happy, totally oblivious to the danger that lurked in this small community. If she made a mistake, if she said the wrong thing, did the wrong thing, she could destroy all that. She'd have to tread carefully and—

"Desmond, I want to go to the mercantile."

Desmond gave her a dubious glance. "Livvie, you've got enough outfits in that wagon to clothe half of Fort Cloud. Besides, I prefer you not look like a field hand."

She waved her hand. "No, no, not for me." She swept aside the curtain and pointed at the boy. "For him. And his friends. I want to buy them some things."

Desmond peered out the window. He studied the boy for a moment then turned to her, his mouth twitching into a smile. "You're going to *bribe* them?"

Livvie shrugged. "I prefer to think of it as scattering happiness to get what I want."

Desmond laughed and shook his head. "I knew you'd come up with something."

"Whoever said money can't buy happiness is wrong. I think I can prove it."

He stood and grabbed his hat from the hook. He held out his hand and pulled Livvie to her feet. She smashed into his body, feeling his heat through the thin cotton of her new dress. His arms wrapped around her waist and pulled her tighter. She peered up at him, loving the smile on his face, the merriment in his eyes, glad he approved of her plan. He stared at her for a moment then leaned down and his mouth covered hers in a soft kiss. For one moment, she relaxed against him, enjoying the feel of muscled arms, the press of hard thighs against her, the lips that stirred her mouth to open to accept his tongue. Her arms lifted to wrap around his neck and pull him tighter.

Her pussy clenched and an ache beat inside. She felt moisture leak between her legs. She had an insane desire to pull herself up, wrap her legs around his waist, and feel the hot pulse of his cock against her.

When she heard movement behind them, a strangled groan caught in her throat. Desmond released her reluctantly and she lurched backward, tugging on her skirt. A hot blush rose in her face as several patrons glanced at them, smiled, and ducked their heads. She grabbed her straw hat and adjusted it, trying desperately to hide her face. Desmond chuckled and turned to Mr. Mercer who stood behind them. She had no idea what they talked about. Her ears roared with the blood consuming her face. When he took her arm and led her out of the restaurant, she heard murmuring and light laughter trailing behind them. She pulled her hat down lower on her head, muttering as Desmond helped her into the wagon.

"Thanks a lot. They'll be talking about that for days."

"You seem the kind of woman who enjoys creating a public spectacle."

"Well, I am…I mean I was, but I'm not used to feeling this way. You do something to me. Something that makes me forget where I am, what I'm doing. I start leaking and…"

She stared straight ahead until he turned her face up to his. "And?"

She signed. "And wanting. You make me want things."

He dropped a kiss on her lips, another public spectacle. "Good. It makes the ruse all the more believable. Now let's go get your bait."

An hour later Livvie had several sacks and crates full of goodies to bribe, entice, compensate, and otherwise get what she wanted. The variety in the mercantile left much to be desired, but she'd done her best. She'd selected candies of all descriptions—peppermint sticks, butterscotch and lemon drops, taffy and caramels. She selected toys for all ages—cups and balls, rag dolls, yo-yos, slingshots, blocks, games for indoor and outdoor use—and whistles, harmonicas and drums. She bought additional slates and chalk, art supplies, several children's storybooks and a collection of dime novels.

As Desmond loaded the wagon with her purchases, he gave her a smile. "Planning to spend any time teaching?"

"Not if I can help it. I'm on a mission, remember?"

Before they left town, Desmond hopped from the wagon in front of the Brandywine. The owner came out and handed Desmond a large wicker hamper. Tantalizing aromas drifted from inside. Even though she'd just eaten, her mouth watered. When she tried to lift the lid, Desmond held it closed. Livvie leaned closer and sniffed.

"It smells like a beef roast."

"It is a beef roast," Desmond said. "With mashed potatoes and gravy. Thought we should all have a meal from the Brandywine. I mean it *is* dinner."

* * * *

Connor got the fire going in the stove to heat his stew then went outside to rustle up a little more dinner. He stepped into the garden and noticed something had been scavenging the vegetation. The scattered dirt and burrows indicated several potatoes and a cabbage had been unearthed. He kicked at the mounds. He didn't mind sharing but he hated a thief.

"Damn prairie dogs."

He'd plucked a couple of tomatoes from the vine when a haze of dust appeared in the distance. He hadn't expected them back so soon. A nice dinner at the Brandywine should have taken a lot longer. He took his greens into the house and prepared a salad then went outside and sat on the porch to wait. When they pulled into the dooryard, delicious aromas drifted around the buggy. Livvie wore a new outfit and she looked good enough to eat, but those smells… He practically tripped over himself to get to them. He tossed paper packages trying to unearth what smelled like a beef roast. He sniffed again. And possibly peach cobbler. A basket had been anchored under the seat. Connor hopped into the wagon to retrieve it as Desmond climbed down from the seat. The wagon swayed when Livvie jumped into Desmond's arms, nearly tipping Connor over.

"You're going to get yourself killed," Desmond said.

"It will be worth it if this is what I think." He hopped from the wagon and lifted the lid, staring at a platter, several bowls covered in cloths and a large dish of peach cobbler. He pulled the aroma deep into his lungs. "I'm going to owe you both for this."

"No," Livvie said. "We owe you for taking care of everything around here."

Desmond gathered the packages from the wagon. "The faster you get it into the oven to warm it up, the faster we can eat."

The prairie dogs could have the cabbage.

Chapter 14

The dinner might have been the most delicious meal Desmond had ever had but he had to admit the company added to the enjoyment. Even after working all day in the heat surrounded by the nauseating aromas of manure and animals, Connor was in great spirits. Livvie laughed and joked about their afternoon as she told of the horrors of Bradley's Clothiers.

"I swear, after an afternoon in that dressing room, I'm ready to be an acrobat in the circus."

Connor hacked off a piece of cobbler and nearly dropped it in his haste to get it to his plate. "Now that's something I'd like to see— Livvie in a circus. You'd look great in one of those costumes."

"I love circuses," Livvie said. "The Fathers took us every year when it came to Maysville. Abbie and Mother ran right to the menageries. My sister became obsessed with large animals. I expected her to travel to Africa at the first opportunity. Jake and Billy always took off toward the clowns." She shook her head. "I never understood their fascination because I found clowns slightly sinister, like they were hiding something evil behind those painted smiles. Billy of course laughed and said they were just good actors who liked the thrill of performing without the restrictions of a director."

"And which part of the circus did you like best, Liv?" Desmond asked.

"Oh, I'd grab Cutter's hand and we'd head for the sharpshooters. I knew he liked that best. If someone was aiming something at a target, that's where we were."

Connor glanced at Desmond. "Is that what you liked best, Liv?"

She glanced down at her plate, toying with the fork. "Well, no, but someone had to go with him, otherwise what fun would he have had?" She shrugged. "I liked all of it anyway and eventually we made it into the tent for the shows. But, I understand how Cutter felt and I admired him for it. Even in what was otherwise a frivolous atmosphere, he needed a purpose. I've always struggled with that. Finding purpose. Cutter taught me it's important to live life outside yourself. I don't think I've done very well with that, but he never gave up on me. It's part of the reason I wanted this assignment and it thrills me he played a part in getting it for me."

"You think there's purpose in this, Liv?" Desmond asked.

"Oh, yes. This is a chance to make a real difference in someone's life. At least I hope it is. I want to succeed. I want to make Cutter proud of me, let him know that he's taught me so much, even surrounded by circus music." She laughed. "Bullets, knives, axes, all finding their way to a target. It's so much more than simple entertainment. There's purpose in it. It's a true skill and one you can use in real life."

Connor nodded and laughed suddenly. "Desmond and Cutter probably have a lot in common. After we went to the circus and Des saw the knife-thrower he wanted to join up. He honed his target skills to perfection, but it sure as hell took a lot of sheets."

Livvie pushed her plate out of the way and leaned forward. "Tell me."

Desmond's gaze swung between the two of them. "Where the fuck did that come from? I've never been to a circus in my life." Desmond peered at his brother but Connor toyed with his fork, refusing to look at him. The smile disappeared from Livvie's face and her brows drew downward. Desmond waited a few moments before he said softly, "Have I, Connor?"

Livvie blew out a breath. "How can you not know if you've been to a circus? It's one of the most memorable things—"

Desmond held up his hand. "Have I, Connor?"

Connor glanced up. "Yes, Des, you have."

"And when exactly was that again?"

"Not sure. About a year before Ma..." He scrubbed at his face then raked his hair back. "We were about seven."

"So tell me," Desmond said.

Connor's glance darted to Livvie then returned to him. "Are you sure?"

Desmond nodded. Livvie looked very confused and he guessed he didn't blame her. The woman remembered everything since she'd popped out of her mother's womb. What would she think when she discovered he'd lost the first ten years of his life somewhere along the line?

Connor rubbed at a spot on his forehead. Apparently he'd developed a headache. Well, that seemed only fair since Desmond suddenly had one of his own. "Do you want me to tell all of it?"

Desmond nodded.

"A couple of older boys had some circus flyers at school. They—"

Desmond dropped back against the seat. "We went to *school?*"

Connor sighed. "Yes, Des, we went to school. I told you that before. Ma walked us there every day when she went to work at the mercantile in town. And old Miss Haggerty, well, let's just say when they invented the word schoolmarm, it was based on her. There has never been anyone marmier."

"Sounds like a real beauty," Livvie said.

"And she was so skinny, it was hard to tell where her arm ended and the ruler began." Connor shuddered. "But we weren't thinking about Miss Haggerty that day. Our mind filled with images of the circus we saw on that flyer. That night at supper you were determined to convince Ma she should take us, but when she glanced at the flyer, she had a sad look and said she didn't know if she could. I put up a fuss. It seemed to be what I did best in those days, but you shrugged and said it was okay. I thought you were crazy. You'd been so fired up to get to that circus, but you were always more in touch with Ma's feelings than I was."

"She couldn't afford it," Livvie whispered.

"No," Connor said, "she couldn't. And Des knew right away and as usual he had a plan. Nothing stops Des when he's on a mission. The next day after school, he dropped his books into my arms and told me to get home and do his chores. When I tried to protest, he gave me such a look I figured arguing with him would be the worst thing I could do. This went on for three days and I'd just about had it by Friday. On Saturday morning, he plopped a pocketful of coins down in front of Ma. He'd been mucking out stalls at Grady's livery. He looked at Ma and said he was taking her to the circus. I don't think I've ever seen a more beautiful smile on Ma than she had that day. While she put on her prettiest dress, we washed the breakfast dishes. We've never done dishes faster in our lives."

Desmond's hands tightened on his thighs. Why couldn't he remember her face? Why couldn't he remember anything about his life with her, what she smelled like, the sound of her voice? She seemed like a woman who'd be impossible to forget and yet—

"So we walked the five miles to the circus. We had the best day— though just about every day was good with Ma. Des had earned enough money for tickets with plenty left over to buy some of the food. Oh, the circus has the best food!" Connor's eyes closed in bliss. "I can still taste it and smell it. I can still hear the music of the calliope and the roar of the jungle cats. And the colors seemed like they'd come from another world. After living day after day in a place of only greens and browns, the streamers fluttering in the breeze seemed like a wonder and the costumes almost hurt your eyes. I felt like I'd been dropped into a magical place that day thanks to Des."

Desmond closed his eyes for a moment, listening to Connor's words, trying to find any shred of memory. It seemed as though he should be able to follow the colorful streamers and the sounds of the calliope, grasp the memory, and claim it for his own. But it remained elusive, like trying to remember a long ago dream fluttering at the edge of consciousness. Connor remembered everything as though it had been branded into his mind, an image he could pull out of his pocket and look at, enjoying even touch, taste, and sound. Desmond could only listen and try to conjure up any image at all.

"I wanted to see everything, experience each performance, hear every song, and sample the food in every booth. All of that wonder and Des wouldn't leave the knife-thrower. He watched him for hours. Ma and I couldn't even get him to move when the main event started in the tent. So we waited for him because he had brought us there. I got a little impatient but Ma just stood and waited, watching Des, talking with me about everything around us."

"And you don't remember this, Des?" Livvie asked.

"No, Liv," Desmond said softly.

"The next day Des wanted to learn how to throw a knife. Ma got an old sheet and drew a target on it with some charcoal. And she offered him a deal. She said she'd teach him and he could practice but only when the sheeting hung on the barn door and she stood beside him."

"Your mother was a wise woman," Livvie said. "Did he stick to the bargain?"

Connor laughed. "He had to. Ma slept with the sheet and carried it with her in a basket when she left the house." Livvie burst out laughing and Connor glanced at his brother. "But Des would have stuck to the bargain anyway. That's the kind of boy he was."

Something slammed through Desmond's gut. He didn't know where it came from but it hit harder than a fist and ground through his insides like a ricocheting bullet. His eyes burned. He needed to get out of the house and away from Connor's voice. He needed to stop trying to picture her because it hurt his head and made his heart ache. He'd give anything to remember.

"Your mother sounds very special." Livvie paused. "How—"

Desmond pushed his chair back. The screech of the legs scraping on the floor thankfully drowned out Livvie's words. He didn't want to hear or answer her question. He ignored the surprised look on her face, grabbed his hat, and headed for the door. "I'll go close down the barn for the night."

* * * *

They hadn't seen Desmond for hours. They'd played a game of chess, but Connor had moved his pieces mechanically without much thought. He thought Livvie probably loved to win but when she put him in check, she'd expressed no joy which surprised him. She'd also been far too quiet all evening though he didn't mind. He feared their discussion about their unique and loving mother had cast a pall over all of them. After she put the chessboard away Livvie settled into his lap and looped her arms across his shoulders. She pressed her lips against his neck.

"You never said if you liked my new dress."

"I didn't? I meant to. Guess I got sidetracked by that basket."

"Maybe you'd like to see the new under things I got too?"

Livvie seemed to have something on her mind. It might have been designed to sidetrack his wayward thoughts but it worked. His cock twitched against her thigh and he moved his arm around her waist.

"What are you wearing?"

"Oh, skimpy airy little things." She trailed her fingers across a breast and watching her touch herself made him harder. "Freda said they're the latest fashion." She laughed a delightful little laugh. "That's debatable of course since Kansas is a little far from New York, but they're very pretty and feel so silky against my skin. Would you like to feel?"

She lifted her skirt to reveal a calf covered in gauzy white fabric. Connor's hand slid down her leg, enjoying the feel of it, but his mind was on something else. He slid his hand under the material and caressed her bare leg above her boot. "They feel very nice. Very soft."

She smiled. "That's my skin, Connor, not the bloomers."

He laughed. "Really? Feels like silk to me."

He ran his hand up her leg slowly watching her face. She tried to keep her eyes focused on him but when he reached her thigh, her lids began to flutter. Her teeth grazed her lower lip. He slid his hand farther, hovering just below the warm, wet pulse of her pussy.

His hand moved up the side of her body and he touched the tip of her breast. Her nipple rose and pressed against the calico. He resisted the impulse to squeeze it because he didn't want to ruin whatever scenario she had on her mind. He appreciated her little attempt at seduction and loved that she'd do that for him. "And what are you wearing here?"

She took a breath and her voice came out in a husky whisper as the hand under her dress dipped a little closer to her pussy. "Oh, a new camisole, in the same material. It's designed to cover but…but doesn't interfere with the lines of the dress. The material of this dress is much thinner than some of my others. You can practically see through it." She sighed. "Though I doubt you noticed with the lure of that beef roast."

"I noticed," he said softly, "even with the lure of beef." He lightly skimmed his palm across her nipple. "Could I see the camisole?"

"Of course." She slowly undid the three buttons on the bodice of the dress, folding down the edges to expose the delicate embroidery that trimmed her silk camisole. It sure was a beautiful thing but he didn't care about a scrap of silk. The swell of her breasts rose high above the neckline, a dark deep valley between them. He wanted to nuzzle his face there and breathe in the perfume of her skin. Connor laid the flat of his fingers on her breast, caressing her lightly.

"So beautiful."

"Are you looking at the camisole?"

His eyes lifted to hers. "Not really. I'm afraid fashion is lost on a man like me, Liv. I'm more interested in what it covers." He tugged at the tie that held the camisole closed and it came loose, opening to expose her breasts. He cupped one in his hand, squeezing and lifting it, ducking his head. His tongue flickered across her nipple and he liked the little shiver that ripped through her upper body. He pulled the nipple into his mouth with a quick tug, sucking hard. She jumped slightly and made a funny little noise. Her hand fluttered near his hair and he knew he'd turn the seduction around when she gripped it in a fist and clutched him closer.

He pressed his thumb against her clit and she sat up straighter, pulling the nipple from his mouth with a suctioning noise.

"Oh, no you don't." He slid his hand away from her pussy.

"Touch me." She dropped her head and her lips touched his hair.

"I want that nipple back in my mouth. Something for you, something for me."

She cupped her breast in her hand and guided it toward his mouth, teasing him by sliding the nipple back and forth across his lips. He swiped it with his tongue and tried to wrap his mouth around it, but she pulled away.

"Touch my clit," she said.

"Yes, princess."

He slid his index finger across her pussy, wetting it with her juices, then found her clit and began to rub it. She brought her breast back to his mouth and he nipped at it. She jerked but didn't take it away. She pushed closer, angling it into his mouth and he sucked it in greedily.

The little nub beneath his finger swelled and hardened with his touch. Her breaths fell across his hair in short pants, punctuated with small moans of pleasure that made his cock throb and his balls ache. He wanted inside her, to feel the soft muscles grip and pulse against his dick and bathe him in the sweet moisture that dripped over his fingers.

His finger dipped inside and her hips rose to meet him. He thrust hard and she held her breath as he angled his finger and caressed the upper wall of her pussy from back to front, searching for that spot he knew would push her over. Her body had begun to tremble and she was close. He sucked on her nipple to match the strokes against her skin. When her body shuddered, her hips jerked up. She collapsed back into his arm and her pussy clenched his finger in a violent contraction. His cock jerked in his pants and leapt toward her. He pushed his finger upwards and her skin quivered under his lips and hands.

When the trembling subsided, he covered her mouth in a hard, deep kiss. She sucked his tongue in greedily, her arms wrapped around his neck. He stood, lifting her in his arms and put her on the floor against the back of the sofa, bending her forward. Quickly he loosened his pants, then flung up her dress and yanked down her bloomers. He grabbed his cock, rock hard and throbbing, and thrust inside her wet pussy. He sank to the hilt in one movement, grabbing her hips and pulling. She lifted on her toes and pushed backwards with a soft cry.

He sought her clit again and rubbed hard as he plunged into her again and again. Her pussy clamped down hard on his cock, the muscles throbbing against his pulsing flesh, milking him. His balls tightened and slapped against her each time he pounded into her, sliding into her damp heat.

She came fast, her body thrusting back against him and burying him deep. The sudden clench caused his cock to explode and his fluid shot out fast, hard, and heavy, flooding her with his seed. Heart pounding, he lowered himself onto her back and kissed her shoulder.

"My new bloomers are going to be all wet," she murmured.

He chuckled. "I'll buy you more."

A muffled laugh rose from the cloud of hair that had fallen over her face. "Not necessary. I already bought six pairs."

Connor withdrew slowly, trying to minimize the mess then grabbed the corner of his shirt. He cleaned up the fluid that leaked from her pussy, gently wiping the engorged area. When he was finished, he lifted her and carried her upstairs. She undressed quietly, watching him as he stripped down. After Connor pulled down the quilt, they settled on the cool sheet to wait for his wayward brother.

Chapter 15

Livvie stared up at the ceiling, waiting for her heartbeat to return to a normal rhythm. She'd set out to sidetrack Connor from worrying about Desmond, but he'd completely stolen her thoughts. Now listening to the crickets outside and Connor's quiet breaths she found them wandering back into her mind and she needed to know the answers. She couldn't help them if she didn't know.

"Why doesn't Desmond remember anything, Connor?"

"I wish I knew."

"How did your mother die?"

Livvie turned and snuggled against him, wrapping her arm around his waist. Connor's chest rose and fell as he heaved a tired and heart-breaking sigh. For a moment, she didn't think he would answer.

"There was an accident, Liv. And it was my fault." Connor turned his face toward the window and his voice fell to a whisper. "I sure as hell didn't mean it to end the way it did. I'd give anything—"

His voice broke and Livvie rose up. She cupped his cheek and turned his face toward her. In the moonlight streaming through the window, she saw the tears that glistened in his eyes. He pulled away and sat up, swinging his legs over the side of the bed. He dropped his face into his hands and Livvie had to strain to listen to each word he forced from his lips.

"I was stupid that day and I pretty much killed our mother and ruined my brother's life. Mine too I guess. Though I don't think about that because I deserve everything I get."

Livvie stroked his back. "That can't be true, Connor."

"Hmm. Well, maybe not. I don't know. I didn't think much in those days. Des did most of that for both of us. But that day I made an error in judgment and I've paid for it every day since. Ma had warned us about old man Murphy's bull. Hell, the entire town knew that bull was crazy as shit and cut a wide path around it when Murphy let it graze. I don't know what the fuck was wrong with me that day. Des kept to the path but I strolled right through the pasture like I owned it. The problem was I didn't. Murphy's bull owned it."

Connor stood up and her hand trailed down to the sheet. He stared out the window and the moonlight reflecting on his face made him appear pale and ghost-like.

"Normally he was a lazy son-of-a-bitch. But for some reason seeing me riled him up that day. He took off after me like a bat out of hell and chased me the whole way home. Ma was hanging the wash when I tore onto the property and Desmond had reached our front door yard. The bull had just about reached the end of its steam, but there was a tough breeze blowing that day. When it saw Ma surrounded by the wash on the line and her dress flapping around her legs that old bull charged with a new burst of energy. One minute my Ma was standing with a wet skirt in her hand and the next—"

"Oh, Connor…"

"He threw her clear over the line and she came down hard. She might have survived that but when we saw the blood we knew…hell, even at eight we knew. But that didn't stop Des. He yelled at me to get to town. He grabbed the wash off the line and started packing it into the wound. I'll never forget the look on his face. He looked like he could keep her alive through his will alone. And believe me, if that would have been possible, it would have worked."

Connor put his hand against the window to capture the moonlight. His fingers slid across the glass as though touching a ghost.

"But of course it didn't work. I'd already learned enough in my short life to know that miracles are few and far between and I sure as hell hadn't earned a miracle that day. For a few hours though I thought Desmond might get one, but even Des couldn't hold her to earth. When I got back with the doctor and a couple of men from town, Ma was gone and the bull was dead on the ground. Desmond had gotten three knives into it. I told you he was good, right? Of course, even that wasn't enough to kill a bull. He'd gotten Ma's rifle out of the house and shot it between the eyes. And Des sat at Ma's side, mopping up blood, talking to her like he did every other day."

"And he doesn't remember any of this?"

Connor shook his head. "I've told him about it. Every spring he brings it up, and he never even realizes it's the day she died. It took me awhile to get him away from her that day. The men were patient with him, almost kind. Of course by then everyone thought we were both as crazy as loons—me for aggravating a deranged bull and Des because he wouldn't talk to anyone but me. I still don't know why he talked to me when…" Connor swung around and faced her. "So after the funeral and a couple days living with Miss Haggerty they shipped us off to Richmond. About two weeks later we arrived in Kansas."

Livvie gasped. "You came out west on the orphan trains?"

Desmond's voice drifted out of the darkness. "Yes, Liv. That's why we're back here now."

* * * *

Desmond didn't like the look on Connor's face. He'd been thinking too much again. Desmond yanked off his boots and tossed them. They thumped against the floor and he heard the sound of the mattress as Livvie rose off the bed. He felt Livvie's light touch settle on his chest. He could control the irregular breathing that had gripped him, but he had no control over the thundering beat of his heart. He'd stood in the hallway for a while listening to Connor's almost fractured voice, hearing the story again, struggling to remember something that existed for him only through his brother's stories. It was hard to live only through someone else's memories, even Connor's. But Connor had to live *with* them. He didn't know which was worse.

He kept his hands at his sides and refused to look at her, staring past her to his brother.

"I wish you'd stop blaming yourself for everything," he said.

A laugh burst from Connor. "You'd blame me too if you remembered."

A quiet sob tore from Livvie's throat. Desmond pulled away from her and ripped off his shirt, tossing it onto the chair. "I know the stories, Connor. I trust that you're telling me the truth. We were little kids when all that happened. Am I supposed to hate you because you were a being a stupid kid?"

"I'd deserve it," Connor said softly.

"Well, you're not getting it no matter how much you beg. You're pretty much all I've had in my miserable life. And I wouldn't even have that if—"

"Not tonight," Connor said.

Livvie turned and faced Connor. "I think we should talk about all this."

Connor left the strands of light and walked into the darkness. Desmond felt the heat of his brother's body as he neared, a body so like his own. He wondered if Connor felt the same pain he did. He thought it might actually be worse for Connor but he'd never know for sure.

"We'll talk about it tomorrow, Liv," Connor said. "I'll tell you how two scared boys rode a train across country with broken hearts, about the foster parents they had, the places they ran from, the beatings they endured and about one horrible night I'd give anything to forget."

Desmond unbuttoned his pants, but paused as Connor continued. He heard pain in his voice, probably as much pain as he'd ever heard in his brother, or at least as much as he could remember.

"But tonight…" Connor put his hands on Livvie's shoulders and guided her toward Desmond. Her naked body collided with his, skin to skin. Her soft breasts smashed against his chest. "Tonight I think we both need to bury our memories. You've already helped me. Now help Des. Can you do that?"

"Yes," Livvie whispered.

Livvie slowly lowered to her knees in front of him. Desmond had only a moment to wonder what had happened when her hand wound around his already hard cock, squeezing, tugging, stroking. Her tongue peeked out and swiped the tip, licking the moisture, then swirling her tongue around the head. He held in a groan as the sharp bite of pleasure gripped him and, though he ached to thrust between her lips and bury himself in her mouth, he kept his hands at his sides. She licked the length then dipped lower and licked his hot aching balls. He reached down and put his hands in the silky strands of her hair, raking through them until his fingers curled around the back of her head. But still he held back.

She wrapped her lips around his cock then slowly drove forward, sliding his cock an inch at a time into her warm mouth. His cock pulsed in a frantic rhythm, waiting for the friction of her lips and tongue. When she began to suck he pulled her head closer. She wrapped one arm around him and with her other hand gently cupped his balls, massaging them to the rhythm of her mouth. She sucked harder and he knew he'd explode. But he wanted something else.

Hard as it was he waited until she slid up his cock and licked the swollen head. Then, he reached down and took his dick in his hand and pulled her to her feet. He locked his hands on her hips and yanked her against him. Her heartbeat pulsed with a chaotic rhythm against his chest. It stirred his senses and broke his heart. Connor still watched them from the shadows.

Desmond pushed his face into her hair and his cock swelled hard between them, lunging against her. "I need to fuck you, Liv. Right now."

Her warm breath flooded across his chest. "Yes, right now."

He swept her up and she wrapped her legs around him. He held her easily, her body so light in his arms, a soft weight that seemed like nothing. She stared up at him with complete trust, her eyes wide, her lips parted. He met Connor's eyes over her head. He nodded slightly and Connor moved closer to them. He pressed himself against Livvie's back.

"Livvie, lean against me," Connor said.

She tilted her head, not quite understanding. Desmond angled his hands beneath her and she tilted backwards against his brother. Her arm lifted and curled around Connor's neck. The other stretched out and grazed Desmond's chest in a soft caress. Connor's hand tucked under her bottom and Desmond took advantage of it to grab his cock. He slid it along her pussy lips, gathering her moisture and wetting her opening. She sighed when the head dipped inside. He felt the soft nip of her muscles against him. When she bit her lower lip, he pushed his cock into her, sinking deep. He almost groaned with the warmth that enveloped him, the gentle folds that spread around him and the pressure of her muscles as she gripped him tight.

Connor began to lift her up and down, gently, slowly. Desmond's cock slid in and out in the rhythm of Connor's movements, a rocking that felt so good and yet not enough. Desmond gripped her hips, tugging harder to increase the pace until his cocked rammed into her, slamming her body into his brother's. Connor swayed with each impact but held steady. Livvie's body tightened and began to tremble and Desmond watched her face as the pleasure swelled through her, the most beautiful thing he'd ever seen. He hoped he could hold to all these memories.

Connor pressed kisses against Livvie's arm and face. She leaned her head to the side to grant him access to her neck, her body trembling. Desmond's balls tightened and his cock throbbed. He wanted to kiss her. He pulled her hips and yanked her forward and down. His cock slammed into her and he came in a hard spasm that shook his body. But in that moment he reached out and grabbed her shoulders, pulling her toward him and smothering her mouth in a kiss. She threw her arms around his neck, returning his kiss, pressing her breasts against his chest. He let himself drown in the softness that surrounded him.

She lifted slightly as Connor's hands slipped away then lowered herself slowly onto his cock, pressing tight against him. She pressed another soft kiss against his lips.

"Feeling better?" she asked softly.

"Much."

She smiled. "You missed seeing my new bloomers."

"Maybe you can show me tomorrow after target practice."

She laughed. "Maybe I can show you *during* target practice. I like to win."

Desmond walked to the bed and dropped her to the mattress. She bounced up with a laugh and just in time to catch another kiss.

"Play time's over," Connor said. "Hit the hay."

Desmond watched the moonlight play over Livvie's face as she rolled her eyes and settled back under the sheet. She crooked a finger at each of them and they joined her. Desmond fell asleep listening to Livvie's soft even breaths and Connor's satisfied snore.

Chapter 16

Livvie tried to concentrate on the target. She pushed at her eyeglasses and twisted her shoulders. They were determined she prove she could keep herself alive. She knew she could do it but her mind whirled with everything Connor had told her over breakfast. Desmond had sat quietly, listening intently like he'd never heard the stories before though it had been obvious Connor had told them many times. After everything they'd been through, these men seemed like a miracle to her. She'd wanted to hear more but Desmond insisted they had work to do.

Livvie pulled the rifle up to her shoulder and aimed at the sheet stretched between two trees across the field. Her shot rang out and a hole appeared near the center of the bull's eye. Connor whooped and hollered like a kid at a county fair, throwing his hat into the air. Practical Desmond refused to celebrate.

"Take another shot."

"Hell, Des, she's a natural," Connor said. "I don't think you could have done better."

Desmond lifted a brow. "Thanks for the critique. It wasn't bad, but that could have been a lucky shot. Liv, this time move back farther."

Livvie gave Connor a quick glance, trying to keep a serious expression on her face. She moved back several paces and adjusted the rifle again. She had no trouble proving a point. When she squeezed the trigger, another hole appeared in the sheet, closer to the center.

Desmond shook his head. "Can you do it without your eyeglasses?"

Livvie eyed the target doubtfully. "I'll be able to see the sheet and maybe the circle, but—"

Connor groaned. "Ah, Des, don't make her take them off. I love those glasses. My dick loves those glasses. In fact…" He took a step toward her and she scurried backwards, laughing.

Desmond moved in front of Livvie, blocking his brother's movement. "Jesus, Connor. What are you? Sixteen? We're working here."

"But the glasses, Des. And it's mighty hot out here. Maybe we could lie under that tree? I'll bet Liv could use a little shade, maybe a little something else to help her relax. You're making this stressful for her. Can't we take a break?"

"No, we can't," Desmond said. "We just started. She can wear the eyeglasses tonight, just for your dick, since you obviously need an added incentive to get it up."

Connor pulled back, making a face. "You're so full of horseshit, Des. Do you actually believe yourself when you talk? I've got a lady here who will testify I don't need *any* incentive to get my dick up."

Livvie nodded quickly, stifling a giggle. Desmond shoved his brother in the chest and Connor flew backwards, laughing his ass off. Desmond frowned. "The lady is mine for the afternoon. Go herd some cattle or something. And bring us back some food. Roast beef sandwiches."

Connor rolled his eyes. "Sure thing, boss." He pointed at himself then at Livvie, mouthing "You. Me. Later." He patted his hand against his heart. She laughed as he backed up and smacked into his horse. He mounted and gave her a leering smile before racing off toward the house.

"What a pain in my ass," Desmond said.

Livvie smiled. "I don't think you could exist without him."

"Some days I'd sure like to try."

"It sounds as though you've both fought hard to stay together and succeeded. Coming here on the trains couldn't have been easy."

"It wasn't." He gestured toward the target. "Keep going. I want to—"

She put her hand on his arm. "I want something too, Des."

He stiffened under her hand, holding his breath. "What?" he murmured.

"I want to know what *really* happened to you. There's more to your story than running away and being returned to bad foster homes. I think there's more here than a couple lashes with a belt, being tired and hungry and working yourself to the bone for ungrateful and uncaring people. There's something Connor didn't tell me this morning."

Desmond ran a hand over his jaw. "Seems he told you just about everything."

"No, he didn't. I could tell by the relief on your face when we left the house. And whatever secret you have between you is the reason you feel compelled to be involved in this assignment. Are you going to tell me or not?"

Desmond took a deep breath. "It's not something I really remember, Liv."

She focused on the target and squeezed off another shot, hitting the target then handed the rifle to Desmond.

"Would Connor tell me if I ask?"

Desmond shook his head. "I'll tell you what I know."

Livvie felt the blood drain from her face as he told her the story of how Connor had saved his life. She listened, knowing Desmond might never remember how truly bad it had been living with Lucas Price. The memories he told, littered with holes, belonged to someone else, a second-hand story that had happened to another boy in another world. The pain etched on his face seemed enough to last a lifetime but it reflected a shared pain with another boy, someone whose memories and life had been torn asunder by a monster. That he couldn't remember seemed almost merciful. His voice fluctuated as he talked, one moment filled with compassion for a victim and the next anger toward an abuser, but never with any kind of personal grief or torment. One thing kept her tears at bay. If she released them, Desmond's story would no longer be a tale that had fueled their commitment to help other boys. Whether he remembered it or not, the reality of it would hit with a vengeance.

When he finished talking, she envisioned two young boys striding on a dusty plain, laughing and planning for their future. Those boys had come far in their journey and the man who stared down at her looked relieved as though he'd shed a burden.

"Is Lucas Price the man Connor killed?" Livvie asked.

Desmond shot a glance toward the target before he nodded.

"Connor made the right decision." She took off her glasses and slid them in her pocket. "Guess we'll see how good I really am."

The circle was a dim outline against the white background but she never doubted she could hit somewhere inside it. And somewhere inside it meant a body hit. That's all Desmond wanted. As she squeezed the trigger, she thought of the man who'd just about beaten Desmond to death. If Connor hadn't already killed him, she'd scour the plains and prairie to find him.

She aimed and fired and, though the shot wasn't near the center, it fell within the boundaries. Desmond shook his head as he slid the rifle into his carrier.

"You're sure you only had two lessons?"

Livvie shuffled her feet then peered at him from beneath lowered lashes. "Oh, I didn't tell you? They have shooting contests at circuses and fairs. Cutter and I had lots of fun duping everyone out of their money. That was our favorite part. Of course after a while people recognized us and stopped betting. We had to travel farther to have fun."

"They have knife-throwing contests at these fairs?"

"Sure. Lots of them."

"Ever throw?"

"A few times."

"Let's go move the target. You can show me."

She wasn't as good as Desmond, but she held her own and they had a wonderful afternoon.

Chapter 17

The next morning Livvie tugged the knot out of her hair for the second time. Curls cascaded around her shoulders. She huffed and raked it back, pulling it tight. She stuck pins into it with shaking fingers.

She moaned at her reflection. "You look like Miss Haggerty."

"Not even close," said a voice from the doorway. She made a face as Connor swung into the room, his hand hooked on the doorjamb. He eyed her green robe, his gaze lingering on the open neck. "Des is hitching up the wagon. You about ready?"

"Not even close." She pulled the pins out of her hair and tossed them on the dressing table. She sank into the chair and dropped her head into her hands. "I'm nervous. I can't even get my hair right." She glanced up at him.

He leaned against the doorjamb. "I think it looks great like it is."

Her eyes widened as she peered into the mirror. "Are you insane? I can't go like this. The entire town will think I'm a harlot."

"You'll have to prove that by me." He laughed and lunged at her, scooping her up in his arms. With two long strides, they came up against the bed and he dropped her onto the mattress. His brows rose and fell as he gave her a leer. "We might as well fulfill the expectations." She giggled as he dropped down beside her and pulled her across his body. Her robe fell open and he yanked her up his body, his mouth locking on her breast, sucking, tearing her apart, and making her mind veer to topics that had nothing to do with school.

"Oh, Connor, this isn't a good idea. You'll make me late for my first day. Desmond—"

"Doesn't know how to start a morning off right." He pressed kisses across her skin. Within moments her body began to long for more. "You're too tense. Let's get rid of a little stress." His hand snaked between them and dipped between her legs, cupping her mound. His other hand wrapped around her shoulders and tugged her closer. "Kiss me good morning, Liv."

She dropped her face and covered his lips with her own, eagerly accepting the tongue that thrust into her mouth. His hand slid lower and he shoved two fingers into her throbbing pussy. An immediate ache spread through her lower half, a hard pounding that begged for release. He pushed deeper and she ground against his hand, riding his fingers until the ache intensified, creating pleasurable waves that pulsed deep inside. Each movement forced her swollen clit against his hand.

She tore her mouth from his to capture a breath and his mouth locked on her throat, pulling and tugging the flesh as her clit tingled in anticipation. The pulses in her pussy matched the pounding of her heart, a deep heavy throb that yearned for release. She ground harder against him, arching her body and scraping against him.

Her limbs tightened. She came with a hard force that caught her breath and her body jerked in a spasm. A tremor rippled through her entire body. Connor's mouth covered hers as his fingers pressed deeper and his palm continued to rub her pussy. More pleasure burst through her and she quivered as the sensations tingled through her.

Finally she slumped against him, her face buried in the crook of his neck. Desmond's voice echoed in the hallway.

"Connor, get your hands off her!"

Livvie groaned and snuggled closer.

"Olivia Raines, get your ass down here *now!*"

"He'll be up here in a minute," Livvie said, "and he won't be happy."

"No, he'll be jealous as hell. But like I said he doesn't know how you should start a morning." Connor grabbed a handful of hair and tugged. "Let's do something with your hair. You look like a harlot."

* * * *

The school loomed one block away. Livvie wiggled in her seat and smoothed the non-existent wrinkles out of her light brown skirt. She looked like the perfect little schoolmarm in her high-collared white blouse, but Connor wondered how long it would be before a few of those buttons came loose. Just a few hours past dawn and already the sun burned hot, the intense heat seeping through his hat. Thank the Lord Livvie had bought that cute straw hat. It shaded most of her face and offered a measure of comfort but she still wiped at a trickle of sweat on her forehead. Or was that sweat caused by her nerves?

Though he wanted time with Livvie, and they had to ensure she got to town safely, he sure as hell hadn't wanted to leave the ranch. He'd left Desmond a list of things to do but he'd much rather do them himself. Desmond had seemed a little distracted this morning. Livvie's satisfied smile and rosy skin had pretty much told Desmond what they'd been up to in the bedroom. He'd seen a pinch of jealousy on Desmond's face. He hated that look, but not quite enough to curb his behavior. He'd take Livvie any time he could get her.

Connor heaved a sigh. "I sure as hell hope this building isn't as bad as I think it might. You'd think a community could take care of their own school."

"Desmond was willing to come," Livvie said.

"I'll bet. He can just stay at the ranch and do some dirty work for a change. I'm ready for a break. Tacking on a few stray roof boards will seem like a picnic." He gave her a sideways glance. "He told you, didn't he?"

"If you're talking about Lucas Price, yes, he told me."

Connor nodded. "I could see it when I got back to the field yesterday with the sandwiches. He looked…hmm, well, I'm not really sure. I could just tell. He looked better."

"It helps to talk, Connor. You two had far too many secrets."

A young girl strolled down the walkway in front of the wagon. A battered school bag swung from her shoulder and a metal lunch pail dangled from her fingers. The sway of her hips told Connor this girl could definitely be trouble. She was one of those girls that caused boys to do stupid things. Waves of brown hair swung loosely down her back and a pretty flowered dress contained a body blossoming into womanhood. As the wagon kicked up some dust, the girl glanced toward them.

A wide smile spilled across her face as she hopped off the planks and skipped toward them. Connor got a bad feeling as he pulled on the reins and murmured, "One of your charges?"

The girl shouted "Morning, Mrs. McBride" and Livvie turned toward her with a smile. Seemingly incoherent words gushed and tumbled between them as Connor studied the girl. Her gaze shot toward him and she scrutinized him for a brief moment, though it took longer than Connor's comfort level could take. A soft smile curved her lips. "Morning, Mr. McBride."

Connor dipped his hat. "Mornin', little lady."

The girl laughed. "Oh, I'm hardly a lady!" She tucked her hands behind her back and swayed slightly on the tips of her boots. She pursed her lips. "And I'm not all that little. Don't you remember me, Mr. McBride?"

Connor drew back and Livvie laughed. "Of course he remembers you, Alice. He's caught up in his own thoughts this morning."

Connor studied the girl from under the brim of his hat. Yep, definitely trouble. He could see it in her eyes. The boys in this town didn't stand a chance. He didn't like the way she stared at him. He felt like an oddity in one of Livvie's fairs.

"Too much thinking is a waste of time, Mr. McBride." She bounced away, shouting, "See you at school!" and ran down the walk.

* * * *

Livvie took Connor's hand and climbed down from the wagon. The children clustered around the parched schoolyard stopped chatting and playing to turn toward her in one movement. Over a dozen sets of eyes locked on her. Alice leaned her head close to the boy next to her—a well-built boy with a shock of sandy hair—and whispered something to him. He nodded with a firm set to his lips.

"Tough crowd," Livvie whispered to Connor.

"Then get up on stage and do what you do, Mrs. McBride."

He gave her a tiny push. *Thanks so much for your help, Connor.* She took a step toward the schoolhouse.

"Morning, children!"

"Morning, Mrs. McBride," they chorused.

She smiled and three small children took a step toward her, smiling back. That encouraged her. She hoisted her sagging book bag on her shoulder and walked up the half-dozen steps to the small porch. When she turned the knob, nothing happened. The door refused to budge. She tried pushing against it with her body. Again, it wouldn't move but a streak of gray dirt ruined her white blouse. With a huff, she glanced over her shoulder. Connor came up the stairs, put his shoulder against the door and shoved.

The door burst inward with an unholy screech. A cloud of dust spewed up and out. Livvie coughed and backed down the stairs. The sandy-haired boy tilted his head and said, "You didn't clean up in there?"

"I'm supposed to clean?" Livvie choked.

"You're the teacher, right?" the boy asked.

She nodded as she wiped the dust from her blouse.

"Well, ma'am," he toed his boot into a pile of dirt, blushing to the roots of his hair, "the teacher does a heck of lot mor'n teach. Don't you know anything about teaching?"

Livvie's shoulders drooped. "Apparently not."

Connor had already gone inside. His boots echoed in the dark interior, a steady clomping as he moved around the building. The sounds alone indicated the ramshackle building held at least a floor which seemed a plus. Livvie peeked in the doorway, squinting in the haze, and barely discerned his shadow moving among the dust motes. Weak bands of light filtered through the tall windows and tracked across a warped wood floor littered with debris, leaves and... Was that a whiskey bottle?

As her eyes adjusted to the gloom, a huge desk appeared in her vision. It dominated the back of the room, centered in front of a large chalkboard. Livvie thought she'd feel like a child sitting in that chair. It looked like it had been designed to hold a king. Low bookcases lined several walls filled with what appeared to be mildewed and water-swollen books that would probably have to be tossed in the trash. Rows of desks and benches for students occupied the middle of the room. A large cranky-looking stove stood in one corner and several empty buckets had been tossed near its base. The room offered nothing but the barest of essentials and most of them appeared worthless. She couldn't imagine spending eight hours inside, let alone expecting exuberant young children to do the same. It seemed a depressing place to trap children all day. An open door led into a dark narrow room. Livvie had no idea what purpose it served but had no desire to see.

She'd never attended school and now she knew why. Her parents would never have subjected her to a place like this.

Connor's hollow voice drifted through the gloom, ticking off things on the disaster list. "We've got a lot of water damage in here. Some of the floor needs replaced, and of course, part of the roof." Each statement wound out of the dull, murky room and stole a bit more of Livvie's hope. How could they fulfill this mission if they didn't even have a proper school? "There's enough dirt to fill a dozen graves. I see a couple of nests. I won't tell you what kind of animals I think they might have held. It would only make you nervous. And, oh, I almost forgot the dead possum."

Livvie's heart sank farther, but she adjusted her bag and stepped over the threshold. The tapping of shoes and clomping of boots sounded as the students followed her up the stairs, eager to see the devastation. When she paused on a creaky floorboard, someone plowed into her back. Livvie glanced behind her and came nose-to-nose with Alice, who peered over her shoulder.

"We ended school early last spring. At this rate I'll never graduate." Alice made a face like she'd eaten a sour apple. "Miss Patterson up and quit then ran off with the mayor to St. Louis. She said she hated Fort Cloud and she hated us."

"That's a terrible thing to say."

"The feeling was mutual," Alice said. "Good riddance."

"I'll try to do better than Miss Patterson."

The boy with the sandy hair grunted. "That won't take much."

Alice laughed. "Sure won't. Of course, it was the mayor's job to handle the school and since he ran off with a lot of the town money… Don't worry though. They'll find him. My mother's on the committee and she hates thieves. We should have mentioned something about the building the other day, but Mother and I were afraid you'd pack up and leave town too."

"It wasn't your responsibility to tell me, Alice. I suppose I should have suspected as much. The letter said some maintenance might be required." Livvie gulped. "I had no idea that meant we couldn't even sit inside." She dropped her bag to the floor and turned to the children who huddled in the doorframe. "But that doesn't mean we won't have school today."

A chorus of ah gees echoed in the interior and Livvie shooed them off the small porch. They backed down into the yard and she waved toward a large oak tree, seemingly the only such tree in Kansas. It clung firmly to its healthy leaves despite the heat.

"Settle down over there. I need to speak with Mr. McBride."

A barrage of whispers followed her as she returned to the building. Connor came out, beating his hat against his pants.

"It's a disaster in there but it can all be fixed. Might take a few days though. I'll run down to the hardware store and order what we need, then stop at the lumberyard and get some men out here. Hopefully someone down there will know who's responsible for this mess."

"Apparently the mayor ran off to St. Louis with the teacher and the entire school budget."

"Great. That would have been nice to know." He looked toward the children then his gaze moved to inspect their surroundings. "I don't like the idea of you being out all day in the open. You'll be okay here?"

Livvie laughed. "Of course. They're just children."

A layer of dust coated his dark hair and when he ran his hand through the strands, a dirty snowfall fell around his shoulders. "I'm not too worried about the kids." He eyed Alice and her entourage. She and a group of older boys lounged on the grass like a queen and her lords. "At least not much. Desmond will pitch a fit you're so exposed."

"I don't think we need to worry with all these witnesses." Livvie glanced at her students. "This has turned out far better than I expected."

Connor grinned. "You're happy about this? I expected you to be half-way to the train station when I came out of there."

"I can hardly teach without the proper tools, now can I? And an adequate classroom is certainly a proper tool." She glanced toward the children, several of whom tossed a ball between them. "Children are so much more relaxed and happy in a less rigid environment, don't you think? I'll have them spilling secrets in no time."

* * * *

Livvie moved her finger to the next name on her list. "Zachary Daily?" She glanced up expectantly, concentrated on the group of boys scattered around Alice. According to her portfolio, Zachary was thirteen and had been indentured earlier in the year by Anthony Pack. Alice's gaze held hers and one of the boys peeked at her from beneath a shock of unkempt dark hair. Livvie glanced at her list. "None of you are Zachary?"

"No, ma'am," the dark-haired boy said.

Livvie smiled. "And what is your name?"

The boy's chest swelled as he took a deep breath, and despite his large size, his voice barely rose above a whisper. "James Keating, ma'am."

"Hmm." James Keating, fifteen, another adopted son of Anthony Pack, the rancher, one of the foster parents to lost boys and possible murderer. Livvie leaned forward, delighted that James had opened dialogue, albeit somewhat reluctantly. "James, do you know why Zachary is absent?"

James ducked his head and that shock of hair covered his eyes. He twisted his face slightly toward Alice. Livvie saw Alice's head dip in a tiny imperceptible nod. "Um, well, ma'am, I suspect it's because Zach's not in Fort Cloud any more."

Livvie consulted her portfolio though she didn't really need to. She'd memorized everything in it. "I've been told that Zachary resides with a man named Anthony Pack, correct?" James nodded. "Mr. Pack had adopted him from the train sometime in the spring. Is that correct as well?" James' eyes widened as he nodded. Livvie tilted her face. "You reside with Mr. Pack also, don't you, James? Is it possible Zachary might have had a problem with Mr. Pack and left for greener pastures?"

"Oh, no, ma'am, he—" The boy's dark brows drew down as a frown skimmed his mouth. He glanced once again toward Alice. Livvie didn't quite understand the look that passed between the children but she suspected by the expression on James' face no one had ever discussed this subject with them before. How was it possible a dozen boys had disappeared and no one thought to ask the children about their whereabouts? What kind of woman had Miss Patterson been that she'd never been concerned enough about her students to ask questions?

Alice leaned slightly closer to James and whispered something. Livvie pretended not to notice but whatever she said seemed to embolden James Keating. He squared his shoulders. "Zach disappeared about a month ago, ma'am. No one knows where he went or why."

"You were friends?"

James nodded.

"I've heard…" Livvie paused as her gaze swept the group of children. They leaned forward eagerly, awaiting a good tale. "There are a few of you that arrived in Kansas on the trains. I'm sure most of you are very happy in your new homes. Is that correct?"

Several heads nodded, some enthusiastically, others with a little more caution. Alice smiled. A couple of the children reached out and took the hand of the child next to them. Livvie was pleased to see her little group held a united front. They looked out for one another.

Livvie locked her gaze on James. "There are probably a few homes, however, that aren't as happy as others. I understand that life can be hard sometimes here in Kansas." James lowered his head. "Are you sure Zach didn't run away?"

"No!" James lurched to his feet and began to pace. Livvie had a hard time hearing his words. "He wouldn't leave me. We talked about it and he said…" Alice rose to her feet and followed him, running a hand down his back and murmuring. The smallest boy in the group, Randy Gerber, put himself directly in James' path. Randy put his hands on the larger boy's shoulder and began to talk, forcing James to look at him. Randy was quickly followed by two boys and a girl—David Mercer, Derrick Spencer and Miranda Loomis.

Worked like a charm.

Livvie clapped her hands to get their attention. Their movement ceased, their mouths snapped shut, and they turned to her at once. Livvie stood and dusted off her skirt. Her gaze moved between the groups but focused on the one she'd already begun to think of as The Half-Dozen.

Mentally she quickly went through her student list. "I've heard Wesley Grimes may have disappeared from Fort Cloud also."

David Mercer, the large, sandy-haired boy, nodded. David was fourteen and the adopted son of the Brandywine's owner.

"Does anyone know the reason why? Can I expect him to come to school in the future?"

"I don't think so, ma'am," David said. "I haven't seen Wes in a couple days."

"And that's unusual?" Livvie asked.

David laughed. "About as unusual at it gets in this town. Wes and I spend a lot of our time behind the Schooner waiting for our old men to come out. Lately Charlie's been there by himself."

Livvie now knew where she'd find her answers but hesitated to push too much on the first day. She also hoped to get some of the younger ones talking. She planned to bring out her arsenal and fatten the kitty. Toys and candy could work miracles. Later, as the children ate their lunch on the grass beneath the oak, Connor returned with a group of men and several wagons filled with supplies and set to cleaning out the school.

Livvie munched on a sandwich and circulated between the kids, listening to various conversations the children held between them. They separated into three distinct groups—The Half Dozen, the girls and the boys. She discovered very quickly that children excelled at resilience. No matter what their standing in the community or their familial circumstances—either adopted or natural children—with a few exceptions, the majority of them laughed and talked openly, enjoying the fellowship the school allowed them. For some of them a day of school offered the best respite they had from the hardships of their lives.

David, Derrick and Randy had a wonderful camaraderie between them. James listened to his friends, nodding occasionally, but rarely spoke. His face, however, held such expression Livvie could almost read his thoughts from a smile that skimmed his face or a raised brow. Miranda, plain and serious, held on to every word that bubbled from Alice's lips yet had few of her own. The girls seemed to have very little in common beyond their ages but an obvious friendship existed between them. Both had arrived on the trains and been adopted by two of the most prominent families in town. They'd been lucky and found acceptance and love both within their town and their families.

She spent the rest of the day asking questions to gauge her students' skills and mentally planning out the tactic she'd use to teach her lessons. Everyone seemed on a different level and she knew she had her work cut out for her. She gained a new respect for Abbie's commitment to teaching. But the gifts worked like a charm. Throughout the day, she'd taken each child apart for a separate interview concerning their home life. She rewarded them with something from her basket.

As school ended for the day, each child returned their toys and books to the basket for safekeeping and she tucked the basket into the narrow little room in the schoolhouse. She discovered it held hooks and cubbyholes and served as a cloakroom for the children's wraps, boots, and books. The room had miraculously escaped the same fate as the rest of the building.

The children stood almost reluctantly and gathered their book bags and lunch pails. None of them looked as exhausted as Livvie felt. She couldn't wait to get home, soak in a hot bath, and get a little adult attention from her men.

Chapter 18

Desmond followed the tantalizing aroma of grilled pork chops. After a day spent surrounded by the pungent smells of ranch-life, it seemed like a bit of heaven. The mouth-watering aroma drifted around the wagon, but under that another smell wafted toward him, this one not so pleasant. What had Connor done all day that he smelled like dog? Desmond reached under the seat to retrieve the basket then drew back.

Connor glanced toward him. "What's the matter? Not in the mood for pork—?"

Connor's mouth snapped close when Desmond unearthed the bloodhound pup and lifted him up. It was the same dog he and Livvie had seen sniffing around near Anna's house.

"What the hell?" Connor said.

Livvie rushed forward, holding out her arms, gushing and cooing. Desmond gratefully deposited the pup in her arms then wiped the drool off his arm with a sound of disgust.

"That's all we need," Connor said. "One more animal to tend to around here."

Livvie lifted the dog in the air and gave him a little shake, ignoring the drool that dripped from the dog's mouth and landed on her shoulder. Desmond shuddered as the ooze tracked down her arm.

"He's just a puppy," Livvie cooed. "Someone's probably worried about him. Oh, look at you. You're just the cutest thing I've ever seen. How'd you get in the wagon, big fella?" She gathered him into her arms like a baby.

Desmond glanced at Connor. "How *did* he get in the wagon?"

Connor shrugged. "No idea. I spent most of the day inside a decrepit old dust-trap planning out repairs. Looks like you'll have a passenger tomorrow." He retrieved the hamper. "I'll take care of dinner while you two figure out what to do with him. I don't— Hey!"

The moment Livvie set the dog on the ground it took off, loping across the dusty yard toward the barn. Livvie lifted her skirt and shot off after the pup. Her hat flew off her head and plopped into the dirt. As Livvie disappeared into the building, a baying sound drifted from inside. Desmond took off running and he heard Connor following. He careened inside to find Livvie hunkered down next to the hound, who stared upwards into the hay loft, whining. Connor slammed his hat down on his head.

"What the fuck? Leave him be. I'm beat. We'll go inside and have a great dinner and…"

Desmond stopped listening. He stooped down, running his hand down the dog's shivering flank. Livvie leapt to her feet and headed for the ladder. Desmond reached out to clutch at her skirt, but he'd have to give her credit. The woman was quick and agile. She was half-way up the ladder before Desmond leapt to his feet.

"Damn," Connor said. "I wish that girl would stand still."

"Liv, stop!" Desmond yelled.

Livvie scrambled higher. "There's something up here he wants. I'm going to find it."

"Jesus, what's up there?" Connor whispered. "Des, I think—"

She disappeared over the lip of the loft, giving them one last glimpse of a ruffled petticoat and showering them with bits of straw.

Connor glanced at Desmond with a sickening look on his face then clamored up the ladder. The dog tried to follow as well, putting his front paws on one of the rungs and staring upwards. Heart pounding, Desmond shot to the back of the barn, ran into one of the stables and rummaged around in the straw. He grabbed the shotgun from its hiding place just as Connor's voice drifted downward.

"She's okay, Des. Give us a minute."

Desmond strained to hear actual words in the voices above but most of the sounds came from Livvie, the gentle, soft murmuring of someone trying to offer comfort. He wondered if they'd found some kind of wounded animal. It would be like her to think mothering a bird would be the right thing to do. He paced the barn floor, listening to the murmurs, his finger hovering near the shotgun trigger. Something wasn't right. The dog continued to hang on the ladder, staring up. His tail wagged from time to time and soft whimpers came from his throat. Finally, after several more moments of excruciating quiet, Desmond heard movement.

Livvie came first, climbing down nimbly, bits of straw stuck in her hair, followed by a pair of legs covered in dirty black pants. Desmond shook his head. Connor had been wearing brown—

A boy dropped off the ladder, hit the barn floor with a loud clomp of heavy boots then swooped the hound up in his arms.

"Oh, I've missed you, boy," the boy whispered. "Thanks for coming."

The animal wiggled with enthusiasm, his long red body shivering with excitement and his tongue lapping at the boy's face. The kid laughed and a smile spread across his broad face. Thirteen? Fourteen? Desmond couldn't really tell much with all that dirt on his skin. The boy buried his face in the hound's neck and his body suddenly shook with quiet sobs.

When Connor hit the floor, Desmond glanced toward him. Connor shrugged. Livvie ran a hand soothingly over the boy's trembling back.

"This is Wesley Grimes and this," her hand reached out and slid across the dog's fur, "is Buster." With that simple statement, she wrapped her arm around the boy's waist and led him out of the barn and into the sunshine.

"Looks like we'll be sharing the pork chops," Connor said.

"Damn it," Desmond said. "I hope you got a lot of them. That boy looks hungry."

* * * *

Livvie filled Wes' plate again. The boy ate like he hadn't had a meal in days though his tall body didn't look in too bad a shape considering he'd probably been in hiding for a while. There was plenty of muscle on his frame. His wide, good-looking face held dark discolorations of old bruises and one eye swelled with a past injury. She'd also noticed as they'd walked from the barn he limped slightly. Questions flooded Livvie's mind, but she forced herself to wait while the boy filled his belly and became more comfortable. Buster hadn't left his side. The dog lay under the table at the boy's feet, seemingly content. His quiet snoring seemed to signal everything was all right with his world.

Desmond and Connor ate with relish, though quietly. They cast glances at Wes but didn't bombard him with questions. When they glanced at Livvie, she gave them a smile and shrug. When the boy pushed his empty plate away, Livvie got him a glass of milk and a slice of peach cobbler. Desmond and Connor had long finished theirs. Desmond toyed with his coffee cup and Connor drummed his fingers on the table.

Connor leaned forward. "Any idea how the dog—?"

"Buster," Livvie said.

Connor sighed and nodded. "Any idea how Buster got into the wagon?"

Wes glanced over the rim of his glass. "No, sir."

"I'm thinking someone must have a pretty good idea you've been hiding out here," Desmond said.

Wes' pale face burst with color as he set the glass on the table.

"Must be someone who cares about you," Desmond said. "Someone who thought you might need some help."

Wes ran his hands through lank blond hair, pulling it tight for a minute. His brown-eyed gaze swept the room, trying to avoid their stares. He put both hands down on the table as though trying to hold himself to earth.

"Any ideas who that might be?" Desmond asked.

"Not really, sir," Wes whispered.

Livvie put her hand over his. "You should tell us, Wes."

Wes released a shuddering breath and tried to meet Desmond's gaze. "It might have been David."

Livvie shook her head. "David said he hadn't seen you in several days."

Livvie leaned back in her chair but Connor leaned forward. He waited until Wes' gaze fluttered to him. "How long have you been here?"

"A couple days."

"Know anything about those prairie dog holes in the garden?"

"I might…"

"Thought as much," Connor said. "So why did you come here?"

The boy chewed on his lips for a moment and finally heaved a sigh. "Someone told me to come here. Said the new teacher'd be coming to town and staying here at the Carpenter place. She…*Someone* seemed to think…" His solemn gaze roamed the table, trying hard to focus on each of them and finally locked on Livvie. A dubious look flickered on his face. "You're the new teacher?"

"Yes," Livvie said.

"You seem kind of young," Wes said. "And not very…teacher-like."

Both men chuckled and Livvie huffed. "I'm old enough, Wes. Why would *someone* suggest you come here?"

"My friend thought you might be here to help."

Desmond's eyes snapped to Connor's.

"Maybe that girl at the school?" Connor asked. "The one that looked at me funny? None of this sounds right."

Livvie studied Wes. So this was the boy Alice had become obsessed with. It wasn't hard to see why—big, strapping, handsome—but Anna had been right. Wes had obviously been a victim of some sort of abuse. Those bruises on his face hadn't been obtained by working.

"How long did you plan to hide on this ranch?" Desmond asked.

"Not long. My friend said Buster would come for me if everything was okay. Otherwise I should get out and run in a couple days." He glanced at Livvie. "Guess they figured you were for real."

"At least *someone's* given us a vote of confidence," Connor said.

"Wes, why would your friend think I'm here to help? Help who?"

Wes held out his hands and his voice shook. "All of us. Hasn't anyone told you that boys are disappearing? I've lost three friends... They tried to take me too." He reached up and ran a hand over the back of his head. "Do you have any idea what's happening here?"

"Yes, Wes," Livvie said, "we do."

"Liv, stop," Connor said. He stood up and went around the table. Buster leapt to his feet and jumped toward Wes' chair, putting his paws on the seat. Connor stared down at Wes and the boy met his eyes bravely. "We don't know anything about this kid."

"Connor," Liv said, "that doesn't seem to matter. He—"

Connor folded his arms across his chest. "Could be a lying son of a bitch. And we might have just blown this entire operation."

"Connor, he's just a kid," Desmond said.

"Yeah, a kid who could have been hired by anyone. Who are you working for?"

Wes lurched back in his seat, the chair scraping along the floor. He stood and glared at Connor, his hands clenched at his side. "Not for you, you bastard. I was *told* you were here to help. I came here to tell you what I know and try to help the others but now I'm not telling you *shit*. We'll find someone else."

He spun around and headed for the door. The dog followed at his heels. Livvie sprang to her feet and tried to head him off but Desmond blocked her way. Connor grabbed Wes' arm, twisted it behind him then patted his pockets. He pulled a folding knife out and held it up.

"Planning to kill us in our sleep?"

"Fuck you," Wes said.

Desmond plucked the knife from Connor's hand. "This is an unusual knife, but I've seen one like it recently. I think he's okay."

Connor released the boy and he darted for the door but Desmond was faster. Desmond leaned back against it, blocking Wes' exit.

"Get out of my way," he snarled.

"I don't think so, kid. Sit down."

"Fuck off, old man."

"Where'd you get the knife?" Desmond asked. "Did you steal it?"

"I'm not a damn thief." Wes tried to shove him out of the way. Desmond stood his ground and when Wes tried again, he grabbed Wes' arms and pinned them behind his back. The boy bent over, groaning and the dog howled then clamped his teeth around the fabric in Desmond's pants. Desmond half-carried Wes across the room, dragging the dog with him and shoved the boy into a chair.

"We're starting over, and this time," he gave Connor a hard stare, "though I appreciate your technique, let me do the talking."

* * * *

"So you came on the train?" Desmond asked.

"Yes, sir. Been here about a year."

"And you were adopted?"

"Not formally, sir. Charlie Stoker took me in. He lives a couple miles south of town. I worked mostly in the fields, tended the animals a little, cooked Charlie's meals."

"Sounds like a fucking paradise," Connor muttered.

Wes reached out and rubbed his hand over Buster's head. "Not much of a paradise, but I got Buster here. Charlie's hunting dog had a litter. For some reason he let me keep Buster. Not sure why. Maybe to make sure I stayed. Charlie's a lazy bastard."

"From the looks of you, kid," Desmond said, "I'd bet he's a mean one too."

"He hits me from time to time, but only when he drinks," Wes said. "Of course he drinks every day. After that last time…well, I had about enough of Charlie."

"So you ran?" Livvie asked.

Wes reached down and lifted the pup into his arms. "No, I didn't. Should have. Would have probably, but I wouldn't have left Buster behind." His gaze slid toward Livvie. "A couple days ago I was waiting for Charlie outside of the Schooner. He likes to go every night. I'd been talking to David Mercer but his old man had already come out and they'd left. Something hit the back of my head. I woke up in a wagon with a whopping headache. I wanted to jump out right then but I was dizzy. So I laid there and kept quiet for a while."

"And what did you find out?" Desmond asked.

"There were two men. I couldn't see anything but their backs. I'm pretty sure one was Anthony Pack. He's a wide fellow and this guy was huge. One of them was drinking whiskey 'cause I could smell it."

"Did they say anything?" Desmond asked.

Wes shrugged. "They weren't real talkative. But one said he had to get back to town fast so they'd better reach the ron…rondy-something before midnight."

Livvie's frowned. "Rendezvous?"

Wes snapped his fingers. "That's it! What is it?"

"A meeting," Desmond said. "Apparently your abductors planned to pass you off to someone else. Any idea where you were?"

"North," Wes said. "I could tell from the feel of the road we were near the Pack ranch. Been there a few times with Charlie. It roughens up right before you hit his place and we passed that by a mile or so. The men were none too bright. They didn't even bother to do more than tie my wrist to one of the planks." He nodded to the folding knife on the table. "But I had that."

"You got the knife from Alice," Desmond said.

"Yes, sir. I managed to cut the rope and rolled out of the wagon when we came to a patch of grass. It took me the rest of the night to get back to Fort Cloud."

"But you didn't go back to Charlie's place," Connor said.

"No, sir. I figured they'd be pretty pissed and just find me again. I hid out in the Bradley's stable. I knew Alice would be in there first thing to take care of Miss Daisy. That's her horse. She loves that horse."

Desmond nodded. "How long did Alice hide you?"

"Just for the day. She brought me some food and I waited 'til dark. Then she told me to get out here because you could help me. She also said she'd send Buster when it was clear to come out."

"And how did Alice know we could help, Wes?" Connor asked.

Wes shook his head. "Not sure. But Alice knows a lot of stuff. She knew about you coming to Fort Cloud. Knew you'd be seeing Anna Glaser. Knew there'd be two of *you*." He glanced at Desmond then his gaze slid toward Connor. "Alice isn't going to be in trouble for this, is she?"

Livvie stood up and paced around the kitchen. "No, Wes, but I can see I'm going to have to make Alice my new best friend."

* * * *

Livvie flung open the window and leaned out, inhaling the warm scent of summer. She ruffled her hair, trying to capture any hint of a breeze to dry her damp curls. She turned as the men came into the bedroom. Desmond flopped onto the bed and Connor dropped the towel around his waist then sprawled in the chair, flinging one bare leg over the arm.

"The kid's washed up and sleeping in my room. My belongings are currently sitting in the hallway. Not sure how all this is going to work. Any ideas, boss?"

Livvie smiled. "You're my husband, aren't you?"

Connor's brows drew down. "Well, yeah, but—"

"Then bring your things in here. Desmond can get his too."

Desmond rose up on his elbows. Connor shook his head as he said, "Oh, no. That can't be a good idea."

"It's the only logical thing to do. I'm a married woman. Married women sleep with their husbands."

"Are you serious?" Connor asked.

Desmond sat up. "You're planning to let him see what's going on in this house?"

"Wes has more important things on his mind than what's happening between us." Livvie put her hands on her hips. "The way I see it, he knows he's safe for now and he's grateful for it. As long as we're trying to help, he's not going to care what the three of us do. Someone tried to abduct him."

"All the more reason for us to keep a low profile in this town," Connor said.

"Which is just about impossible since we've been the talk of this town since before we arrived." Livvie moved closer to the chair, her mind suddenly on things besides abduction and the children of Fort Cloud. "Besides, I'm not exactly the low profile type." She loosened her robe and let it slide down her arms. The fabric fell into a silky mound at her feet.

"Looks like someone has their confidence back," Desmond said.

Livvie ran her hands down her thighs. She loved the way Desmond tracked the movement. "I was scared out of my wits for a while there. And the condition of the school almost made me panic. But I'm feeling better now. A *lot* better."

"Glad to hear—"

She dove toward him and he caught her, flipping her onto her back. The wet strands of his hair slid across her face like satin. "We're going to do this, Des. I don't have any doubt in my mind. As soon as I—"

He captured her mouth in a kiss that stopped her words then made her forget them altogether. He slid his arm under her waist and slowly moved her until her head rested on the pillow. The mattress sagged for a moment with Connor's weight and her thighs were pushed apart. As Desmond began to suckle her breast, Connor's mouth latched onto her clit.

Both mouths felt amazing but she couldn't concentrate on either one because each sent a ripple through her entire body. She just allowed the sensations to swamp her, enjoying the flickers, the tremors, the vibrations that flowed beneath her skin and made her pussy pulse in anticipation and leak moisture into Connor's mouth. He lapped it up greedily.

Desmond's tongue circled her nipple while his hand tweaked the other one then pinched it between his fingers, rolling and pressing until her pussy clenched with the same rhythm.

"I need one of your cocks in my mouth right *now*."

"Give the lady want she wants, Des. I'm planning to put mine in her pussy. I've got it just about as wet as I want it."

Desmond got to his knees and straddled her face, dipping low. She grabbed his cock, running her hand up and down the smooth hard length, pumping as she watched his face. The musky scent of his arousal surrounded her and made her mouth water. She licked her lips and Desmond lunged, driving his cock into her mouth.

Connor rose to his knees and hooked her knees over his arms. She couldn't see his face but she felt the soft prod of his cock at her entrance. It slid softly over her folds, dipping and bumping against her flesh. She wiggled slightly, wanting it inside. Connor took the hint and slammed into her. He gave an exaggerated groan. Livvie giggled.

"Can't say that I like the view of Desmond's ass," he said, "but I can see his cock sliding in and out of your mouth, Liv, and I gotta say...*damn* that makes up for it."

She would have said something but her mother had always said not to talk with her mouth full. She giggled again at the thought then the giggle died in her throat as Connor's began to finger her clit, rubbing gently as he rocked into her body.

Desmond's cock swelled in her mouth. Her tongue traced the engorged veins, licking and feeling the pulse of his blood through the taut flesh. She sucked harder, knowing he was almost ready to come and reached between his legs to cup his balls and squeeze gently. Desmond's fingers dug into her upper arms and her mouth flooded with the salty taste of his cum. She swallowed several times then continued to suck, enjoying the way his cock softened in her mouth. When he pulled out and fell to her side, she turned her face for a kiss. His mouth swooped onto hers just as the orgasm built within her.

Her legs tightened in Connor's arms and she arched upwards, grinding her clit against him. He pumped harder, rougher. Desmond sat up and watched as his brother's cock slid in and out of her.

"Talk about sights. Her juices are all over you. Lucky bastard."

Connor's words came out in a rough whisper. "Damn right."

He straightened, yanking her tight against him. Her orgasm exploded and shudders racked her body. Desmond caressed her breasts as heat engulfed her, sending ripples of fire from her pussy through her limbs and into her face. Her nipples peaked and Desmond took advantage to pull one into his mouth and suck. The draw of his mouth sent another spasm through her and when her pussy clenched down on Connor's cock, he came with a spasm of his own. His body shook and jerked against her then he collapsed forward. Desmond lurched away just before Connor landed on top of Livvie with a grunt.

"I gotta say I like married life," Connor murmured.

"Seems you gotta say a lot tonight," Desmond said.

"Next time we'll switch. She can eat my cock and you can eat her pussy."

"I'm not fussy," Desmond said.

"Neither am I," Livvie said, "but breathing would be nice."

Connor rolled to the bed and gave her a smile. "You're a demanding little wife, you know that?"

"You wouldn't have it any other way."

"Sure wouldn't," Connor said. "But I am glad I have ranch duty tomorrow. I need a break."

Chapter 19

The workmen managed to get the schoolhouse in a semi-state of repair by the end of the week. Livvie had managed to get Alice aside to tell her Wes and Buster had been reunited. Alice had smiled and hadn't made any comment beyond "Good. Now what are you going to do to help us?" With that, she had flounced away. Livvie's jaw had dropped.

The next week the interior had been swept of debris and everything had been cleaned. The windows sparkled and sunlight filled the room. Livvie moved her students inside. After she'd given a short test to determine their aptitudes and depth of knowledge, her rational part told her the students should sit according to their educational levels. Some of the older boys had been exposed to far less education than even the youngest of her students. Their erratic pasts had played havoc with their education. James Keating barely knew his alphabet while Tyler Talbot, the six year old, could already read.

But she wanted them to be comfortable and content, and more importantly, happy. In her heart she thought these children would thrive if allowed to progress at their own pace surrounded by their friends. Pointing out their shortcomings and segregating them from their fellows did not seem the way to challenge them to excel. She allowed them to take their choice of seat and saw that they divided up in their natural way. Alice and her group filled the back row, the younger boys fanned out in the center and the smaller girls sat in the front.

Livvie spent the morning reviewing the basics of reading with the entire class. Several of the younger children were bored, scribbling on their chalkboards. Alice and Miranda whispered quietly in the back of the room. But the majority sat enthralled as she explained the concept of alphabetical symbols, the sounds they represented and how those sounds coalesced into a spoken and written language.

When lunchtime came, she hustled them outside to eat at the new tables Desmond had ordered for the schoolyard. She noticed James talking excessively, his face animated, his body thrumming with excitement. When she passed by their table, she heard Alice's exasperated breath and her weary, "Yes, James, I'll help you. But I'm sure Mrs. McBride would be willing to give you extra instruction. Why don't you ask her?" Livvie felt a sense of pride burst through her.

Desmond came at lunch, carrying a basket from the Brandywine. He spread a blanket under the tree and they settled down to eat.

"Get any more out of Alice yet?" he asked.

"No, I haven't had the chance." She rolled her eyes. "Seems I'm actually supposed to teach here and some of them want to learn. Imagine that."

Desmond eyed the girl. "I don't think she knows anything about these abductions. I think if she did, the problem would have been solved."

"She does seem like that kind of girl, doesn't she?"

Desmond smiled. "She's definitely a ball of fire. Like someone else I know."

Livvie rummaged through the basket and pulled out a tin. "Well, this little ball of fire is about ready to burn out. I have some students who are so enthusiastic I can't get a break. I really need to—" She twisted off the lid. "Eeww, milk?"

Desmond took it from her hand. "That's mine. There's tea in there for you."

After she'd taken a long drink of the cool tea, she perused her students. Several of them had finished and run off to play a game of bowling, a classroom gift for taking her little test the week before. James was hunched over a reading primer with Alice at his shoulder. He listened in rapt attention, and as she read, he moved his finger across the lines.

"I kind of like teaching," she said quietly. "And I've discovered I kind of like children."

"That doesn't surprise me at all," Desmond said.

"Really? I thought I'd be thoroughly unsuited to do this."

Desmond winked at her. "You've got a lot of compassion wrapped in that cute little package. You like to help people, Liv. It's in your nature. And you're good at it." His gaze slid away from her. "I'm living proof."

She leaned across the blanket and kissed him, a soft gentle kiss. But even that was a mistake because when his hand came up to cup her head and draw her closer, she found herself pulled to his heat. She couldn't stop the small moan that escaped her lips. Several of the children snickered and she jerked away.

"And I'm living proof I can't be too close to you," Livvie said.

"I like you close to me. Connor can have the ranch life. I prefer hanging around the schoolyard. I kind of like the teacher."

Livvie shrugged. "Connor seems to prefer it this way. I guess he's claimed the ranch as his domain. And with Wes to help him we might actually pull this off." Livvie licked her lips. "Wes is a great cook too."

"I promised him I'd stop by the butcher before I left town. He wants to make fried chicken and I'm not objecting. Charlie Stokes might have actually done him a small favor. I'm thinking once this is over and the poor kid can come out of hiding, the Brandywine might hire him."

"*After* he gets an education," Livvie said.

Desmond nodded. "Already on it. Since he's in hiding, I've been working with him at home. He's quite bright and seems to have a pretty good knowledge base. I knew you wouldn't want him to miss all this."

"Really? That's the sweetest thing I've ever heard."

"That kid deserves a break in life. He sure hasn't had one up 'til now."

"And who gave you a break, Des? After everything you and Connor went through, it's obvious you got one somewhere along the line. Who offered you aid, comfort?"

"Anna," he said quietly.

A wave of something like jealousy rushed through her, but it seemed foreign and unnatural. She had no right to be jealous of something she'd never been a part of until recently.

"Oh. Yes, of course, that explains…everything." She tried to keep the emotion off her face. She wasn't even sure what emotions suddenly whirled inside of her. She needed to do something with her hands. They trembled now and she didn't understand it at all. She began to gather up napkins and tins, stuffing them back into the basket.

"It's not what you think, Liv."

She swallowed hard, but still couldn't seem to find her voice. She tucked a strand of hair behind her ear and slapped the lid closed on the basket. "I wasn't thinking anything at all." She struggled to her knees but he grabbed her hand.

"Will you sit down and let me explain?"

Unable to look at him, she murmured, "I have to get back to the school. The children—"

"Are fine." He nodded to the group clustered around the bowling game.

"It's really none of my business. You don't need to explain."

"But I want to. Please." He nodded to the blanket and she sank down helplessly beside him, steeling herself to listen. "I never slept with her."

"Okay," she said softly.

"I'm not sure about Connor. You'd have to ask him."

"I won't," she whispered. "I don't need to know. It's all in the past, isn't it?" When he didn't answer her right away, she glanced up. "Isn't it?"

"Yes, it's all in the past, at least as far away as we can put it. We have a pretty long history with Anna." She signed heavily, unsure she believed him and knowing she didn't want to know anything about their past with Anna Glaser. "We met her on the train."

"Anna came on the orphan train too?"

He nodded. "I don't really remember her from the train but Connor does. She was a year or two older than we were. We got on in Richmond. When we changed trains in New York, she was there. She didn't know much about her circumstances but apparently her father had recently died. He'd been wealthy once but Anna was left with nothing. She got adopted out a few stops before we did by a farming couple who just wanted a child. She was one of the lucky ones. Years later, we found ourselves in her area and Connor managed to find her. We worked for her old man for about a year. Guess we were about fifteen then. He taught us everything we know about farming, about animals. Anna taught us to read and write and, for a while, how to be happy. We almost forgot we weren't part of the Glaser family."

"They gave you a great gift."

"We were grateful. It's probably the most stability we've ever had. We were there when...when Anna had her accident. She fell out of the loft and tore up her insides. Before Anna fully recovered, Mrs. Glaser told us to leave. The old man was sorry for it, but that woman ruled the homestead and she wanted Anna married off. She knew it wouldn't happen with us around."

"Anna was in love with one of you."

Desmond laughed. "Connor has a way with women. Always has."

"It's not so hard to imagine."

"He didn't want to leave her, but we wanted a good life for her and we couldn't offer that. Our departure though had the opposite effect. I'm sure Mr. Glaser never really forgave us for it because Anna got angry with her mother and ran off."

"With…what? A gambler? A gunslinger?"

"Well now, that man couldn't be pigeon-holed. He'd do just about anything for money. When we hooked up with Anna again in Tulsa, Gregory Powers was running with a gang of outlaws and I suspected he wasn't long for this life. Turns out, I was right. Anna, by then, had discovered another way to support herself."

"From the look of her home, it's fairly lucrative. What does she do beside play Good Samaritan?"

"That's not for me to say." He lifted his chin toward a buggy that ambled slowly down the street. "You can ask her yourself."

Livvie clamored to her feet, cast a quick glance toward her students then walked to the edge of the school yard. She tried to press the wrinkles out of her skirt. She felt like a child caught lazing away an afternoon while she should be studying. She'd been in that position more than once. Anna stepped out of the buggy like a vision dressed in a beautiful day dress of rose-colored cotton. She shaded her eyes against the sun as her curious gaze inspected the building, the new tables, and the group of children thoroughly enjoying their bowling game.

"Things certainly look cheery around here," Anna said.

"It took us a while," Desmond said, "but the work's paid off. We have a working school again."

Anna smiled then focused her gaze on Livvie. "I'm assuming you've used the time to your advantage?"

"You knew how bad this place was?" Livvie asked.

Anna laughed. "Intimately. I'd been down here several times in the summer. At first, I thought to tell you but then reconsidered. It looks like my instincts worked. I hoped to provide a more enjoyable venue to get to know them. The children seem happy, content… probably malleable."

"I'm gaining their trust, trying not to push too hard." Livvie took Anna's arm and led her a slight distance away. She told her about Wes and Alice's involvement. "Alice refuses to discuss it. Any ideas how she'd come by her information? It's incredibly accurate."

Anna's peal of laughter caught the attention of the children. All of them waved to her. "That's easily explained. You've met Freda of course. The woman never stops talking. But you don't know what Karl Bradley does." She leaned closer. "He's the telegraph operator at the station. Alice does occasional deliveries for him. I'm sure the Bradley household fairly rings with gossip and half-truths."

Livvie stared at Alice with a new perspective. The girl may have used information she'd learned, but she'd kept it as quiet as possible, sharing it only with several of her friends who were either involved directly or might be able to offer help. Alice Bradley was definitely a bright, resourceful girl, and obviously knew instinctively who to trust.

"I hear my own share of gossip," Anna said, "and I'm here to share as well. Stanley Mercer is being pressured about that note on his property and his agitation level has increased. He wouldn't tell me specifics, but he's been offered an alternative. He thinks he can meet their demands."

"You think one of the boys is the alternative?" Desmond asked.

"Yes," Anna said. "Obviously he gave them Wes. Since that has backfired, I'd suspect he's willing to sacrifice David."

Livvie's heart lurched. The man would willingly give away his own son? David had been adopted by the family three years before and had bonded with the Mercers' natural children, Lisa and George. She glanced across the yard where David patiently held George's arm, trying to teach him how to aim a slingshot.

"Oh, no, that's not going to happen," Livvie said. "I won't let it. How did you come by this information, Anna? Someone must be trying to divert attention, or throw suspicion."

Anna shook her head. "No, Olivia. I spoke with Stanley myself."

Livvie leaned closer, trying to keep her voice down, which was incredibly hard. Her ears thrummed with the hot blood bursting through her veins. "And he just blurted out he's going to exchange his own son for the note on the hotel?"

"No," Anna said. "He didn't mean to tell me I'm sure. But when Stanley drinks he gets…maudlin sometimes. And when he's offered comfort he practically crumbles."

"You offer…comfort?" Livvie shook her head. "What does that mean exactly? Are you a nurse of some kind? A minister?"

Anna shot a glance toward Desmond. "She doesn't know?" When Desmond shook his head, Anna closed her eyes wearily for a moment. "Olivia, I swear you must be the most naïve woman this side of the Mississippi. There are several names for what I am, but I actually prefer courtesan, if it's all the same to you. I'm fairly exclusive in my clientele. Men come from miles away to…receive my brand of comfort."

Anna Glaser was a whore, a prostitute? It just wasn't possible. The air whooshed out of Livvie's lungs and heat engulfed her face. She knew her mouth had dropped open when Desmond's fingers tucked beneath her chin and clicked it close.

"I'm…I'm sorry," she stuttered. "I had no idea. I hope I didn't—"

Anna laughed. "Offend me? My dear, offending me is the toughest job on this planet. I love what I do and I make a damn good living. But I'm not above using my…connections to help a greater good. Now what do you plan to do with my hard-earned information?"

Livvie lifted her chin. "Stop him of course."

* * * *

Connor watched as Livvie climbed nimbly up the fence and perched on the top railing. He moved around the wagon to remove the other side of the harness from the horse. "So you're going to stop Stanley Mercer. Sounds admirable, but just how do you plan to do that?"

"I haven't exactly figured that out yet. Mainly because I haven't figured out what he might be planning."

"It doesn't seem to take a whole lot of planning," Connor said. "Grab a boy, make him disappear and chalk it up to an unstable home life."

"That's going to be hard for Mercer to do. I've watched David for over a week. He's a happy, healthy boy. He has good friends and gets along well with his siblings. From what I've seen there's absolutely no reason for him to run away. He has a future here."

"Not if Stanley Mercer has any say in it."

"No one would believe David Mercer just picked up and left town. It's not possible."

"Then, that's a big hurdle to overcome, unless Stanley Mercer wants to bring suspicion upon himself. With his rather dubious finances and his visits to Anna, I imagine he'd want to avoid people asking questions about his life." Connor glanced toward the other side of the corral where Wes tossed a ball and Buster raced across the dirt to retrieve it. Wes continued to pump water into the trough until Buster returned and dropped the ball at his feet. When Connor turned back, he saw Livvie's furrowed brow as she studied the boy.

"They may have asked for David, but Mercer gave them Wes," Livvie said.

Connor nodded and hoisted the harness gear onto the fence post. "Seems a logical thing to me. Wes' abuse is common knowledge in town. People wouldn't question the likelihood he'd run away. Charlie Stoker would never question it and wouldn't make an issue of his disappearance. It's not in his best interests. And it sure as hell wouldn't surprise him."

"And Wes and David spend evenings together outside the Schooner. If Pack questioned Mercer, it's an honest case of mistaken identity. The boys are similar in build and coloring. But I doubt Pack would question him, because Mercer's deal is to deliver a boy. It hardly matters who it is if he meets his obligation."

"Wes' little disappearing act created a problem," Connor said, "which is why Mercer is panicking."

Livvie hopped off the railing. "If he panics, he might get stupid."

"We can't count on him getting stupid. Mr. McBride might have to go drinking tonight." He grabbed her wrist and tugged her until her body came up against his warm heat. He leaned down and nuzzled his face into her neck. "I'm going to need a real reason to drink. Fighting stirs up the blood. Care to rile me up?"

Livvie laughed and tugged away. "I could rile you up plenty, but I doubt you'd get out of the house afterwards."

"I have a better idea."

They both whirled to find Wes standing behind them, tossing a ball from hand to hand. Buster, apparently realizing the boy had business to attend to, dropped to the dirt and laid his head on his paws, waiting patiently.

"What do you have in mind?" Livvie asked.

"Let me go back to the Schooner."

Connor shook his head. "Not a chance in hell, kid."

"Look, I'm not just a kid." Wes squeezed the ball in his hand. He glanced down then tossed the ball away. Buster scrambled to his feet and burst across the corral.

"We're dealing with dangerous people here," Connor said.

"Anthony Pack's a fat old man."

"Who might just be a murderer." Livvie reached down and took the ball from Buster's mouth then tossed it away again.

"Pack's blind as a bat. He couldn't hit something with a Winchester and a target lit in flames."

"The murderer didn't use a rifle, and it might not have been Pack," Connor said. "Someone used their fists."

The boy lifted his chin. "I can handle myself."

"Not against a man with no boundaries you can't," Connor said. "I can pretty much guarantee it's going to take a lot more than a folding knife to get away the next time."

Wes kicked at the fence post. "It sounds like Mercer's going to be in deep shit if he doesn't deliver someone soon."

"Looks that way," Connor said.

"Then David's in real trouble. I can't let that happen to him. He deserves a lot better than that."

"You all deserve better than that, Wes," Livvie said. "And we aim to see you get it."

Chapter 20

While Livvie cleaned the kitchen and Wes read one of the dime novels she'd purchased, Desmond sat on the porch and wondered how they'd keep the kid from running off the minute they closed their eyes that night. He suspected Wes had enough loyalty to David Mercer to put himself in the direct line of fire with or without their blessing. Connor seemed to think he would.

After he'd done a routine check of the property, he went back to the house, and he and Livvie played a game of chess in the parlor. Wes watched them, his face filled with agitation and his body wound tight. He wondered around the house, tinkered with the piano—and played surprisingly well—picked up several books just to toss them back down and finally returned to the kitchen.

When Livvie went to bed and Wes had pulled some charcoal and paper out of Livvie's book bag, Desmond rummaged through the bookshelves. He finally chose *Ben Hur*, which seemed large enough to outlast Wes' dogged determination to wait him out. He settled himself in the dining room where he could see all the doors in the house. He'd just become immersed in the tale when Wes' head finally hit the table. It had just passed midnight. Desmond closed his book and went out to the porch to wait for Connor.

Two hours later, he heard the sound of Connor's horse. When Connor returned from the barn, he fell to the top porch step and leaned against the railing.

"Damn, they pour strong whiskey at the Schooner."

Desmond laughed. "Sorry you had to make that sacrifice."

"You go next time. Another night like that will kill me. But I made a few dollars playing poker, with Stanley Mercer of all people."

"How'd he seem?"

"Jumpy. Nervous as hell."

"And David?"

"I had a clear view out the window from my table. The kid sat outside on the bench for hours waiting for his old man. Poor kid. I suspect Mrs. Mercer worries her husband might pay Anna a visit after his evening out. I followed them home and waited outside for a while. I don't think anyone would be stupid enough to abduct the kid from his own house."

"You might be surprised how stupid people can—" Desmond stopped and glanced at his brother. "Do you hear—?"

The sound of a rifle blast burst through the night as the railing above Connor's head splintered and cracked, showering shards around them. Both men dove for cover. As Connor threw himself off the porch and sprawled in the dirt, Desmond fell backward, rolling over the rough porch floor and peering into the darkness.

"Nice job of noticing a tail," Desmond muttered.

"Fuck you," Connor whispered. "I'm drunk as a skunk. I rode home half-asleep."

Another shot rang out as the kitchen door flew open. When the screen door slapped closed, Buster began to howl. Connor leapt to his feet and hurled himself over the garden fence, diving for a shape in the darkness. Desmond heard their bodies hit the ground on the other side of the house.

Wes' voice quavered. "What the hell was that?"

Connor's hand slapped over Wes' mouth just as the front screen door burst open. Livvie rushed out in a swirl of blanket, her hair a cloud around her face. As the blanket slid from her shoulders Desmond caught of flash of pale skin in the moonlight and knew he had only a second. He bolted to his feet and tackled her as another shot punctured the quiet night. Her scream caught in her throat. He rolled as best as could to shield her body and they fell to the porch planks, their foreheads smacking together with the impact. He rolled again until she was tucked beneath him.

Her muffled voice became lost in his chest. "Oh my god, what—"

"Shh. Not a peep."

Desmond heard Connor say, "Stay put," and then saw a glimpse of Connor's white shirt as he wiggled on his belly through the garden. Desmond hoped their assailant didn't have the same vantage point. A moment later he heard the imperceptible squeak of the kitchen screen followed by "It's okay, buddy. Let's put you in the wash room." The light winked out in the kitchen. Another shot rang out and the glass of the window exploded in a starburst. He heard a groan from the other side of the yard and a howl from inside the house.

"Wes?" Desmond whispered as loud as he could to get the boy's attention.

"I'm fine." His hushed voice held a ragged edge. "Just scared is all."

Another few moments and the parlor light winked out as well. More rifle fire scattered around them, tearing into the railings and clapboard. The front window shattered and glass twinkled around them. Desmond lowered his head and clutched Livvie tighter. He waited in agony until heard the slide of a rifle barrel through the opening in the door.

"Can you see anything?" Connor whispered.

Desmond could barely hear him over Livvie's ragged breaths in his ear.

"No, but there's a horse out there. I can hear it. About twenty yards directly ahead of you."

"We need you on the end of this gun," Connor murmured.

"You're better with a rifle. Handle it."

"Jeez, Des, I don't need you bitching at me 'cause I missed. I'm a little drunk here."

"And I'm a little busy here, Connor. Just handle it."

"Why do you get all the best assignments? I'll trade—"

"Just shoot the bastard," Livvie whispered furiously. "I'm hot as hell in this blanket. And there's a rock pressing into my ass."

"That's probably Des' hand," Wes whispered.

"Um, could we focus here, people?" Desmond muttered. "Gun fire, bad guy—"

Livvie jerked beneath him, her body going rigid, as Connor opened fire, squeezing off six shots in quick succession. One bullet ricocheted off something metallic then a scream pierced the night. Desmond heard the sounds of a muffled thud as something hit the dirt and a horse galloping in the opposite direction. He raised his head and peered into the yard.

"Could be a trick."

"We won't know 'til one of us checks," Connor said. "Heads or tails?"

Desmond chuckled when Livvie bristled beneath him, her small body wiggling. Her breath burst against his neck as she raised her head, trying to push him off. "Oh for crying out loud, let me up. I'll go."

"Stay put," Desmond said. "Rifle."

He rolled off Livvie and caught the rifle Connor tossed in his direction. Connor disappeared into the interior and he pounded up the stairs to retrieve another weapon. The vegetation rustled on the other side of the porch.

"Wes, you stay put too," Desmond murmured. "One hero per night. I've drawn it tonight."

Desmond slid down the porch steps on his belly and started to slither across the dooryard, aware of his clothing rasping in the dirt. But beyond that sound was another—a soft moan, low to the ground and not too far away. Having focused on the horse, he'd misjudged the distance of the man. He struggled to see anything in the sparse moonlight that filtered through the cloud cover.

Damn. The man couldn't have worn a white shirt?

The breathing got louder and within another moment, he realized this was not a trick. Connor had hit the shooter, possibly numerous times. He smelled the cloying metallic scent of fresh blood. His body slid over an object on the ground and his hand reached out to trace the shape of a rifle barrel. He rose to his feet, giving the rifle on the ground a kick behind him then trained his own on a huddled shape.

"I can kill you before you move a muscle. Got any other weapons?"

The man released a ragged breath. "No."

"Get to your feet. Slowly."

Desmond watched the shape form into a smaller man as he struggled to his feet. When the man raised his face, he recognized Stanley Mercer. He'd been at the Brandywine enough to know the owner.

"Where are you hit?"

"Shoulder, thigh..." Mercer gasped. "Wrist's broken I think. Bullet knocked the rifle out of my hand."

"You'll probably live, at least 'til my wife gets her hands on you."

"There's no question about that." Livvie stepped out of the darkness followed by Connor and Wes.

Wes reached down and collected the rifle from the ground. He hefted it in his hand. "Nice weapon. I've always wanted my own Winchester. I'm keeping it."

"You've earned it," Livvie said. "Call it retribution. I have a few questions for Mr. Mercer and we won't be exchanging pie recipes. Move it, Mercer. Welcome to the McBride homestead. We can guarantee you an interesting evening."

Desmond reached out and gripped the back of the man's neck, pushing him forward. Mercer uttered a soft cry and stumbled toward the house.

* * * *

"I wondered where that little bastard had gotten to when he disappeared out of the wagon," Mercer mumbled.

He glared at Wes who lounged in a chair, his leg slung over the arm. He brushed a cloth across his new Winchester, then raised it up and pointed it toward the man.

"Want me to finish what Connor started?" Wes asked.

"The house has enough bullet holes, Wes," Livvie said.

"Believe me, I wouldn't miss."

Livvie put her hand on the barrel and pushed down gently. "Perhaps not, but put the gun down anyway." She whirled around and tapped her foot. "Mr. Mercer, you're not making friends here and I can't keep three of them off you forever."

"We're not the threat." Connor nodded toward Livvie. "You don't want to piss her off. Just tell her what she wants to know and you might make it through the night."

Mercer pressed a hand against his bandaged thigh. He grimaced as blood seeped through the cloth. He ran a hand through strands of stringy brown hair. "You going to let me see a doctor?"

"Don't need a doctor," Desmond said. "I can take out a bullet. Better start talking soon though. That shoulder wound looks pretty bad. Might be bone fragments in here. They can play hell with movement if—"

"Okay, okay. I'll talk. I saw you," Mercer's rather glazed stare darted between Connor and Desmond, "*one* of you following us home. I knew something wasn't right about this. Everything seemed just a little bit too tidy. You—one of you, both of you, I'm not even sure what's going on here—aren't a typical rancher type. And I sure as hell have never seen a teacher like looks like *her*."

Livvie huffed. "What does that have to do with anything?"

Wes laughed. "If you'd ever seen Miss Patterson you wouldn't have to ask."

"So how did you figure it out?" Mercer asked. "You haven't done my son any favors by interfering in this."

"Your *son*, Mr. Mercer?" Livvie's voice shook with her anger.

"I was never going to give them David!" Mercer cried. "I love my son."

She struggled with the impulse to grind her finger directly into the wound in his shoulder. "What kind of man turns *any* boy over to an unknown future in exchange for financial freedom?"

"I didn't know what else to do," Mercer said. "They threatened me, they threatened David. I can't lose everything I have. I planned to… I had to give them someone. So I gave them…"

"Someone who didn't matter." Wes angled the rifle against the chair and stood up. Buster got to his feet and rubbed against Wes' leg before Wes slowly walked toward Mercer who cringed backwards in his seat. A shudder ran down the boy's back. Wes' body vibrated with fury, but his quiet voice seemed so soft Livvie had to strain to hear him. "I wish people would stop deciding how much value I have because I'm an orphan. I matter, damn it. Maybe not right now…" His voice broke as he struggled with his next words. "But someday I'll matter. I'll make sure of it."

Livvie put her arm around Wes' shoulder. The boy tried to jerk away but she held tight. "You matter now, Wes. To David, to Alice, to us…" She swept her hand out to encompass Desmond and Connor. "And we're going to make sure you all matter and that you all get the future you deserve. Go to bed now, Wes. I want you to come to school tomorrow."

The boy nodded, shot another angry glare toward Mercer then turned. He grabbed the rifle and went up the stairs quickly, Buster loping at his heels. Livvie stared at the staircase for a moment, blinked back sudden tears then turned back to Mercer. She quickly explained what they knew, pacing back and forth in front of him, while the McBride brothers stared out the windows keeping a watchful eye out for more trouble.

"And now you're going to tell us what *you* know."

"I can't do that," Mercer said. "It's a death sentence."

Livvie ran her fingers lightly across the man's shoulder. She watched a trickle of sweat drip down his forehead to the bridge of his nose. "Yes, we've heard it can be dangerous around here to ask questions. We know about Frederick Skylar. What we don't know is who killed him. Was it you?"

"I'm not a killer," he said softly. "I only came here to scare you, to warn you not to interfere. You need to get the hell out of Fort Cloud."

"We're not going anywhere and we aren't scared," Livvie said. "But you are, Mr. Mercer."

A burst of laughter shot from Mercer's mouth. "With good reason. You'd be too if you knew what I know."

"Then tell us," Livvie said.

Mercer shook his head. His hair flew around his face then stuck to his sweat-dampened skin. "I can't," he squeaked.

She let her fingers slide toward the bloody spot on his shirt. "Are you sure, Mr. Mercer? Because there might be consequences to your reluctance to help us. Was it Anthony Pack? Is he the one who beat Frederick Skylar to death?"

Mercer took a deep breath. "Pack's a fat pig. He doesn't have the energy to raise his voice let alone his fists."

"So it was his partner? Robinson Booker?"

Mercer drew back and more sweat dotted his brow. "You don't want to talk about Robinson Booker, girl. That's a sure way to get yourself in bigger trouble than you already are."

Livvie waved a hand. "He's just a man. If you tell us how to find him, we can cut a great chunk of the fear out of your life, Mr. Mercer. Now tell us about the rendezvous. Where is it and what happens to the boys when they're delivered?"

Mercer's eyes closed for a moment. "No. I won't tell you."

"Are you sure about that?" Livvie's fingers trailed over his shoulder again. Mercer shivered. She glanced up to find Desmond and Connor both staring at her with a horrible fascination. When she reached the wound, she rammed the tip of her finger inside. Mercer screamed and she continued to dig deeper, twisting until Mercer dug his teeth into his bottom lip deep enough to draw blood.

"Jesus, Livvie," Connor whispered. He took a step away from the window.

"Let her go," Desmond said.

"The rendezvous, Mr. Mercer." Livvie pushed her finger farther. Mercer's head dropped down and a jagged moan tore through the room. She put her hand under his chin and lifted his face. "Look at me." Glazed with pain, his eyes tried to focus on her, blinking rapidly. "Talk."

"North," Mercer gasped. "About two miles north of the Pack ranch. There's a lean-to there in a stand of trees. Three days. I'm to deliver a boy in three days. Booker sells them to a miner in Idaho. That's all I know."

"Thank you, Mr. Mercer. Now I'll have Desmond take a look at those wounds." Livvie wiggled her finger and it popped out with a squishy sound. She held up a piece a metal. "And look, I've already managed to remove one of the bullets." Mercer's head drooped forward.

Connor gripped his hair and tilted his head back. Mercer's eyes rolled back. "He's passed out."

Livvie dropped the bullet down onto the table then wiped the smear of blood on Mercer's shirt. "Good. I was tired of him anyway."

"You're a dangerous woman, Livvie," Connor said softly.

"He pissed me off. He shot up my house, broke a boy's heart, and is league with the devil." Livvie glanced down at her skirt and threw her hands up. "And he's gotten blood on my skirt. If I didn't have to set him free to catch this god-damned Booker I'd let him bleed to death."

Desmond unwrapped the strip of bloody cloth from Mercer's leg. "Where did you learn your torture tactics?"

Livvie touched her chin. "Hmm…I'm not sure. It just came to me. I really wanted that information and I hate wasting time."

Connor laughed. "You have the instincts of a professional. You'd do your fathers proud."

"One of them anyway," she murmured.

Desmond glanced up. "Which one?"

She shook her head. "It doesn't matter. Just fix the bastard up so he can be useful to me in the next few days. I can't use him like that."

"You're the boss," Desmond said.

Chapter 21

Livvie struggled to lift the cast iron skillet. She had to admit it would make a great weapon, but it seemed a little too heavy for cooking eggs. She wrapped a cloth around the handle and moved it from the burner as a cloud of smoke rippled toward the ceiling.

"You're getting better at that," Desmond said.

Livvie waved her hand to clear out the air to get a breath. "Just takes a little practice. Another couple years and something might even be edible." She swung around and grabbed a stack of plates as another burst of smoke plumed up. She turned to see Connor pulling the pan of potatoes from the stove.

"Half of them are still white, a definite improvement." He leaned down and dropped a kiss on her nose. "You look incredibly good for a woman who got an hour of sleep. Look at those rosy cheeks, that sparkle in your eyes..." He stared at her for a minute then he shot Desmond a dirty look. "Damn it! He touched you this morning, didn't he?"

Livvie laughed. "There might have been a little touching. There actually might have been a *lot* of touching."

"Fuck, fuck, fuck," Connor said. "Damn, I'm sick of drawing the short straw."

Desmond snorted. "Draw? Like you'd ever draw."

"You could have touched me all you like," Livvie said, "but you spent the whole night prowling around down here."

"Someone," Connor shot another pointed look at his brother, "had to keep an eye on our hostage. What do you plan to do with him today?"

Livvie glanced at Desmond. "I hadn't really decided. What do you think?"

"He's going to have a tough time explaining two bullet wounds and a sprained wrist."

Connor laughed. "And a tougher time explaining to his wife why he didn't come home last night. Iris Mercer doesn't seem the forgiving type."

Livvie nodded. "Probably best we keep him here until the rendezvous then." She shoved the plates into Desmond's hands, marched to the kitchen door, and swung it open. "Wes, move your ass!"

Desmond set the plates down to pick up the art supplies Wes had left on the table. As Wes trudged into the room, wiping his eyes, Desmond glanced up. He shuffled some of the pages he held in his hands and held up a portrait. Livvie grabbed it out of his hand and stared. It was a portrait of her, full of smiles, dancing in a field of flowers followed by Buster who leapt through the tall grasses.

"This is wonderful, Wes. May I keep it?"

"Sure, if you want it. I was really just scribbling."

"Where'd you learn to draw?" Connor asked.

"My dad," he murmured.

"You sounded pretty good on the piano last night," Desmond said. "Did he teach you that too?"

Wes nodded as he slid into a chair. "He taught at a boys' academy in Vermont and I went to school there. When he got sick and died, I worked in the kitchen for a while, but eventually someone came, took me away and I ended up here. I'd kind of been hoping for Colorado. I like the mountains."

Livvie went into the dining room to put her portrait in the sideboard drawer for safekeeping, talking as she moved in and out of the swinging door. "Kansas may not be what you hoped for, but I can guarantee we can make it better for you. I'm glad you're coming to school today. The children will be so excited to—" She paused with her hand on the door then let it swing shut. "Des? Something wrong?"

"I'm not sure." His quiet voice scared her more than the trembling hand holding the sheath of papers. For the first time since she'd known him, Desmond looked pale. He tugged his lower lip between his teeth. He laid one of the drawings down on the table. "Who is this man?"

Wes glanced at the paper. Livvie took note of a beefy face, lank hair and a pair of beady eyes that held a cold, calculating intelligence. "It's Anthony Pack. I thought you'd need to know what he looks—"

"And who is this man?" Desmond hesitated a moment then laid another sheet down. The man who stared from the portrait held little humanity in his gaze. It seemed the glare of a predator with thoughts of destruction, pain, brutality. Wild strands of scraggly hair surrounded a wide face and a full beard covered the lower half. Livvie shuddered wondering how much damage a man like this man could do in his lifetime.

"That's Robinson Booker," Wes said.

Desmond shook his head. "No."

Connor shook his head and rubbed his hands over his face. "That's not fucking possible." He turned and vomited into the sink.

"It *is* Robinson Booker," Wes insisted. "I've met him. I never forget a face and I can draw from memory. Have I done something wrong?" His terrified gaze swung from Connor to Desmond.

"No, of course not," Livvie said.

Connor heaved again and Livvie ran across the room, grabbing a cloth and pumping cool water over it. She ran it across the back of Connor's neck, watching as Desmond's hands curled into fists.

"Desmond, I don't understand. Do you know—?"

He backed toward the door, his eyes locked on the paper. "I'll go hitch the wagon. We've got to get to town." He slammed his hand against the screen door and vanished.

Livvie's breath caught in her chest and Connor pumped water into his cupped hand. He splashed it over his face then stood. A stream of water dripped down his face like tears.

"Connor? What is it? What's wrong?"

"The man in that drawing is Lucas Price," he said softly.

Livvie shook her head, whipping it back and forth, struggling to understand. "That isn't possible. Lucas Price is dead. How could Wes draw a man who died twenty years ago? You said you killed him." She grabbed the front of Connor's shirt, but Connor stared at the floor. "Look at me!" When Connor lifted his face, she yanked him down. "You said you *killed* him. How can it be Price?"

"I don't know...but it is."

Connor leaned against the sink then slid to the floor, his head dropping onto closed fists. She crouched down beside him, pulling damp strands of hair away from his face.

"Fuck," Connor whispered. "I killed him. I *know* I killed him. The knife went into his neck. He fell to the floor. There was blood, so much blood."

"Go talk to him, Connor."

Connor's face twisted toward her. The sorrow etched in his face broke her heart. "I can't, Liv. What will I say?"

"You'll figure it out. Don't let him deal with this alone. I have faith in you to make it right. Go."

* * * *

Desmond tightened the harness strap, refusing to look up. "Remind me again who you killed, Connor, because looking at that drawing, I'd say Lucas Price is alive and well and roaming free in Kansas."

"How the fuck would you know? Thought your memory had blanked out."

"Apparently it's back." He moved around to the other side of the wagon, ignoring the shadow that crept closer. "And I gotta tell you, now that it is, I wish you'd done the job right the first time."

"I thought I had," Connor murmured.

"Christ," Desmond murmured. "I'm right, aren't I? It's Lucas Price."

Connor appeared next to him and Desmond risked a glance toward him. When his brother nodded that cold fear spiraling through his body tightened harder. Desmond rubbed his lower arm as a pain tingled though it. His body didn't like the memory either.

"The knife hit him in the neck, Des. I saw the blood. I saw him hit the floor. Then I ran."

"Jesus, Connor, you were never any good with a knife. Fuck." He grabbed the reins and gave a tug. "Come on, Pretty Girl."

"Des, wait."

Desmond paused and the horse came to a halt. Desmond stared out into the yard then lifted his gaze to the darkening sky. It would be a wet ride home later in the day. He felt Connor slip up beside him like his own shadow.

"I shouldn't have run. I should have made sure he was dead."

"We'll make sure this time. I'll take Fort Cloud today. You stay here with our guest. If he complains, shoot him. You're good with the Winchester."

* * * *

"Wes!"

Alice shot toward the wagon, laughing. The wagon dipped precariously as Wes hurtled from the back then sprang up, rocking Livvie in her seat. He swept Alice up in his arms and spun her in a circle. Her brown hair swirled around like a cloud caught in the wind. As he placed her on the ground, the children pressed toward him, laughing and talking at the same time. As Livvie took Desmond's hand to climb down from the seat, fat heavy drops of rain splashed on her skin.

Desmond helped Buster down from the wagon. Several of the children ran towards him and Buster eagerly greeted them with licks to their faces and slaps of his tail. Miranda swooped the dog up in her arms and a dozen hands gave him enough pets to make him happy for a lifetime.

Desmond glanced at the sky. "I think I'll get the horse in the shed and stick around for a while. You get them inside. This weather doesn't look good."

Excited chatter followed Livvie as she hurried to unlock the door and usher the children inside before the rain began in earnest. Already the sky rumbled with thunder and lightning flickered in the swollen clouds, casting an eerie green glow across the sky. The sounds made her shiver with an unusual nervousness. She rubbed her arms as gooseflesh peppered her skin.

As the children gathered in their seats, still bombarding Wes with questions, Livvie worried about Desmond. He'd been very quiet on the trip to town. He'd agreeably answered most of her questions but those answers had been mostly a string of I don't knows. When she broached the subject of the drawing, he refused to discuss Lucas Price. She wondered how one drawing had unearthed his buried memories but she feared, as they poured through him, it might be too much too fast. Even now as he stared upward with his mouth set in a hard, firm line, she knew thoughts he couldn't possibly understand must be whirling through his mind. She wished she could have spent a little time alone with him and forced him to discuss whatever preyed on his mind.

Buster stared out the open doorway. A low growl rumbled in his throat as he watched Desmond moving the horse into the shed. The thunderclouds churned overhead in the darkening sky, twisting and spiraling into a collage of black, gray, and dirty white that moved swiftly across the sky like waves rolling on the sea. The rain pelted the ground in heavy drops that left holes in the dirt and splattered the ground in a tiny shower of muddy dust pellets. The air around her seemed heavy and oppressing and she had a hard time pulling breath into her lungs.

Livvie shook her head then turned to her students. Her gaze flickered over each smiling face then her brow furrowed.

"Where's James?"

Randy Gerber turned toward her. The smile lingered on his face for a moment, but soon settled into a frown. "We haven't seen him this morning."

"He might have work to do," David said. "Sometimes Pack keeps kids at the ranch if there's too much work."

Livvie strode to the front of the room. "That's not acceptable. James needs to be in school. I'll send Mr. McBride out to discuss that with Mr. Pack."

"It won't do any good," Randy said. "Pack makes his own rules."

"We'll see about that. Mr. McBride can be very persuasive."

She glanced to the window where drops of rain slammed into the glass and lazily slid down to the sill. She couldn't send Desmond out in a thunderstorm, but the timing of James' absence caused some concern. Even if they couldn't get him back to town, she really wanted to make sure he was okay.

Desmond hadn't moved from the spot in front of the shed, but he pulled off his hat and ran a hand through his hair still staring toward the horizon. In that moment Buster let out a bark, bolted out the door and Livvie watched as his squat body angled toward Desmond. Desmond stiffened and ran toward the school house at the same time huge chunks of hail began to pound against the windows and roof. She watched them strike and burst against the glass. A horrible, almost mechanical noise rumbled through the building and the floorboards vibrated beneath her. She stumbled for a moment and clutched the edge of the desk for support.

The children stood up in one motion as Alice yelled "Cellar!" They moved toward the front of the room as Livvie stood immobile trying to figure out what had happened. The noise intensified until she thought her head would split in two. Someone tugged on her dress and she glanced down to see Lisa Mercer pulling at her.

"Come on! We've got to get to the cellar."

Lisa clutched her hand and began to tug just as David tore to the back of the room and swept his little sister up in his arms. Livvie's gaze ripped throughout the room. Several of the children were already outside. Desmond herded them toward the back of the school and she watched them racing around the side of the building. Wes lingered near the door, pushing some of the younger girls outside. When George Mercer tried to backtrack toward his brother and sister, Wes shoved him outside.

"Come on, Mrs. McBride!" David ran up the aisle while Lisa's eyes remained locked on Livvie over David's shoulder.

"What's going on?" Livvie shouted.

"Tornado!" Wes yelled.

He gestured wildly, trying to get her to move forward but Livvie's feet seemed anchored to the floor. Tornado? Outside the window had become ominously dark and lightning flashed in the distance. That horrible noise grew closer, sounding like something hurtling toward them from hell. The raindrops continued to splash at the glass and the hail tapered off into an occasional clunk and knock as the last remnants of ice dissolved. Fascinated, she watched as a dark cloud seemed to drop out of the sky, lower and lower until it grazed the prairie at the edge of town. She'd never seen anything like it in her life. The beautiful black spiraling cloud swirled and swooped, dipped and swayed in a random dance of flickering colors. Flashes of lightning sparked within its depths, causing pulses of white within a pallet of muted shades. Huge plumes of dust spun in an ever-widening circle and suddenly poured upward into the swirling cloud that shaped itself into a funnel. As it skipped and skittered, touching the landscape in random dots of movement, brush and grass tore from the land and disappeared. Lightning shot from the cloud and trees burst in sparks of fire.

"Get to the cellar, Wes." Desmond's shout pulled her gaze from the window in time to see him give Wes a push out the door.

Desmond ran toward the back of the room, his gaze focused out the window. He clutched her arm and yanked her hard enough that she stumbled into the desk.

"Livvie! Let's go!"

"What is it? Wes said—"

He didn't answer her question. His arm slid under her knees and the next thing she knew he carried her out the door and they stepped into another world. The wind tore at her hair and that screeching-tearing-ripping sound ground through her head until her ears burst with the pressure. Her skirt whipped around her body when Desmond set her down near the corner of the school and the gusts pulled at her, tugging her until she nearly fell.

"Cellar! Now!" Desmond said.

Stupidly she stared at the last of the children as they vanished into a door set into the ground. Funny she'd never noticed that door before. She grabbed the hair that twisted around her face, but her gaze kept returning to that black swirling mass of cloud that skipped closer to them even now. It looked powerful, hypnotizing, devastating. It leapt on a small tree in the distance and the tree spiraled into the cloud, whirling and spinning higher and higher until it dropped out of the sky and smashed to the ground in a mangled mass of dead wood.

Her eyes widened and then she realized just how much danger they were in. Desmond's hand pushed hard on her back, almost shoving her in his desperation. She started down the steps into the dark interior, trying to see through her tangled web of hair. Several pale terrified faces stared up at her and Wes plowed into her as he barreled back up. He yelled for Buster as she lost her balance and stumbled into the rough wall. Her blouse caught on something, ripped and she fell down the last few stairs.

David helped her struggle to her feet and she turned just in time to see Desmond grab Wes' arm, shout into his face then twist his body around. Desmond shoved him inside, waited until he'd taken three steps then the door slammed closed and left them in total darkness. She waited an excruciating moment, the pressure in her ears building, her ragged gulps of breath pulling and catching in her lungs. Suddenly colder than she'd ever been, she crossed her arms over her chest, praying the door would open and Desmond would come through. Instead, the hatch rattled on its hinges, lifting and dropping with a thunderous pounding rhythm that forced Livvie to cover her ears. It seemed as though a mythical monster tore at the door, battering away until the wood caved. It would sweep into their lair to devour them in huge powerful teeth. How could a cloud have so much power?

She backed away until she felt two small bodies press against her. She sank to the floor and pulled Tyler Talbot and Moira Wilkins into her lap, holding their trembling bodies and trying to still her own.

Chapter 22

"It's very quiet. I think it might be over."

Wes' voice wrapped around her. It was the first coherent sound she'd heard in what seemed like hours. Hearing a human voice after the ungodly noises earlier forced her to awareness and snapped her out of the trance. She blinked and realized she could see much better as weak lines of sunlight flickered through the cracks in the door. She gave Tyler and Moira quick kisses on the tops of their head and struggled to her knees, lifting the two youngest children with her. Alice pulled them into her waiting arms.

She walked closer to the stairs where Wes stood staring up at the door, David Mercer at his side. The boys started up.

"No! Wait!" She grabbed each boy by an arm. "I should go first."

"You won't be able to lift the door by yourself," Wes said.

Livvie nodded. "Right. You're right. You and I will go. David, you stay here with the children. Keep them safe until we say it's clear."

"Yes, ma'am."

"If something happens…" Livvie turned and studied David's face.

He gave her a quick smile. "I've been through this before. You go check. We'll wait here."

David herded the children into the deepest part of the cellar. She watched until they disappeared then turned to Wes, taking a deep breath. He gave her an encouraging nod and they started up the stairs, each echoing footstep causing another cramp in her gut. Somewhere beyond that door was Desmond and she had no idea what kind of world she would find. She reached out and wound her fingers through Wes'.

"It's going to be okay," he whispered.

"Yes, of course it will. It has to be."

Wes slid one bolt then another. She hadn't even been aware he'd locked them inside. The slide of the metal sounded loud in the confining space. The sound of something that could change her life. She and Wes pressed against the wood. The door lifted an inch at a time until Wes put his shoulder against it and gave a mighty shove. The door flew up and sunlight flooded across their faces as the door banged against its hinges, throwing aside the small tree that had blocked it.

Tears blurred her vision as the sudden brightness of the light stung her eyes. She squinted and blinked rapidly to clear them, trying to take in everything in one glance. Wes stepped over the lip of the door and held out his hand to help her over some rubble.

Miraculously the school still stood. Livvie had expected a pile of kindling and had already mourned its loss. Several of the windows had blown out and some of the clapboard siding had been torn loose. Shingles and slats of wood littered the yard. The large tree where she'd held her lessons remained upright but large branches covered the ground and the yard was a mess of leafy and brushy debris. The small stable seemed intact, though its door hung by one hinge. Livvie heard Pretty Girl inside nickering softly. She caught her lip between her teeth.

"Where's Des?" she whispered.

"We'll find him. He's here somewhere…with Buster." Wes turned and yelled into the cellar. "David, it's over. You can all come out. Help the little ones. There's a big mess up here."

Livvie took several steps forward, wanting desperately to start looking yet so afraid of what she might find. She tripped over the broken remains of one of their picnic tables. Her entire body trembled and she bit her lip because tears threatened and she didn't want to cry in front of the children after they'd been through so much. But it seemed impossible to hold them in. Already they tracked down her cheeks. She felt the warmth on her face.

She counted the children as they filed out of the cellar. Wes scoured the yard, lifting boards and limbs, shoving debris out of his way as he searched. He finally shouted "Over here!"

They all raced toward him where he stood by an upended table. Livvie dropped to her knees and peered underneath. "Oh God, it's Des!" She scrambled to her feet and grabbed the edge of the table.

"Help us!" Wes took a place next to Livvie and gripped the edge with strong hands while David, Derrick, and Randy grabbed the lower end. With a mighty heave they flipped the table over where it smashed against a downed limb. Desmond lay face down in the grass, his arms tucked beneath him.

Livvie reached out and swept a trembling hand over his hair. A large lump knotted the back of his head. She leaned down and pressed her nose against the side of his neck, feeling the warmth and more importantly the strong beat of his pulse. She let out a shuddering breath then turned to them with a smile.

"He's alive."

Alice slid to the ground, dropped her face into her hands, and began to sob. Miranda wrapped her arms around her friend and began to rock her gently.

"Help me turn him over," Livvie said. "Be very careful. He's hurt the back of his head and I'm not sure what else."

The four older boys knelt down and gently maneuvered Desmond onto his back. Scratches and cuts marred his pale face and a large bruise had already formed on his forehead. His eyes were closed, his lashes fluttering. But he breathed in even breaths and clutched in his arms was Buster.

"Oh, buddy," Wes whispered. "Come here, boy."

Wes gently lifted the limp pup into his arms, cradling him loosely, and nuzzled the side of his face while Livvie inspected Des, running her hands over his body, feeling his heart beat. She cupped the side of Des' face and turned to Wes.

Livvie struggled to find her breath. "Des seems okay I think. Is Buster…is he…?"

"He's breathing." Wes' soft voice trembled. "A little. Come on, buddy. Wake up. Let me see those pretty brown eyes."

Livvie ran her fingers across the smooth hair on the dog's head, willing him to open his eyes, to lick the face he loved so much. The dog's body shuddered beneath her hand and for a moment, her heart stopped as a huge sob tore through Wes' body. Alice moved towards them on her knees and leaned against Wes' back.

"Come on, Buster," Wes said. "I need you. Open your eyes, buddy."

Buster's eyes fluttered then opened. He shook his head beneath Livvie's fingers and then his tongue peeked out and slid against Wes' cheek. All the children laughed and several of the older boys cheered. Derrick slapped Randy on the back. David dropped to his knees and gave Wes a bear hug from behind. The boy clutched the dog tighter then turned to Alice and practically fell into her arms.

"I think…" Desmond's voice pulled her away from the cheering children. Tears dripping down her cheeks, she cupped his face. He licked his lips and tried to smile but his eyes flickered shut with the effort. "I think…I think I fell."

"I don't think you fell. I think a table dropped on you."

"Guess I'll be ordering some new tables." He took a deep breath then pressed a hand against his chest. "Might have busted a rib. Is Buster okay? I think I knocked us both out."

"You probably saved his life," Livvie whispered. "What's a little knock-out between friends? Oh, Des, I was so worried about you."

"I'm…good." He tried to sit up but a slice of pain rippled across his face. He turned his face toward the children. "Everyone okay?"

"Yes, we're fine. We were scared, but they seemed to know exactly what they were doing. I'm very proud of all of them."

"It's Kansas, Liv. Kids learn fast here."

"I'm beginning to understand that. I'm just glad I have all of you to teach me. I think...I froze in there, Des. If you hadn't come back in—"

"Someone else would have pulled you out. They love you, Liv. They're not going to let anything happen to you."

She smiled. "And I'm not letting anything else happen to you. I seem to bring nothing but trouble to you, Mr. McBride."

Desmond chuckled softly. "Isn't that what a new wife's for?" He stared at her with those incredible blue eyes, slightly dazed but so full of emotion. Her heart skipped a beat when she realized how close she'd come to losing him. His gaze darted away from her for a moment. "Look's like we have company."

The residents of the entire town seemed to be on their way up the street. Several women ran forward and clutched their children while the men offered quick hugs then hung back inspecting the damage. Anna maneuvered through the crowd, and between them, they managed to get Desmond to his feet. He seemed a bit woozy and Livvie took advantage of it to wrap her arm around his waist. Just as she thought another person couldn't possibly fit into their school yard, a cloud of dust appeared as a horse galloped down the street and careened to a stop, inches from Desmond's feet.

Connor jumped down and grabbed his brother, peering into his eyes. He touched some of the cuts on his face. Desmond jerked and moaned under his fingers. Connor's hand cupped the back of his head watching as Desmond grit his teeth.

"Easy, big brother, I've got a whopping headache and..." He winced as Connor pressed one hand on his chest and one on his back. "Ouch."

"A busted rib? One, two?"

"I think one."

Connor continued his inspection, his hands sliding down Desmond's arms and legs and cupping the back of his head again. He peered into Desmond's eyes for a long moment. "You look like you'll live. We'll wrap you up and you'll be good as you ever were. That bump's going to hurt like hell for a while though. But you kept everyone alive so a headache seems like a fair exchange. That was a big one. I watched it moving. It formed, dissipated, re-formed. It skipped the ranch. We're fine there, but I knew...I watched it..." He ran his hands over his face. "Christ, I was scared."

"Hmm, Connor?" Desmond's brow rose. "What did you do with our, um, guest?"

"I tied him to the piano. Figured he'd never manage to move it. Who the hell cares about him anyway? I was worried about you, you ungrateful son of a—"

"I'm grateful," Desmond said quietly. "Not sure I've seen you move that fast in your life."

"I can't lose you, Des. You're like a bad habit. I need you to feel alive." He frowned suddenly and his gaze flickered to the left, then the right. He leaned a little closer and whispered, "What's everyone staring at?"

Most of the children were still gathered around Wes and Buster, laughing and talking, but Livvie had been so occupied with her men she hadn't noticed the entire town had stopped talking with Connor's arrival. They had moved to gather around them in a circle. Some stared outright, others murmured among themselves. A few faces held smiles and some frowns.

"I think they're staring at us," Desmond said.

"Why?" Connor asked.

"Cause there's two of us. And one of her."

Freda Bradley bustled forward. She waved her hand. "Looks like your little secret is out of the bag. That's going to be a lot easier on some of us. Of course it leads to a great many questions," she winked at Livvie, "but now's not the time. We obviously have work to do around here."

Livvie and the McBride brothers watched in amazement as Freda clapped her hands and took charge. She directed several of the men to clean up the debris and two others to measure the windows. Two men were instructed to go to the lumberyard to obtain shingles and replacement boards. When she had everyone working, she whispered for a few minutes to Iris Mercer then turned back to Livvie.

"A telegram went out last night. Anthony Pack came into the station and sent one to a town in Nebraska. I suspect that's where you'll find your other culprit, this Booker fellow no one seems to know. The message was short and sweet. Said there was trouble, he'd be arriving shortly, and they needed to clear out. I've told Iris to keep her mouth shut for now. We can deal with Stanley later when the sheriff arrives."

Livvie shook her head as the words gushed from Freda, trying to comprehend everything she said. "You know about Stanley Mercer, Mrs. Bradley? How—"

"Freda, dear, call me Freda. I have my ways and Alice has hers." She glanced to where Alice and Wes sat, their heads together, whispering. "Together we seem to know everything in this town. Now the problem is the sheriff won't be arriving for a while. I've already had Karl check the lines. Some of them went down with the tornado. So a telegram is impossible."

"Don't you have a—"

Freda interrupted Connor with a wave of her hand. "Of course we have a lineman, but he has a long route and it will take him several days to get back here. And I suspect he'll find some more damage along the way."

"Can you—?"

She nodded to Desmond. "Of course we'll send a rider to the sheriff's office, but it will still take several days for him to get here." She fingered Livvie's blouse and stuck a finger into the rip where she'd caught herself on the nail. "If you bring that by the shop later I can sew it up for you good as new. I swear we need to fix that cellar.

The children say it's scary as hell. I think I'll go talk with Mr. Loomis right now and see what we can do about it." She scurried away, calling over her shoulder "Remember to bring the blouse!"

"She'd make a good mayor," Desmond said, "but she wears me out."

"Doesn't surprise me," Connor said. "You look like hell. You could use an afternoon in bed. Any takers?" His brows rose as he turned to Livvie.

"I'd love that, Connor, but…" She pursed her lips as she watched the activity around her. "I'm afraid we have another problem."

"We don't need any more problems," Connor said. "I'm worn out. Emotionally exhausted. Tornados do that to me. Come on, Liv, let's take a break."

"James didn't come to school today."

"Leave it to Livvie to find the biggest problem possible," Desmond said. "Looks like we better head home and make some alternate plans with our guest."

"We don't have time for that." Livvie spun around. "Freda!"

Chapter 23

Livvie twirled in front of the full-length mirror then put her hands on her hips. "I love this, Freda. Thank you." She stared at her reflection admiring the way the buckskin molded to her curves yet gave her plenty of movement. She'd worn pants a few times in her life, much to her parents' dismay, but she'd never felt so comfortable in them. Not only did she look good, as Connor had told her, buckskin was great for traveling on horseback.

Freda put her hands on Livvie's shoulders and twisted her this way and that way, plucking at seams, running her hands down the arms. "I wasn't sure it would fit. I made it for one of the boys in town, but Derrick hasn't collected it yet. I'll make him another. This should suit you fine for your ride north. Now if those men of yours would get back with the supplies, we could get them outfitted as well."

Livvie laughed. "Don't let them hear you say that. Men don't wear outfits. They wear clothes."

Freda waved her hand and puckered her face. "Don't let them fool you. Have you seen some of the dandies in this town? That Stanley Mercer is the worst. It's a real shame what's happened to that family. Who would have thought Stanley would be involved in anything like this? But don't you worry about that now right now. When Tad Wilkins and his men come back with Stanley, they'll head for the livery. Tad's got a couple of storage rooms there and he's our unofficial law here. We can lock Stanley up tight until the sheriff collects him."

The bell tinkled above the door and Anna stepped over the threshold. She took one look at Livvie and a smile spread across her face. "When I recommended Bradley's, I assumed you'd be buying dresses."

"Oh, I have, believe me! But dresses will be a hindrance where we're going."

"So you're heading out today?" Anna asked.

"We don't have a choice. I'd planned to use Stanley Mercer as bait and set a trap, but Pack has seen fit to tamper with my schedule and up the ante. Another boy went missing. We're still hoping to have this situation taken care of in a few days."

"You've made great progress, Olivia. You should be congratulated."

"I've had a lot of help."

Anna picked up a small reticule from the counter and ran her fingers across the beads. "True enough and their hearts are certainly in this mission. I've never seen the McBride brothers so focused...particularly with such a pretty distraction." She turned, leaned against the counter, and let her gaze wander down Livvie's body. "Have you made your choice yet?"

"Anna Glaser!" Freda cried. "Even I haven't asked that question yet."

"Really?" Anna laughed. "Then I imagine I've completely overstepped my bounds."

Freda huffed and puffed, her face turning a hot shade of red. She stuttered for a few moments then clamped her lips in a firm line.

"Freda, do you think you could go fix my blouse?" Livvie asked.

"Certainly, dear." She stepped backwards and narrowed her eyes at Anna before she turned on her heel and marched into her sewing room. Immediately the whirring drone of the sewing machine filled her void.

Livvie stared after her, shaking her head. "You left her practically speechless."

"And you're avoiding my question. Have you made a choice?" Anna asked.

"Do I have to choose?"

"Not if you want to live a life like mine, but frankly, Olivia, you don't seem the type."

Livvie ran her hands down her thighs, loving the feel of the buckskin. She turned to the mirror once again. "You seem to enjoy your life, Anna. Have you reconsidered settling down?"

"I've always had a mind to but I'd like to settle with a man who doesn't search for a compromise with a loaded Winchester. I like more finesse, someone with the skills of a diplomat, unfailing loyalty, a charming sense of humor, unique intelligence… Oh, there I go day-dreaming again." She laughed, a delightful sound that made Livvie smile. She came up behind Livvie and met her eyes in the mirror. "Let's say I'm always looking for the perfect man. I just haven't found him yet."

Livvie studied her friend in the mirror. "There are some out there. I know several."

"Then you're luckier than most."

"Are you sure Connor isn't the right man?"

Anna blinked then sighed. "I assumed they'd told you about that. What happened between Connor and me happened in a different lifetime. I wouldn't give up those memories for anything but there's nothing between us now, hasn't been for a very long time." She caressed a strand of hair on Livvie's shoulder and gave her a smile. "I just wanted you to know, in the event he's your choice." She toyed with the curl, adjusting it across the buckskin with the skill of a hairdresser. "You can't go wrong with either one. They're both good men."

"I know," Livvie said. "That's why I intend to keep both."

Anna's mouth dropped open.

Livvie frowned. "If they both want me that is."

The bell tingled as Desmond and Connor ducked their heads and came through the door. When their eyes found Livvie across the room, wide smiles lit their faces.

Anna sighed. "There doesn't seem to be any doubt about it. You're a lucky woman, Olivia."

"Yes, I am."

Desmond tipped back his hat. "I don't think I've seen buckskin look better on anyone."

Livvie's brow rose. "Ever looked in a mirror? Or at your brother?"

Livvie laughed when both men blushed, but she was happy to see the color back in Desmond's face.

Anna gave each man a kiss on the cheek. "I think I'll wish you luck and leave you three to your preparations. Besides, I have some studying to do. Apparently I'm teaching school the next few days." She waved to Livvie as she walked through the open door.

Freda whirled out of the back room at the sound of the bell, muttering as she hurried toward the counter. "Some people in this town have no common sense and way too much nerve for their own good. Stirring up gossip, asking questions..." She ran her hands over several shelves, flipped through some garments, and pulled several items down and slapped them on the counter. She waved her hand, gesturing them toward her.

"Come on, gentlemen. We haven't got all day. The lady's in a hurry. Strip down and get outfitted. My buckskin is the finest quality. Don't worry about me. I won't peek." She chuckled as she headed to the back room. "At least not for long."

"Do what she says," Livvie said. "You'll never fit in the dressing room. We need to get out of town and find James. Did you get everything?"

Connor dropped his pants and kicked them away. He grabbed a pair of buckskins off the counter and pulled them up his legs. "Got the bedrolls, extra cartridges, some canned food, canteens, rope..."

Half-listening Livvie watched as Desmond pulled off his shirt. She reached out and trailed her hand over his bandage. "Does it hurt?"

"Only when I breathe," Desmond said. "Or move…or when my heart beats fast." He pressed a hand against hers. "Like right now."

"Anyone interested in how I'm feeling?" Connor asked.

"Get caught in a tornado today?" Desmond asked.

"No, but—"

"Then, no, we're not interested."

Connor stripped off his shirt and Livvie's gaze darted between them. Identical but for the bandage around Desmond's chest—wide shoulders, strong, muscled chests with that sprinkling of dark hair, and all hers. Both of them. Anna was right. Could a girl get any luckier? She sighed.

"I'm going to tell you anyway." Connor's voice became muffled as he pulled on his shirt. "I'm feeling like I should head out alone. It seems—"

"No," Livvie and Desmond said together.

When he pushed his head through the neck hole, he frowned. "Why the hell not?"

"Just forget it," Desmond said. "It's not going to happen."

Connor gave his brother an incredulous look then turned to Livvie and spread out his hands. "We have to face facts. Desmond's all busted up—"

"I'm not *all* busted up," Desmond growled. "I could still whip your ass."

"Not today you couldn't. And you, Liv," Connor held up his hand when Livvie opened her mouth. "You're a woman, small and pretty and soft…" He let his stare slide up and down Livvie's body then he smiled. He reached out and ran his hand down the soft buckskin sleeve. "I have to say you look good enough to eat."

"Don't get sidetracked, Connor," Desmond said. "What's your point?"

Connor's glance snapped to Desmond. His smile dissolved. "My point is I can't risk… I won't be able to take it if…" He rubbed his fingers against his forehead. "Look, I just don't want either of you to get hurt."

Livvie lifted her chin. "We appreciate it but you can forget it. We're a team and I'm in charge."

Connor rolled his eyes. "There she goes with that again."

"Well, I *am* in charge. Caroline said—"

Connor shook his head and glanced at Desmond. "She's forever trotting out these connections of hers." He put his hands on Livvie's shoulders. "You heard Mrs. Harrison, plain as we did. Issues of safety are in our purview. And I want you to stay here. For your safety. Des, back me up here."

Desmond dropped his pants to the floor. "I can't." When Connor's jaw dropped, Desmond refused to look at him. "It's her mission. She's entitled to see the end of it."

"Are you insane?" Connor grabbed Desmond's arm and jerked him away from her. Desmond stumbled with his pants trapped at his ankles and shuffled across the room.

Livvie tapped her foot while they discussed her in hushed, angry tones and watched as a woman strolled toward the shop window. She came to a complete stop and peered inside. Her eyes widened then lingered on Desmond's almost completely naked body. Livvie didn't blame her in the least. It was quite a tempting sight. When the woman saw Livvie watching her, she lowered her head and quickly turned and moved up the walk.

Connor's argument hadn't come near to ending. His voice rose as Desmond shook his head. Livvie spun around and stalked to the counter. She let her hand trail on various fabrics, wondering if she could learn to sew when this was over. Maybe Freda would give her some instruction. She paused on some sturdy fabric in a dark blue color, fingering the cloth.

"Freda, what's this blue cloth? It's kind of rough and—"

The whir of the sewing machine stopped. Freda's voice drifted out of the back room. "It's called denim, dear. I just got a shipment on the last train. It's been quite popular in other towns around here. I thought I'd expand a little."

"It would be perfect for working around the ranch. Do you think you could make trousers from it?"

"Of course, dear. We'll measure your men when you return."

"Measure me too! I want some!" She heard Freda chuckle. She patted the cloth then moved her gaze to the shelving. "Freda, can I have any hat I want?"

"Of course, dear, help yourself! I'd recommend one from the third shelf."

Livvie pulled down a floppy brown hat and dropped it on her head. Nice and loose with a wide brim to keep the sun out of her eyes. She cast a quick look toward the men still involved in their discussion then peeked in the mirror. She liked it. And she really liked these clothes. She twisted to see her ass. Connor had apparently reached the end of his rope. She turned to find him pacing.

"Oh, for Christ's sake, Des. We'll lose her completely if she ends up fucking dead." He slammed his hat on his head. "And we'll be shit out of luck keeping any friends in Kansas if that happens. I wanted to stay here, damn it."

"She deserves it, Connor, and it's what she wants."

"I don't give a damn what she wants. I fucking *hate* this."

Livvie's breath hitched. *Lose me?*

Connor yanked open the door. "I'll be down at the livery, packing up the horses. Make it quick." He slammed the door behind him. The bell jangled furiously.

She ran to the window then stood still for a moment, watching Connor stomp across the street. Several people scurried out of his way. Finally she turned to Desmond, who pulled on his trousers. "What did he mean, Des? Lose me?"

"He's talking out of his ass."

"Tell me."

Desmond glanced out the window. "Connor thinks I'm caving in to avoid a temper tantrum, because I'm afraid you'll get on the next train and vanish from our lives."

Desmond winced as he tried to put his arm in the sleeve. Livvie reached out to help. She smoothed the fabric across his shoulders. "He should know me better than that."

"He does. Don't pay any attention to him."

Suddenly she was afraid to meet his eyes. "Is that really what you think would happen? That I'd just give up and go home?"

"No, Liv, that's not what I'm afraid of and it's not what scares him either."

"What is it then?" She peeked at him from beneath her hat.

He cupped her face in the palm of his hand. "What do you think?"

"I'll be as careful as possible," she whispered.

"I know you will and you've got the skills to back you. But Connor is right. This is going to be dangerous."

"I won't do anything stupid," Livvie said. "If you're not afraid I'll leave, why are you in favor of letting me come with you?"

He grabbed his hat from the counter. "Because you've earned it, Liv. You deserve to see justice done."

"Everyone deserves that, Des."

"It's not always possible," Desmond said, "but we can give it to you. You've done a good job here. Your father would be proud."

Livvie laughed. "Which one?"

"If it doesn't matter to you, it doesn't matter to me." He reached toward her and Livvie stepped into his arms as his mouth covered hers. She pressed herself gently against him, careful to avoid causing him pain. He moved his mouth from her lips to her throat and whispered, "Never hold back with me because of a couple scrapes." She wound her arms around his neck and pressed tightly against him, enjoying the feel of his hard thighs and the rigid cock pressed against her. When Desmond pulled away, he set her back firmly on her feet.

"Damn. I sure wish we had a free afternoon."

"Me too. But I plan to reward you both for your services later."

She winked. Desmond laughed as she picked up the scattered clothes and tossed them on the counter. She grabbed a satchel Freda had packed for her. "Thank you, Freda!"

Freda poked her head out of the back room. "Happy to help! Now get on with you. Don't worry about Wes. Iris will take good care of him. You keep yourself and your men safe, Olivia. I know you'll do us proud."

Her final words were almost lost in the tinkle of the bell. "I'll bill you!"

* * * *

They made poor time on the journey north. This area had seen a deluge of rain. The horses were forced to plod slowly, their hooves sinking in the swampy mess that had once been a dirt road. The tornado had transformed it into a soupy quagmire of mud, leaves, sticks, and other debris. Downed, twisted trees occasionally blocked the road, and several times, they had to veer their horses off the overgrown path and wade through the swampy fields. Livvie would never get used to what passed as a road in Kansas. Puddles of standing waters littered both sides of the road and huge mounds of mud rose in the flat plains, dropped there by the force of the winds.

After their incredible luck against nature in Fort Cloud, the amount of tornado damage shocked them. They passed several homesteads that had taken massive hits. Broken boards and rubble in the distance indicated a home had once stood there. After seeing several cows milling around without a structure in sight, Livvie imagined these farmers had simply abandoned their property and headed for a town. She'd not seen any refuges in Fort Cloud and they'd not met any on the road. Fort Cloud obviously wasn't the town of choice in this area of Kansas. She couldn't imagine why. Fort Cloud had everything a person could ever need.

Desmond pointed west and Livvie had to shield her eyes against the lowering sun until she saw the dark shadows in the broken flattened grassland. Several mounds rose in the distance beyond a ripped and shredded barbed wire fence. It took her a moment to realize the jumbled heaps she saw were steer carcasses, probably dropped when the tornado touched down. She shivered to think how close they'd come to disaster and death in Fort Cloud.

"I'd say we're getting close to the Pack ranch." Connor glanced toward the setting sun. "I'd hoped to get to it before nightfall. Not sure that's going to happen dealing with all this shit."

"They have to deal with it too," Livvie said.

"Not if there's less damage in the direction they're headed," Connor said. "They might be thirty miles ahead of us by now."

Livvie shrugged. "Then we'll hook up with them in Meridian. That's where the telegram went."

Connor groaned. "Damn it, Liv. Use your head. Do you think Price is stupid enough to meet up with Pack in Meridian? This isn't some Maysville garden club meeting. Jesus Christ."

Livvie dropped her face, heat blazing across her skin.

"Lay off, Connor," Desmond said.

Connor's heated gaze swept between them. "Do you two have any idea what we're riding into here?"

"I don't think you have to ask me that, Connor," Desmond said quietly. "What exactly is wrong with you today?"

"With me?" Connor's voice rose and his hands clenched on the saddle horn. He tossed a nod in Livvie's direction. "She's read too many dime novels. She thinks we're off to some kind of fun mountain rendezvous."

Livvie's jaw clenched. "I don't think that at all. I know—"

Connor punched his finger toward Desmond. "And you seem to think we're going to get out of this alive."

"We will," Desmond said, "if you'd get the bug out of your ass."

"What the hell does that mean?"

Desmond lurched across the distance between them and yanked the reins out of Connor's hands. He pulled on both sets and the horses came to a stop. Pretty Girl pulled up short behind them. Desmond stared at his brother until Connor shifted his gaze toward him. "I know you're scared, Connor. I also know you're hurting like hell that you think you let me down."

"Oh, for Christ's sake, Des, I don't—"

"You did the best you could, Connor. You were ten fucking years old." Desmond rubbed his arm then continued quietly. "I remember all of it now. Every miserable hour, day and week I spent with that man in that god-awful place. I was barely alive half the time, but I managed to live. Do you know how?" He waited for Connor to shake his head. "I lived by thinking about you. I stayed sane and pulled myself out of misery for those nights I could get to that cave. You were the only thing that kept me going. And when that night came... Well, I remember every hit, every punch, every kick. I don't understand what motivates a man like Lucas Price. I hope I never can. But I know he couldn't stand to look me in the face one more minute knowing he couldn't break me."

"You can't be broken, Des," Connor said quietly.

"Not sure about that. He would have succeeded if you hadn't found me. That was an amazing thing you did for me, Connor."

"I didn't do enough," Connor said. "I thought I had. I thought you were safe, that we both were. But I made a lot of mistakes that night."

Desmond smiled. "You only made one mistake."

Connor lifted a brow. "What was that?"

"You forgot I throw a knife better than you do. You should have taken me with you."

"I can still kick your ass with a Winchester."

Livvie heaved a giant sigh. When they turned to her, she pursed her lips. "Oh, you two do go on and on. You're worse than Freda. Can we move along, gentlemen? I have a culprit to catch and daylight's a wastin'."

Connor rubbed his forehead. "Who put her in charge any way?"

Desmond burst out laughing. "Someone with a lot more sense than we have. You've got to hand it to her. She's single-minded when she sets her mind on something."

Livvie smiled. "Not entirely single-minded. They'll be a surprise in it for you later if we can get to the crossroads before dark." She glanced down at the muddy path. "I'd race you but I don't think that's possible on this…road."

"Hardly matters who wins," Connor said. "I have a feeling we'll both be getting that surprise."

"You can count on it," Livvie said.

"I'm going first," Connor said.

Livvie smiled then a blush rose in her face at the thought but she said it anyway. "No one needs to go first…if you both go at the same time."

"Jesus Christ," Desmond whispered.

Connor glanced at his brother. She'd never seen Connor look more serious in his life. "Heads or tails?"

"Either side's a winner," Desmond said.

Connor nodded. "You're right about that."

Chapter 24

They managed to find a relative dry spot near the remains of the lean-to Stanley Mercer had told them about. A creek flowed nearby so while Connor filled their canteens, Desmond made a fire and Livvie prepared their camp for the night. After checking for rocks and other debris, she spread out a tarp and arranged the bedrolls. Not exactly the comforts of home but she was in the wilds of Kansas, camping under the stars with two men who'd given her the best couple weeks of her life. Despite the danger that lurked ahead, at that moment she wouldn't have wanted to be anywhere else.

Desmond passed out hunks of bread and tins of beef.

"Not exactly Brandywine fare." Livvie made a face as she spooned more of the hideous concoction into her mouth.

"I hear they've had a menu change," Desmond said.

"Stanley Mercer may be scum," Connor said, "but he sure could cook a beef roast."

"Ma could make a good beef roast too," Desmond said.

Connor glanced up from his can. "You remember that?"

Desmond tilted his head and smiled. "Yeah."

"Anything else?"

"She made some kind of cherry dessert..."

"That she sold at the mercantile in town," Connor said.

Desmond nodded. "And she wore a hat..." Desmond circled his forehead with his hand. "A straw one with a blue band that matched her eyes." He turned and flicked his finger at the brim of Livvie's hat. "Kind of like that cute one you bought at Bradley's. That's about all I remember...so far."

Connor nodded. "It's a good start. Keep working on it."

Desmond licked some coagulated beef off his spoon and grimaced. "You know, if things work out the way we've planned, and Wes is working at the Brandywine when we get back, maybe he'll make us more of that fried chicken."

"Livvie could always get a job there. Her cooking's not quite as bad as this." He held up his can then ducked as Livvie swung her arm to cuff the back of his head.

"Keep it up, big guy, and you won't get your surprise."

"Now, Liv, you promised," Connor said.

She grabbed the can out of his hand and tossed it into the darkness. "And I intend to keep it."

* * * *

Desmond made his decision quickly before things moved out of his control. Usually Connor took the lead in initiating the love play the few times they'd taken a woman together. But those women had not been their Kentucky princess. Livvie might think herself a cosmopolitan city girl and an experienced woman, but her naiveté hovered around her like an aura, a gentle breath of innocence that clung to her and sparked happiness in everyone around her. He refused to take a chance with her well-being. Most of all he refused to damage that vivacity that made Olivia Raines who she was. Connor was an enthusiastic and considerate lover, but Desmond couldn't trust him with this. Their lives together, their future, might depend on this night and if something went wrong, Connor wouldn't be able to handle any more guilt.

After Livvie tossed the can, she laughed and pounced toward Connor like a kitten toward a ball of string. Desmond stood and lunged forward. He wrapped his arms around her waist, and snatched her backwards. She smashed into him, the air exploding from her lungs in a surprised gasp. Connor's eyes widened but for once he kept his mouth shut. Desmond would thank him for that later. At the moment, he had something else on his mind. He ground his swollen cock against Livvie's ass, noting the way she giggled as she twitched her lower body away from him. He slid his hand between her legs and yanked her back tight against him. She sucked in her breath and stiffened. Connor continued to watch him like he'd lost his mind.

He pressed his cheek close to hers. A shiver moved through her body. He hoped he wasn't making a mistake here. He really wanted this. They needed this. The huskiness of his voice surprised him.

"You sure you know what you're doing here? Taking us both on?"

She murmured something unintelligible and he tried again.

"Do you know what kinds of things two men do to a woman that offers something like that?"

"I'm a big girl," she murmured. "I can handle it."

"But do you know what they *do*?"

Desmond lifted his eyes to peer at Connor. Connor looked ready to leap off the blanket and join in but that slight bit of confusion on his face kept him anchored.

"Yes, Des," she said quietly, "I know what they do."

"Then tell me. So I know you understand."

He felt the hot blush that flamed in her face. He wondered for a moment if he should just take a walk, leave Connor alone with her for awhile then come back and forget this crazy idea.

You're an ass, McBride. Are you willing to give up everything you want?

"You'll fuck me at the same time. In two places," Livvie said quietly. She held up her hand as he opened his mouth. "And I know one won't be my mouth. I'm not sure exactly how this all will work, but I think between the three of us, we can come up with something. I know you're worried about me, Des, but I trust you, and I planned for this. If you let me go for a moment, I'll prove it."

Desmond's brow furrowed. He glanced at Connor who mouthed, "let her go". His arms dropped from her body and she stepped away, reaching for her satchel. She rummaged around for a moment, pulling out hankies, a camisole, hair pins, a pair of socks, and finally held up a small jar with a flourish.

Desmond scratched his jaw. "You're going to put on face cream?"

Livvie huffed and gave him one of her looks. "It's not for my face, silly. I assume this isn't going to be the most comfortable thing ever at first. The cream's to help things…slide a little better. It's all I could see on Frieda's shelves I thought might help. I hope she wasn't suspicious when I asked for it."

Connor laughed. "She's thought of everything, Des, as usual. What are you going to do about it?"

"You know the answer to that," Desmond said. "I'm going first."

* * * *

Des had Connor scared for a minute. The most perfect night of their lives had been spread out before them like a gift and he'd thought for a minute his brother would ruin it all to hell. No one could turn into a wet blanket faster than Des. He worried too much, or thought too much, or something. Connor knew Livvie better than to think she'd do *anything* she didn't want to do. But things had begun to look up and Desmond seemed to be looking forward to this, maybe even more than Connor did. And, their little Kentucky princess, though she looked a little bit nervous, might actually be in charge right now. Connor planned to enjoy the ride and go wherever Livvie took them.

Connor stood up and stretched. "I'm pretty sure I let you go first last time."

Desmond gave him an almost goofy grin. "Can't say as I remember that."

"You can't pull the memory excuse any more, little brother." He gave Livvie a wink. "We're on to you now."

Desmond shrugged. "Then let's just say I'm insisting."

"Well, if you're going to put it that way…" Connor waved his arm and backed up a step. "Then I am graciously getting out of your way."

Connor didn't give a damn. If this worked out to his satisfaction, they'd have the rest of their lives for him to get a turn, maybe even several. Livvie had already taken off her boots and Desmond had started on his. Damn, Livvie was good for Des.

Livvie and Desmond stared at one another as they stripped out of their clothes, mirroring each other's movements. As Livvie unlaced her shirt, Desmond unlaced his. Des paused for a minute as glimpses of Livvie's pert rosy breasts came into view and Connor had a hard time taking his eyes away as well. When she gripped the edge of her shirt and began to tug it upward, Desmond whipped off his shirt and flung it into the scrub, his gaze never leaving her body. Livvie smiled as her hair clouded down around her shoulders and across her back. She took a deep breath then ran her hands from her hips bones to her abdomen then cupped her breasts, squeezing and lifting.

"I love being naked," she whispered. "Don't you?"

God she was perfect. Desmond didn't say a word but Connor couldn't resist another minute. He dropped to his knees and tugged her forward, taking her nipple into his mouth. He held back with everything he had from simply devouring her then suckled her gently. Her hands came up to rest in his hair, pulling strands through her fingers as she made small noises in her throat. Connor unfastened her pants and pushed them down her hips. He needed to feel the soft globes of her rounded ass, the smooth skin of her thighs. Her scent enveloped him, the intoxicating aroma of a seductive, desirable woman and the pure innocence that was all Livvie. Behind him, he heard Desmond's pants drop to the ground.

"You're falling behind here, Connor," Desmond said.

"Just give me a minute." Connor dipped slowly and swiped his tongue across her pussy. Her hands tightened in his hair and her hips angled toward him. "She's so wet, so hot." He took another taste, spearing his tongue into her warm haven and licking across her pussy lips. When he fluttered his tongue across her clit, she shivered and mewed like a kitten.

Then he backed away because he had definitely fallen behind. He ripped his shirt off and almost fell trying to get out of his pants. Desmond didn't waste time. He fell to his knees in front of her and began to eat her pussy. Connor watched each nuance of Livvie's face as the pleasure wound through her. He studied each tremor that shook her body, each quiver that touched her limbs, each spasm that tore through her. He'd never seen anything more beautiful in his entire life.

* * * *

When she and Abbie had discussed boys, fucking two men at once had never been one of the topics that had come up. Livvie vaguely wondered what an older sister was good for if she couldn't be counted on for sexual advice. They'd discussed kissing, caressing, orgasms and actual fucking, but surprisingly, two men had never been in the scenarios.

Scenarios change, Liv. Just enjoy it.

Abbie obviously had no imagination and less experience.

When Desmond's tongue flicked across her clit, her legs threatened to give out beneath her. His touch electrified her, sending hot pulses zinging through her. Her body quivered with anticipation as strong, hot hands roamed down the backs of her thighs and up again. A thick finger slid between her cheeks, lightly stroking skin that had never been touched. She clenched instinctively as he prod gently, pressing against the small hole of her ass.

Tonight meant something and she knew her future hinged on what happened between them. Win or lose, she decided Connor and Desmond would leave here with an experience to remember and know that no matter what happened tomorrow she loved them tonight. What else could she give them? They hadn't discussed their feelings, their relationship, or their future. If this was their last night as the McBrides, she intended to brand her mark into their hearts and minds.

Now if someone would only tell her what she needed to do...

"Just relax, Livvie," Desmond murmured. "Trust me."

Connor stroked her hair and through half-closed lids, she watched Connor hold the open jar toward his brother. Desmond dipped his finger into the cream then a cold wetness spread between her cheeks. She slivered slightly and gasped when Desmond's tongue traced a path over the slit of her pussy. Her knees buckled but Desmond tightened his hands on her. She held her breath, feeling the long, smooth, rhythmic strokes of his tongue. The flesh between her legs pulsed and tiny flutters twitched the muscles inside. His mouth felt wonderful on her hot skin, easing the ache of the throb between her legs, dipping into the wet warmth that seeped from her. Her pussy was damp, hot, and swollen. The ache turned into a burning itch and her breasts throbbed. She reached up and cupped her hands around them, rolling her nipples until she felt Connor's warmth behind her and his hands cupped the full aching flesh that throbbed, needing the touch of a man. Not just any man—one of the McBrides, her men.

Desmond thrust his tongue inside her pussy. His finger slid between the cheeks of her ass and she felt the tip of his finger penetrate a fraction of an inch. Her lips pressed into a tight line and her jaw clenched. She steeled her legs, trying desperately to stay on her feet. His mouth settled on her clit and sucked. Her hand strayed to his face and cupped along his jaw. His muscles flexed with the movement of his mouth and Livvie caressed the stubble on his face, the scratchy rough texture against her hand. Once she had wished that mouth sucked on her and now...

"Oh, Des..."

She bowed toward him as she shuddered. Shivers ran rampant through her body, and Desmond held her hip tight as his mouth continued to devour her flesh. She wanted him inside, needed him inside, wanted him… She wanted the thick, hard, swollen pulse of his cock in her, anywhere he wanted to put it.

Her stomach muscles clenched and tightened as she came. Moisture flooded from her pussy. She bit her lip to stifle the sound that threatened to explode from her and a sharp ache tore through her body. She wanted it hard, deep… Her body shuddered violently. Connor's hands tightened on her breasts. Desmond's mouth continued to torture her clit and his finger slid farther into her ass. She felt the pressure of the invasion but the pleasure sweeping through her body blanketed any pain. As his mouth continued to suck on her, his finger pumped in and out of her ass in short gentle strokes.

"Oh! Holy moly…"

Her head fell forward and she tried to talk but her words became lost in the web of hair that cascaded around her face. Her eyes closed and she floated in all the sensations that coursed through her. The muscles inside her throbbed with a deep pulsing rhythm, clenching and releasing to the beat of her heart. Uncontrollable shivers racked her body and she nearly collapsed. Connor gripped her shoulders and held her steady.

Desmond withdrew his finger and for a brief moment disappointment flared through her until she felt the gentle press of something larger. Two fingers. She forced herself to relax and leaned back against the warm security of Connor's chest. Desmond continued to thrust his fingers into her, deeper and harder with each stroke. Connor kissed her face, her jaw, her earlobe while smoothing damp hair away from her brow. Three fingers now speared inside, widening her channel, stretching the tight hole for something larger. She breathed in and out, concentrating on each breath as Desmond's fingers held her hostage in something that was part pleasure, part pain.

His mouth searched her pussy again, his tongue flicking over her clit like flashes of lightning caught in a swirling funnel cloud. Hot, restless anticipation danced through her limbs and her inner muscles pulsed with need. A shudder ripped through her body and she jerked against Connor. Her eyes flew open and her head lowered just as Desmond raised his face and those midnight eyes clashed with hers.

"Are you okay, Liv?"

"Oh yes…" Her sigh seemed to fill the prairie. "Now, Des. I want you both now…" She reached up and wound one arm around Connor's neck while she caressed Desmond's face with the other. "Fuck me… both of you. Right now."

Desmond rose to his feet, his naked body sliding hot against her. He stared down at her, his eyes full of secrets, mysteries, emotions that she couldn't begin to comprehend.

"I need to kiss you, Liv," he said softly.

"Yes," she whispered. "I need that too."

His hot mouth pressed against hers like a gift, his tongue plunging into her mouth with hunger, ache, and a driving urgency. He wrapped one hand around the back of her neck and cradled her head, tilting her face higher as his lips devoured hers in a crushing, bruising kiss. She sucked in his tongue, caressing it with her own. Her lips caught at his again and again until she couldn't pull another breath into her lungs. He pressed hard kisses against her throat, his lips sucking her flesh.

When his mouth came back to hers, she wrapped hers around his lower lip and tugged it between her teeth. She sucked, nibbled, and nipped it gently, then slid her tongue across the fullness of the most seductive mouth she'd ever seen. When she drew away, Desmond smiled and gazed at her curiously. She whispered, "You have an adorable mouth. I've wanted to do that since that night I saw you."

His hand drifted up the back of her head to play in her hair. "You can do it any time you like."

Connor cleared his throat. "Excuse me. Can I do anything?"

Desmond gripped her shoulder and spun her around. Livvie lifted her face to meet his twilight blue eyes and the amusing smile on his face.

"You can fuck me if you like," Livvie said.

Connor laughed. "Now we're talking."

Desmond put his hands on her waist and lowered her to her knees on the blanket. He followed her down and the coarse hair of his thigh brushed hers as he separated her legs, pushing them apart. He slid his finger between her cheeks and coated her skin with more cream and the hard length of his cock poked against her ass, pulsing and eager. Connor dropped to his knees and pushed two fingers into her pussy. He slid them in and out in an excruciating rhythm. Already pleasure coursed through her, little tingles that nipped at her skin and vibrated through her muscles. Connor rubbed her clit with his thumb, sending bursts of sensations through her pelvis. Her pussy clamped down on his fingers as he pulled them out. She almost groaned with the loss.

She wrapped her hand around Connor's cock and lifted her face.

"What are you waiting for?"

"Not a thing."

Connor plunged his cock into her pussy, sliding in one smooth stroke to bury deep. Livvie sighed and wrapped her arms around his shoulders. He rocked into her several times then reached between them and pinched her clit between his fingers, rubbing with soft gentle strokes until her breathing became tiny, needy pants. He withdrew and glanced over her head.

Desmond moved the soft, velvety tip of his cock up and down between her cheeks in caressing strokes. The pulsing tip touched her opening and Desmond spread her cheeks with his hands. The head of his cock nudged her ass and she pressed back slightly. He slid in, slowly pushing deeper. Livvie concentrated on the feel of Connor's thumb and the grinding ache that wound through her pelvis. As Desmond relentlessly drove farther, Connor leaned down and locked his mouth on hers, until she knew instinctively that Desmond had gone as far as he could. He released an exhausted but satisfied sigh.

Desmond's back settled flush against her own and his hands clamped on her hips. Connor rammed his cock deep into her, rocking her against Desmond. She nearly moaned with the pleasure.

Slowly they began to move within her, one pumping in while the other withdrew. Livvie found it nearly impossible to concentrate on any one sensation. Her entire body swelled with hot, pulsing waves of pleasure. Two mouths spread kisses over every inch of skin they could reach, two tongues left searing trails of heat on her flesh and the friction of two cocks nestled within her body sent alternating courses of fire over her clit and through her pussy and ass.

Their sweat-slicked bodies rubbed and slid across each other. Livvie's hands roamed over every muscle and limbs she could find and her lips pressed burning kisses against Connor's chest and Desmond's face when he leaned into her. She alternated between gripping Connor's ass and yanking his cock deeper and grabbing Desmond's hips to drive his cock harder. Their balls slapped at her flesh, causing ticklish sensations that spiraled and joined the almost painful ache that needed to be appeased. Caught between them she couldn't breathe, she couldn't move and she didn't want to do either.

Her body trembled violently under their hands and mouth and finally, she could do nothing more than clutch them both and surrender to the lure of the orgasm that threatened to consume her. Her pussy pulsed and contracted, gripping Connor hard. Connor's head dropped against her hair and his warm breath exploded around her. Her ass clenched in response and Desmond groaned behind her. She let go in a violent shudder and her men both slammed into her wet, throbbing holes, squeezing her between them as their bodies' spasmed simultaneously. Hot jets of cum spurted into her and their bodies trembled against hers, quaking and quivering in their arms. Two sets of arms wrapped around her and squeezed.

The pleasure swept through her in an intense storm of flickers and pulses, flashes and grinding heat. Wave after wave poured through and swamped her senses until her body went limp against them, held up only by the weight pressed against her on both sides.

Connor kissed the top of her head as Desmond kissed her shoulder. Desmond withdrew first with a heavy sigh and fell to the blanket. Connor lowered her gently to the ground, his cock sliding out slowly with his movement. Livvie's hands fluttered, trying to find them both with her eyes closed. Connor slipped next to her, tucking his head near her shoulder. Desmond dropped a kiss on her forehead and his warmth suddenly vanished.

"Be back in a minute."

She heard the sound of a canteen being opened.

"Now *that* was something," Livvie whispered.

"The best I've ever had," Connor said.

Desmond ran a cool wet handkerchief over her sweaty skin then between her legs. Livvie opened her eyes and met his midnight eyes.

"And what did you think?"

"It was more than I ever hoped for." He gave her a smile then winked. "And I'm already looking forward to the next time." He grabbed another hanky and wet it.

Connor rose up on his elbow. "I get that beautiful ass next time."

Desmond threw the sopping cloth at him and Livvie laughed when cool drops of water splashed on her skin. Connor sputtered when it hit him in the face. The men began to argue back and forth. Livvie stared at the scattering of stars above, barely listening to their words but taking comfort in the comfortable and playful banter and the camaraderie that existed between them. Between all of them. She felt content, cherished, and protected. She felt at home.

"Isn't Kansas beautiful?" she murmured.

"It's just about perfect," Connor said.

"*She's* just about perfect," Desmond said.

"Hardly perfect," Livvie said. "But tonight...you made me feel that way."

The men settled down on the blanket, snuggling close to her.

"Stay put," Connor said. "No gallivanting around during the night."

"You're the boss," Livvie murmured, squeezing his hand.

"Ha!" Desmond said. "That'll be the day."

Chapter 25

My head really hurts.

Livvie remembered walking down to the creek. Although Desmond had done a pretty good job of cleaning her up, her skin felt sticky and she continued to leak between her legs. She'd listened to their breathing and thought she could sneak off for just a minute and they'd never even miss her. So she quickly threw on her clothes and practically tiptoed the short distance to the creek. She didn't remember slipping or falling but she must have hit her head on something because an ache throbbed at the base of her neck. The rock pressing into her butt didn't help. She blinked several times but she felt woozy and disoriented. Why hadn't the men come looking for her? Maybe she'd only been gone a few minutes. She tried to stand up and couldn't move her arms or legs.

Damnation. Now what?

Both her wrists and ankles were bound, and someone had enough forethought to tie her to a small tree. She attempted to call out but the sounds she heard were muffled. Bound, gagged, and obviously out of commission. Okay. So she hadn't slipped. Someone had hit her in the head and abducted her.

Great. Very professional, Liv. You will never live this down. If you survive…

She'd damn well better survive. Her parents would kill her if she didn't.

She sat still, allowing her eyes time to adjust to the dark, and waiting for the spinning in her head to stop. She felt like she'd just taken a ride on a carousel, and she'd never handled carousels well.

She usually puked. A dying campfire sparked and sizzled about thirty feet away. She flexed her hands, trying to get some feeling into her numb limbs. Shadows emerged on the other side of the camp, three of them—one very fat, one very large, and one fairly small. A nice little set of villains, and one for each of them.

If they find you.

They'd find her. They had to. Her parents would kill them if they didn't. She knew Connor and Desmond would be searching for her now but she had no idea how far they'd come and how long it might take to find her. She'd been at the creek and if they'd carried her through the water, there would be no trail, no tracks to follow.

Another man emerged from behind the bushes.

Damn it. There are four men. Well, I'll just have to take out two of them.

She heard a soft sound beside her, the rustling of movement in the grass. Probably just a prairie dog, or with the kind of day she'd had, a snake. But, she wanted to know for sure before something slithered into her lap. She wiggled, turning her body slightly so she could see to her left. She squinted and made out a shape against a neighboring tree. She held her breath and strained to hear anything else but the hushed whispers on the other side of the camp and the crackling noises as the fire consumed its last bit of fuel. Just as the last of her patience and air ran out, she heard a soft intake of breath. She wiggled a little more, turning her body in a semi-circle until she confirmed that the shadow against the tree was a person. Unfortunately, the shadow couldn't help her because she saw the arms had also been pulled back behind the trunk.

She murmured a muffled noise behind her gag. James Keating shifted against the tree and returned her muffle with one of his own.

The men sitting around the fire completely ignored them as though they had no concern they could escape or be saved. She wondered at their conceit but planned to use their misplaced estimation in her favor.

They seemed to be involved in plotting out the rest of their conspiracy. They murmured among themselves and she managed to hear Nebraska, apparently talking about their rendezvous point. It became clear who was in charge when a voice rose and the largest of them stood up and glared down at the others.

Lucas Price was a bear of a man. He would have appeared menacing and terrifying to anyone under any circumstances, but knowing his history and disposition, added to the amount of intimidation he exuded. His stern face, huge body, and powerful movements forced Livvie to cringe back farther against the bark of the tree.

She couldn't see Price's eyes from the distance, and she thought that might be the only thing keeping her from passing out. Knowing Desmond had barely survived his encounter with Price caused an anxious apprehension to twist through her nerves. That she and James were at the mercy of a man like Price caused a cold sweat to dot the back of her neck. She had to get away from this place and she had to take James with her.

She rubbed the back of her head against the tree, trying to dislodge the gag which was a mistake because it hurt like hell. The lump where she'd been hit throbbed in aching protest, and it became clear she also had a laceration because hot searing agony shot through her entire head and down her spine. Her body trembled and she gritted her teeth against the pain and nausea that rippled through her body. Beads of sweat burst out on her forehead.

Livvie sat quietly, willing the nausea away and stifling a groan as waves of sickness churned in her stomach. She closed her eyes and took several deep breaths, blinking back tears of frustration. If she couldn't get loose, she couldn't help James. If she couldn't help James, she'd fail.

The only solution was to get loose. She flexed her hands again, gauging the strength of the rope and the tightness of the bond, trying to get some leeway in the knots. But these damn kidnappers knew how to secure a hostage to a tree. She imagined they'd had plenty of practice in the last year. She bent her wrists, twisting them slightly, but already she felt the burning prick of raw skin against the rough rope and knew with even a little more movement she'd be bleeding.

Her shoulders ached from the strain and the pain in her head made it difficult to turn her neck. But she turned it anyway, hearing the creaking protest of her muscles and tendons as she angled her face toward her shoulder. She lowered her head as far as she could until the edge of the dirty gag touched her shoulder then she slid her chin up slowly, trying to pull the cloth down. More sweat broke out on her face. Her shoulders screamed in complaint and her scalp tingled as the hair trapped in the gag stretched and tugged. She stopped for a moment and let her head fall back against the tree, ignoring the flare of pain. She pulled several shattering breaths into her lungs. Hot tears tracked down her face. She could feel James watching her.

Stop being a spoiled brat, Liv. There's no one to fix this but you, so fix it.

She closed her eyes and tried to relax. She envisioned herself in a circus. She entered the center ring amid a roaring crowd that met her with cheers and stomping feet. Wrapped in a flowing confection of emerald green, because Desmond liked green, she raised her arms in thanks for their appreciation. She flung off her silky cape to reveal a costume the color of buckskin that molded to her frame and flexed with each graceful movement of her muscles. She was limber, supple, her body primed to do anything and everything she demanded. She could stretch and bend, twist and turn, roll and tumble, climb and caper. The audience applauded and cheered as her tendons stretched, her muscles contracted and her limbs contorted to follow her commands. She entertained the crowd with unparalleled skills they'd never witnessed before. This was her life. She was an acrobat. And a piece of cloth on her face would not present a problem.

She dropped her head to her shoulder once again, scraping the cloth against the buckskin and within a moment, the rag slipped down her chin and fell to her neck.

"Now for the ropes," she murmured.

The ropes fell from her wrists and her arms dropped to the ground. Her upper body fell forward before she could even wonder what the hell had happened. She jerked upright and twisted her face. A hand clamped over her mouth and her heart lurched as she raised her eyes.

David Mercer put a finger to his lips. She smiled beneath his hand and nodded. When David removed his hand, she twisted her face to see Wes come around the tree. He sliced the rope that bound her ankles and gave her a grin before he moved toward James. A pair of paws settled on her upper arm as a little body wriggled against her. She leaned down to receive Buster's drooling kiss on her cheek.

She slowly rose to her feet, her back pressed against the trunk to control her trembling limbs. She waited for a moment as dizziness swamped over her like a wet blanket almost knocking her off her feet. She kept her body flattened against the tree then slid in a circle until she faced a small nest of scraggly shrubs. The three boys looked ready to bolt, but Buster pressed against her shin then plopped down on her foot and laid his head on his paws.

David glanced around the tree. "We've got to go."

She tried to focus on Wes. She saw double so she scrubbed her hands over her eyes and tried again. She held out her hand. "Give me the knife."

Wes shook his head.

"Give me the knife then get moving."

"No," Wes said, "you're coming with me now or I'm not going."

Livvie clenched her jaw against the pain that swelled through her head.

"Connor and Des can handle it," Wes whispered.

"These men could be miles away before they get here. There are other boys' lives at stake. Zachary Daily for one."

"You're going to pass out, Liv," he argued.

"I'm fine. Just give me a minute." She swallowed the bile that rose in her throat. Her lashes fluttered and she willed her eyes open.

James raked dark hair away from his face and stared toward the fire. "If it's the same to all of you, I'd like to see them dead before we leave. I'm not much in the mood to be a mine slave in Idaho." Even in the gloom, Livvie saw the purple stain of the bruise on his face. He took a step toward the camp. "If you can hit one with the knife, I can probably take down one of them. I'm pretty strong. That only leaves two." He glanced toward Wes and David.

"I don't want any of you in that clearing," Livvie said.

"They have guns," David whispered. "I can see two rifles and a shotgun. Plus one of them is wearing a holster."

"Do *we* have guns?" Livvie's brow rose as her gaze slid toward Wes. He reached toward the ground, grabbing the Winchester. "Then our problem is half-way solved. Can any of you shoot?"

All three boys nodded, but David looked terrified. The son of a hotel owner probably didn't have much reason to practice his shooting skills. She had no idea what kind of life James had led since he arrived in Kansas, but with her luck lately, Pack probably hadn't let him near a gun. That left Wes. His bravado in front of Stanley Mercer could have been feigned, but he looked comfortable with the rifle in his hand.

Livvie thought her best chance lay with Wes. "Wes, I'm going use the knife and aim for the man on the right. If I can take him down before the others realize what's happening, we have a better chance. I want you to aim for Pack, shoot him dead then hand me the rifle. Can you do that?"

"Yes," he murmured.

"If someone makes a break for it, let them go. If someone gets their hand on a gun, I want all of you to run."

David looked conflicted, but reluctantly reached into his pocket. "I have this." He dangled his slingshot between his fingers.

Livvie smiled. "And you're good with it. I've watched you. Let's see if we can find some rocks. David can take one side of camp, James the other. Throw then move somewhere else fast. Got it?" She glanced between James and David. They both nodded and dropped to their hands and knees.

Livvie leaned her head back against the tree. Her hands trembled. She didn't know if it was nerves or the headache that still ground through every inch of her body. It didn't seem to matter. She needed to control it. Wes curled the folding knife in her hand. She hefted it for a moment. It was so light, and the moveable handle caused an instability she didn't like at all.

Livvie sighed. *Something to remember: Never get abducted without your eyeglasses.* Slowly she turned and leaned around the tree. Thirty feet away—less than ten yards—and easy pickings with her glasses in the daylight, possibly even without. But the dark and the wavering heat and flashes of light above the camp fire played havoc with her eyes. The bump on her head hadn't helped either. The blurred vision would be a problem. But she'd hit within the target before and a hit in a target meant a hit to the body. She just had to do enough damage to keep the first one down.

Buster lifted from her foot and let out a low growl. One of the men had moved to the other side of the fire and appeared to be coming in their direction.

Time's up.

"They're coming," she whispered. "Go!"

James and David hunkered down and bolted in opposite directions. The man's head snapped up at the sudden rustle in the trees and he lurched forward. Livvie darted around the tree and let the knife fly as Buster shot forward into the clearing. A dark stain spread across the man's neck and he fell to his knees, his hands flailing toward his face. Livvie heard the gurgle in his throat before he dropped face-first into the dirt.

Buster skirted the fire and leapt toward the group as Wes fired his rifle. Anthony Pack spun around, clutching at his shoulder then dropped as a barrage of rocks rained down from the left. Price and the other man jumped to their feet and reached for rifles then dropped down aiming toward the trees where Livvie and Wes stood. Wes tossed the Winchester at her and Livvie caught it, trying to aim for Price. A rock came from the left and hit Price's accomplice in the side of the head. He listed to the side, fell, and lay still just as Buster launched himself at Price's legs and knocked him over.

Pack staggered to his knees, reaching for his pistol, and Livvie aimed directly at his chest. As he drew the side arm from the holster, she pulled the trigger and his body blew backward slamming into a large rock. Price struggled to reach again for his rifle, kicking at the dog fastened to his leg. Another rocky missile came from the right and hit his leg. Price screamed in fury and kicked out harder, spending Buster spinning toward the fire.

Wes shot out of their hiding place and raced across the clearing.

"No!" Livvie shouted.

Already half-way across Wes ignored her and leapt over the fire in time to scoop Buster in his arms. Price gripped the rifle and aimed it at Wes who dove to the ground and rolled. Another rain of rocks showered Price and he staggered backwards still trying to aim his weapon. A rock flew from the right and hit the barrel, knocking the rifle aside as he pulled the trigger. The shot went into the bushes. James' shadow darted farther to the right and Livvie waited an agonizing moment for the scream of a boy. When another barrage of rocks came from the right, she shot forward and went down on one knee.

Price stood now and had his rifle trained directly at her.

Just hit the target, Olivia. Any hit is a body hit.

But of course the best scenario ended with him dead. She squeezed the trigger and a starburst of blood flared from his forehead. His body swayed, his eyes focused directly on her then he pitched forward. She lurched to her feet and ran toward him, kicking the rifle away. She pushed hard and flipped him over, just to be sure. Dead as the proverbial doornail.

"Bastard. That was for Desmond."

A quick check on Anthony Pack proved him dead as well. All in all, a good night.

Wes headed for the first downed man and yanked the knife from his neck. He wiped the blood on the man's shirt then moved quickly to the second man, who had begun to groan. David had done an excellent job of knocking him out with the slingshot. Wes leaned toward the man, the knife aimed toward his throat. Livvie put a hand on his shoulder.

"I need one of them alive."

Wes folded the knife and slid it in his pocket. "You're the boss." He squatted down and pulled Buster into his arms, and got rewarded with a lick to the face and a smattering of drool.

James and David cautiously entered the clearing. James found a length of rope and set about tying their captive. Wes nodded toward the man on the ground. "Think he'll know anything?"

Livvie studied the man. "He better because it's the only thing saving his sorry ass. I heard Nebraska, but I'm hoping he has a more precise location and a name. It's all the information I need to turn this case over to the authorities and end this."

The man groaned again. His lids fluttered open and locked on Livvie. His eyes widened and he tried to raise his head.

"Morning, sunshine," Livvie said. "You're in a world of hurt right now."

James slammed his fist into the man's face. His eyes rolled back and his head clunked to the ground. James glanced at her and shrugged. "Just putting him out of his misery. Besides I hate this son-of-a-bitch."

"Whatever makes you happy, James." Livvie turned to Wes. "Where exactly are we? Any ideas?"

"We're a couple miles west of the Pack ranch. They hadn't gone very far. I think they hoped you'd bypass them."

"Which we had," Livvie said. "The tornado didn't make tracking easy. How did you find us anyway?"

Wes smiled. "We didn't expect to find *you*. That was a bit of a surprise. But we had this." He reached into his back pocket and pulled out a small reading primer. "Alice suggested it. I had to break into the school to get it. James' scent is all over it. Buster didn't have a lick of trouble tracking him even after the tornado."

Livvie knelt down and ruffled her hand across Buster's head. "You all make one hell of a posse. I couldn't have asked for a better team."

"Fuck...that."

Livvie whirled around at the sound of Connor's voice. He staggered between the trees then leaned down, his hands on his knees, his breath heaving. He pulled in another huge gasp of air and sank to his knees.

"I heard the rifles...and ran the last mile. Ever try to run through mud? Not fun."

She squealed and ran towards him, nearly knocking him over when she dove into his outstretched arms. He pulled her tight and devoured her mouth in a kiss that seemed both desperate and perfect. When he let her up for air, she planted kisses all over his face.

"Jesus, I'm going to have to get a leash for you. You need to stay put when I say so." He glanced over her head. "Save me anything to kill?"

"Meant to, but it was taking you too long to get here." Livvie lifted to see over his shoulder. "Where's Des?"

"Hopefully not realizing I sent him in the wrong direction," Connor said. "He's gonna be pissed."

"I am pissed." Desmond reeled into the clearing and fell back against a small tree. He pressed his hand over his chest and twisted his face toward his brother. "Care to explain how I ended up going east? Damn…I think I'm having a heart attack." Connor rolled his eyes and Desmond narrowed his.

"Now, Des," Connor said, "I tried to—"

"Save the martyr bit and stop worrying about me all the time." Des slid down the trunk and landed on his ass. "I figured it out pretty quick. I backtracked and followed you."

Connor shrugged. "Then no harm done."

Livvie wiggled in Connor's arms and he released her. She crawled across the distance between them and curled into Desmond's lap.

"When I heard that first shot…" Desmond stared over her toward the burning embers of the campfire. He glanced at her and gave her a weak smile. "I see you didn't need us."

"I always need you," Livvie said.

Desmond cupped her face and his mouth covered hers in a sweet kiss. "That's for taking care of Lucas Price."

She smiled under his lips. "I went for the kill instead of the body shot. I wanted to get it right the first time."

He kissed her again, one that held every feeling he'd ever had and made her body press against him hard, wanting to feel the heat, the fire. When he reluctantly peeled his mouth from hers, he murmured, "I missed you, Liv. That was for me."

"I could tell," she whispered.

He smiled then flipped her over on his lap and swatted her ass.

"Ouch!"

"That's for ruining what was otherwise a perfect night." She shrieked and wiggled until he released her. She scrambled backwards, laughing. He stared at his hand. "Great. I'm not dirty enough? Now I have mud all over my hand."

She leapt to her feet and twisted around. "I have mud on my ass? Oh, someone is going to pay for that. I love this outfit."

Chapter 26

They plodded into Fort Cloud, hungry, filthy, and tired, but Livvie had never felt better in her life. They had a name, a location, and a date for the rendezvous Lucas Price had planned with his contact in Idaho. Once the sheriff arrived and the telegraph had been repaired, Livvie knew they'd see the end of the mission and the return of the boys to their respective towns to be adopted.

When they arrived at the school, Livvie gratefully slid off the horse. She had one moment of peace before Anna came to the door and let the students converge on her. Soon the yard filled with the citizens of Fort Cloud, eager to hear about their adventure and success.

After Tad Wilkins carted their captive off to the livery, women began to arrive with food. The new tables the townsmen had crafted in their absence filled to the brim with an array of meats and vegetables, desserts and cheese. The owner of the Prairie Schooner brought some jugs of whiskey and cider and slapped them down on the table, realizing he'd have no patrons that day. A few of the men gathered fiddles and pipes and played throughout the afternoon. The smaller children joined them with harmonicas and drums from the school. Her young heroes—Wes, David and James—sat in a cluster of the older children, telling and re-telling their story. Alice and Miranda hung on every word. Buster slept on Alice's lap.

As people filled plates and cups and settled down for a picnic, a lone horse raced down the dust of Main Street. Livvie shielded her eyes against the sun as the shadow approached. When she saw the rider's shock of unruly dark curls she shrieked, jumping up and down, and rushed into the street. Martin leapt from the horse before it stopped and gathered her into his arms.

"Oh God, Liv, I am so glad to see you alive."

He hugged her so tight she could barely squeeze in a breath. She laughed and finally managed to extricate herself from Martin's arms.

"What are you doing here? Didn't you get my letter?"

He ran his hands through his hair. "I don't know. I spoke with Caroline a few days after you left. A man was *killed* here, Liv. They didn't tell you that and I—"

Livvie nodded. "Yes, I know. But that—"

"I came to take you home. They will never forgive me if something happens to you. We need to go now. Someone can send your things. I've arranged for tickets to the next town. We'll wait there for a train back to Cincinnati." His gaze suddenly lifted and scanned the crowd behind her. "What's going on here?"

Livvie reached up and cupped his face. She forced him to look at her. "We're celebrating. The mission is over. We've been successful and everything is okay. I'm fine."

Martin blinked. "What?"

She wound her arms around his neck and pulled him into a hug. "My Galahad. I love you so much, Marty." She pulled away and took his hand. "If you want to hear about our adventure, I know three boys that would love to tell it one more time."

"I'd love to hear it, because I've moved beyond worried into confusion."

"If you were worried, why didn't you just send me a telegram, Marty?"

He smiled. "Because I knew you'd ignore it. I figured I might have to carry you away from here kicking and screaming."

"Who's your friend, Olivia?"

Livvie turned at the sound of Anna's voice. Anna's brown eyes rose from hers to the man behind her. A soft smile lingered on her lips.

"Anna Glaser, meet my brother…er, my uncle, Martin Travers."

Anna laughed. "That sounds fairly suspicious, Olivia. Which is it exactly?"

Martin held out his hand and smiled. "I'm her uncle actually, but in our family it's incredibly hard to keep track of things like that."

Anna took his hand. "You must have an interesting," her gaze caressed Martin's face, "and beautiful family, Olivia. I assume everything is okay at home?"

"Yes, Anna. Martin just…just wanted to see Kansas for himself."

Anna tucked Martin's hand into her arm. "I know you're exhausted after the last few days, Olivia, so I'd be more than happy to show your uncle around our little town. Mr. Travers, let me introduce you to some of the greatest cooking this side of the Mississippi and some of the nicest people. Hopefully we can convince you to stay awhile."

"That shouldn't be too hard, Anna." Martin took a backwards glance at Livvie and laughed. "Nice outfit, Liv, but did you know you have mud on your ass?"

She made a face at him and headed for the shade of the tree. She leaned back against it, enjoying the sounds of happy chatter and laughter and the music that filled the yard. She closed her eyes until two darker shadows fell over her. She opened one lid then patted the grass on either side. Connor and Desmond settled beside her.

"Martin heard about Skylar, huh?" Connor asked.

"Yes, but I think I convinced him everything is fine."

Desmond glanced to where Martin and Anna sat at a table, their heads close together. "I'd say if he's not convinced yet, he will be soon. I'm glad someone new arrived. Maybe everyone will stop looking at us so funny." He turned to Livvie. "How's the head?"

"Still spinning a little," Livvie said, "and more so now that Marty's arrived."

"Once it stops, let us know," Connor said.

Livvie tilted her face toward him. "Am I getting a surprise?"

Connor shook his head. "No, you're getting your ass kicked."

"For what? I solved the crime, killed some bad men, completed the—"

"And scared us half to death," Desmond said.

"Well, I didn't mean to do that. Getting kidnapped wasn't anywhere in my scenario."

"Scenarios change," Connor said.

"I've certainly learned that," Livvie muttered.

"We can't lose you, Liv," Connor said.

"And I don't want to be lost," she whispered.

"The next time we say stay put, listen to us," Connor said. "Sometimes we know—"

She held up her hand. "Stop right there." She pushed off from the ground. She whirled around and glared at Connor then let her gaze slide between them. "I'm supposed to just *listen* to you? What gives you the right to tell me something like that? It's not exactly like you're my real husband. *Either* of you. And even if you were, what makes you think I'd listen just because—"

Desmond had mumbled something under his breath and she missed it. Damn she needed to learn to quit talking.

She put her hands on her hips. "What did you say?"

Desmond shrugged. "I said we can fix that."

Her heart fluttered. "Fix what?"

"Fix not being your real husband."

"That's not possible," she whispered.

"Why?" Connor asked.

"Well, because…" She glanced back and forth between them. "Because there are two of you and one of me and…"

"You have two fathers, right?" Desmond asked.

"And your mother is married to one, but loves them both, right?" Connor asked.

She nodded.

"And you've told us she loves them the same," Desmond said.

"She does," Livvie said.

"Do you love *us* the same?" Connor asked quietly.

She shook her head. "I'm so confused. Where is all this coming from? We've never talked about...love."

"Since when is talking necessary between us?" Connor asked.

Her lip thrust out in a pout. She knew it was a childish gesture but couldn't stop it. No one had ever mentioned the word love to her and now they wanted her to admit her feelings? No, no, no. They didn't get to make the rules. "What makes you think I think I love you at all?"

"Just answer the question," Desmond said. "Do you love us the same?"

She sank to the ground and nodded. She had no idea what she should say, not really any idea of what they were telling her. Her heart pounded so loudly she could barely hear her own thoughts.

Desmond reached out and took her hand. "We love you the same too, Liv. We are both madly, passionately, desperately in love with you. We don't want you to choose between us. We want you to take the package deal. Two McBrides for the price of one. You may be the product of two different fathers, but we have a feeling you've learned to love from your mother. Is that true? Are you truly your mother's daughter?"

Livvie said. "It sounds like you two have already discussed this."

"We have," Connor said. "We know what we want, but we need to know what you want."

Livvie smiled. "I can't imagine spending one day without either of you in it. I want you both. I love you both."

"Good then," Connor said. "We'll have to plan some kind of wedding, in case there are children."

"There he goes with his damned logic again," Desmond said.

"There *will* be children," Livvie said. "I insist on it. And I don't care which of you marries me as long as I become Mrs. McBride for *real*."

"I'll do it," Connor said. "I'm the oldest."

Livvie smiled. "You'd sacrifice yourself for me? How sweet of you."

Desmond frowned. "Not good enough. It's just his insatiable need to be first."

Connor's brow furrowed then he snapped his fingers. "C comes before D."

Desmond grunted. "I'm glad to know you've finally conquered the alphabet, but it's still not good enough."

"It's two more reasons than you've managed." Connor reached into his pocket and pulled out a coin. "Heads or tails?"

Desmond smiled. "Not gonna happen. I'm marrying her."

"On what grounds?" Connor asked.

Desmond glanced at Livvie and winked. "I saw her first."

Livvie smiled. "I think we have a winner."

She wrapped her arms around her two men reveling in the wonder and possibilities of love. "I love being my mother's daughter." She leapt to her feet and grabbed their hands, tugging them to their feet. "Let's go get some pie. And I'd really like to try some of those barbecued ribs. Glory makes the best ribs, but these looked pretty damn good. I wonder if anyone brought champagne... I love it. I really have to warn you though. I get a little grabby with champagne."

THE END

ABOUT THE AUTHOR

Amber Carlton's love of historical romance began when she read *The Passionate Adventures of Angelique*. Amber is entranced by all things historical, but has a special fascination with English and American history. She lives in the present but loves to write about being "elsewhere".

Her obsessions include the writing of Stephen King, Philip J. Fry and his friends on Futurama, the world of Buffy the Vampire Slayer, and things that go bump in the night.

Amber has two sons and currently lives in Ohio with her boyfriend and dog.

Siren Publishing, Inc.
www.SirenPublishing.com

Breinigsville, PA USA
28 December 2009
229906BV00004B/11/P